The CHILDREN OF THE WIND quartet is a sweeping
Irish-Australian saga made up of Bridie's story, Patrick's
story, Colm's story and Maeve's story, four inter-linked
novels beginning with the 1850s and moving right up
to the present. The first in the series, *Bridie's Fire*, was
published in 2003.

Bridie's Fire
Becoming Billy Dare
A Prayer for Blue Delaney
The Secret Life of Maeve Lee Kwong

KIRSTY MURRAY is a fifth-generation Australian whose ancestors came from Ireland, Scotland, England and Germany. Some of their stories provided her with the backcloth for the CHILDREN OF THE WIND series. Kirsty lives in Melbourne with her husband and a gang of teenagers.

OTHER BOOKS BY KIRSTY MURRAY

FICTION
Zarconi's Magic Flying Fish
Market Blues
Walking Home with Marie-Claire
Bridie's Fire

NON-FICTION
Howard Florey, Miracle Maker
Tough Stuff

KIRSTY MURRAY

Children of the Wind

Becoming Billy Dare

ALLEN&UNWIN

First published in 2004

Copyright © Kirsty Murray 2004

Allen & Unwin
83 Alexander Street
Crows Nest NSW 2065
Australia
Phone: (61 2) 8425 0100
Fax: (61 2) 9906 2218
Email: info@allenandunwin.com
Web: www.allenandunwin.com

National Library of Australia
Cataloguing-in-Publication entry:

Murray, Kirsty.
Becoming Billy Dare.

For children.
ISBN 1 86508 735 1.

I. Title. (Series: Murray, Kirsty. Children of the wind; bk. 2).

A823.3

Designed by Ruth Grüner
Set in 10.7 pt Sabon by Ruth Grüner
Printed by McPherson's Printing Group, Maryborough, Victoria

1 3 5 7 9 10 8 6 4 2

Teachers' notes available from www.allenandunwin.com

Contents

Acknowledgements

As with each of the books in this series, there are countless people who helped me bring Paddy's story to life.

In Ireland: Father Padraig O'Fiannachta, Con Moriarty, Gerry O'Leary, the Clarke/O'Neill family, Alice Perceval, Margaret Hoctor, Ruth Lawler, Angela Long, Paddy Hines, Patrick Sutton, Colm Quinn and Oliver P. Murphy.

In Australia: Judy Brett, Graham Smith, Joanna Leahy, Peter Freund, Jocelyn Ainslie, Ben Boyd, Don Blackwood, Reuben Legge, Matthew Taft, Penni Russon, Sarah Brenan, Rosalind Price, and with loving memories of Helena Holec.

The list of authors and historians whose understandings of the past I depended on is too long to detail but I would particularly like to acknowledge the work of Michael Cannon, Andrew Brown-May, Mark St Leon and Margaret Williams.

For enriching my research by making their archives and collections available I would like to acknowledge the State Library of Victoria, the Caroline Chisholm Library, the Performing Arts Museum, All Hallows College, Dublin, the National Library of Ireland and Belvedere College.

The poem that John Doherty and Mr Maloney teach Paddy is 'The Stolen Child' by William Butler Yeats. The poem that Paddy translates from Latin is an eleventh-century Invocation by Bishop Patrick that was sourced from *The Writings of Bishop Patrick 1074–1084*, ed. Aubrey Gwynn, and translated from the Latin by Ben Boyd. The song that the shearers sing with Paddy and Violet is from *Waratah and Wattle* by Henry Lawson. On page 223, Paddy also briefly quotes Macbeth.

I would also like to acknowledge the support of the Australia Council.

And to the thieves who stole the first draft, thanks for teaching me that a good story is more than simply words on a page.

Every book is an adventure, a trial and a great joy. Thanks to my family for sharing the ups and downs of this one: Ken, Ruby, Billy, Elwyn, Isobel, Romanie and Theo.

To Theodore William Harper,

philosopher, actor and inspiration

I

Goodness

Paddy opened the carriage window and stuck his head out, feeling the cold wind whip his face.

'You daring me still?' he called over his shoulder. 'You know I'll prove you wrong, Mick.'

Mick stepped away from the rush of cold air. 'I dare you then. Go on,' he said, his teeth chattering.

'Pull the blinds down in the compartment,' instructed Paddy, 'and if the conductor comes by, mind you don't let him shut the window.' He undid the buttons of his soutane, and shoved the long black robes into Mick's hands. The ground rushed away beneath him as he slipped through the narrow opening, reached up to the edge of the carriage and hoisted himself onto the roof. The smell of coal was strong. He had to stretch his arms wide to keep himself from sliding sideways. For a moment he lay flat on his belly, his eyes stinging from the smoke and wind. He pressed his cheek against the cold metal and thought of that moment at Gort when he'd hugged his mother one last time, feeling the smallness of her, like a frail bird.

The whistle blew as the train veered around a bend and Paddy found he was sliding towards the edge. His shirt rode up and his bare skin scraped against the metal. He could hear Mick calling and he groped for a hand-hold, curling his fingers over a narrow ridge.

'Sweet Jesus,' he muttered, as he lowered his legs over the side, 'please don't let him have shut the window.' Then his feet found the ledge and he scrambled back inside, laughing with relief.

Mick sat down on the dark leather seat, put his head in his hands and groaned.

'Sure I thought you were dead, Paddy Delaney. And how was I to be telling my parents that the little priest had jumped out a window!'

'I didn't jump, I'm not a priest yet and you owe me sixpence.'

Mick sighed. 'My good pennies for America wasted on a mad Irishman.'

Paddy buttoned up his soutane and sat down beside Mick. 'How can you be grudging me sixpence when you're about to have the time of your life and I'm bound to studying for years and years?'

'And how will you be taking a vow of poverty and obedience, when you've always been the one for taking a dare and robbing an innocent soul of his pennies?'

'That was the last bet you'll ever lose to me, Michael MacNamara. I'm turning over a new leaf. I promised my mam I'd be good. I'm giving up playing the devil.'

'So you say,' said Mick, handing over the sixpence. 'But the devil is good to his own.'

'God's truth!' swore Paddy, 'Once I'm in Dublin, I'm going to be a new man.'

Mick folded his arms across his chest. 'Well now, if

that's the last bet I'll be losing to you, I'll wager I can beat you in a wrestle.'

Paddy laughed and jumped on Mick. 'We're not in Dublin yet!'

The engine blew a blast of steam into the chill afternoon air. Paddy studied the faces of the people hurrying along the platform, wondering how to find his uncle, but when he saw a bald man with intensely blue eyes and a face as red as scoured brick striding towards him, he knew it had to be Uncle Kevin. Hurrying to catch up was a small, brown-haired woman.

'Patrick Delaney, is it?' Uncle Kevin clamped a thick hand on Paddy's shoulders and turned him sideways and then straight on, as if he was a prize specimen.

'You're a big lad for your age,' he said. He gestured to the woman. 'This here is your Aunt Lil.'

'It's grand to meet you, Aunt Lil. My mammy sends her kind regards.'

Aunt Lil stared at him, her expression startled. 'Sure but we're glad you've come at last.' Her hand trembled a little as she reached out and touched Paddy's cheek and then his hair. 'No one warned us you'd be such a handsome one! Bless you, look at this hair, Kevin, it's like pure gold!'

Paddy smiled. 'I used to have curls, but a boy can't be going to school with curls, so Mam cut them off on my last night home.'

'It must have broke her heart to see those golden locks fall.'

'Sure, she was crying as she swept them up,' said Paddy, grinning.

Uncle Kevin snorted. 'Don't be fussing now,' he said gruffly. 'You'll make the boy as vain as his father.'

Paddy fought down the sharp reply that leapt to mind. He'd promised his mother he would give up answering back to his elders, along with all his other bad habits.

Uncle Kevin turned and led the way, shouldering through the crowd like a bull amongst cattle. Outside the station, he hailed a cab, driven by a man in a battered top hat. Paddy's bad mood dissolved as he leant out of the window, excited by his first sight of Dublin with its clattering trams and streets thronged with people. When the cab crossed over the Liffey River, Paddy leant so far out that Uncle Kevin grabbed him by the scruff of the neck and hauled him back in.

'You're not a wild goat from the Burren any more, young man. You're a seminary boy, or soon enough will be. They won't be standing any nonsense at St Columcille's.'

Paddy slumped in his seat and eyed Uncle Kevin with annoyance. It was obviously going to be harder to be good when Uncle Kevin was around. He was relieved when the cab pulled up outside a tall, narrow shop with a canvas awning and wooden trim painted dark green. Above the door, in gold lettering were the words *K.M. Cassidy, Tobacconist.*

Paddy jumped out of the cab and stood staring through the plate-glass window at the display – pipes with carved ebony bowls, pipes with bone handles, tobacco tins of all sizes, boxes of cigars, and even special knives for cutting tobacco. When the door of the shop swung open, a rich, heady scent drifted into the street. Paddy breathed deeply, savouring the aroma. It reminded him of his father. The only memory Paddy had, from when he was very small, was of a man lying down beside him on a big bed beneath a window and the scent of tobacco was all around them.

A maid took Uncle Kevin's hat and cane from him as they entered the flat above the shop, and then disappeared with Aunt Lil. In his study, Uncle Kevin settled down in one of the deep armchairs before the coal fire and gestured for Paddy to take the other. The odours of old leather and stale smoke were thick in the air. Uncle Kevin pulled out a pipe from his pocket and began packing it with tobacco.

'This is a great day, Patrick, a great day.'

Paddy wasn't sure if he was meant to say anything. He wriggled uncomfortably in the deep armchair. Uncle Kevin leant forward and rested one hand on Paddy's knee.

'What is the happiest moment in a man's life?' he asked.

'When he receives his first communion?'

'Aye, that's the happiest moment.'

Paddy tried to think back to his first communion, but all he could recall was the cake that his mother had made for the celebration. Uncle Kevin took a silver-framed photo from the mantelpiece and handed it to Paddy.

Two pale-eyed boys, as alike as any human beings could be, stared out at Paddy. They were dressed in dark clothes, and their faces were as still as corpses, their figures shadowy against the faded background.

'That's your Uncle Patrick and me on our happiest day. And there's only one day that would have been happier. If Patrick had lived to take his vows, sure that would have been a blessed occasion and we would already have a priest in the family. You know, your Uncle Patrick told me he could hear the voice of God calling him. If he had lived, he would have been the finest priest in all Ireland. A bishop, an archbishop even. Perhaps, Rome.'

He took the photo from Paddy and placed it reverently back on the mantelpiece.

'And now we have you. Your mam has said you were for the church ever since you were born. And here you are, off to St Columcille's, the first step on the great journey. Sure, your Uncle Patrick never had such a grand opportunity. The Jesuits will make a great man of you, Patrick.'

Paddy pulled at the collar of his soutane and frowned. He hated being called Patrick. It made him feel as if he were living in the shadow of his lost uncle. He wished Aunt Lil would call them for tea.

Uncle Kevin crossed the room and pulled open a drawer in his desk.

'There's something here I want you to have, Patrick. Something I've been saving.'

Paddy stood up and Uncle Kevin took his hand, turning his palm over and then folding it shut on a string of well-thumbed coloured-glass rosary beads.

'They were your Uncle Patrick's,' he said, his blue eyes growing watery.

'Thank you,' said Paddy, uncomfortably. There was something macabre about the touch of the cold rosary beads. It was as if he was putting on a dead man's shoes. He shuddered and slipped the rosary into his pocket.

2

Into the dark

Paddy was glad when Aunt Lil pushed the door open and came in with the tea things.

'Sure, Aunt Lil, this is a feast!' he said.

Aunt Lil laughed. Over tea, she asked him all about the long journey from the summer fields of the Burren and laughed again when he described the hapless Liam O'Flaherty and his broken-down cart struggling to get them to Gort in time for the train. She urged him to eat up, pressing more cream biscuits on him.

The shop bell rang and Uncle Kevin stood up.

'You can stop your fussing, Lil. John's here to take the boy,' he announced.

Down in the street, Uncle Kevin slung Paddy's bag into the old cart parked by the kerbside.

'This here is John Doherty.' Uncle Kevin nodded at the driver, a long-faced man with black hair cropped close under his cap. 'I can't be leaving the shop, so John will be taking you out to St Columcille's. Every Sunday, after mass, he'll bring you to us for your dinner and then return you to college in the evening. You're to mind him, boy. Mind John on the journey, and mind the Fathers and the Brothers at the college. And remember us in your prayers.'

Aunt Lil tapped Paddy awkwardly on the arm. 'Sure, but we'll be looking forward to next Sunday, Patrick.'

Paddy could tell she wasn't used to hugging children. He thought of his mother and the way she always hugged him before they parted, even if he was only heading out to play.

'Hurry along then,' said Uncle Kevin. 'Don't be keeping John waiting.'

The cart moved out into the city traffic. They crossed the Liffey again and Paddy twisted around to stare back at the statue of a man who stood watching over Sackville Street.

'Who's that monument of, then?' asked Paddy.

'Who else but the great man himself, Dan O'Connell,' replied the carter.

'He was a great man, it's true,' said Paddy. 'I'm hoping to be a great man myself one day – a priest.'

'A priest, you say?' John Doherty turned to smile at Paddy, his brown eyes creasing. He pulled out his pipe, stuffed it full of tobacco, and lit up.

Paddy put his elbows on his knees and leant forward in his seat, staring at the road ahead. 'One day, I'm going to be a missionary. I'm come from Clare to study for the priesthood. My mam says there's a million heathen in Africa that need saving so I'll be off in Africa, sailing the rivers and slashing through the jungles.'

'Wisha, if one of my little nephews were to be a holy priest, I'd be right proud that he'd been called.'

'Well, I haven't exactly been called yet. See, I was the

first and the only one of my mam's boys not to die. All the others, seven of them, they all went to God, and Mam promised him that if I was to live, then the Holy Church would have me.'

'Your mother's a good woman, to be parting with her only child.'

'Oh, there's still my sister Honor at home. She's been away in Belfast since I was small but she's come back now to be with Mam. Mam says my dad and all those dead brothers that are with Jesus, they're watching over me and on account of them, she says I'll be saving souls in Africa.'

'Africa, you say,' said John Doherty, and he laughed, a short bark of a laugh that quickly turned into a hacking cough. He spat a wad of dark spit onto the road and wiped his mouth on the back of his sleeve.

'Sorry, lad,' he said as he continued to cough, his breath coming in short gasps. Paddy took the reins until John's breathing settled to a steady, wheezing rhythm.

'It's good to see the open fields,' said John, waving his hand.

Paddy nodded and handed back the reins.

'At home, I like best to be out of doors, under the open sky.'

'Ain't it bleak, all that stone and wind on the Burren? Sure this soft green is sweeter,' said John.

'No, it's not what you think. The granite is grand to climb and the wind blows off the sea and round the grey hills and you can run wild across the stone. On a clear day, you can see the Arran Isles and they look like fairy kingdoms. It's not bleak at all.'

John Doherty nodded. 'Mr Yeats, he's a poet that writes

about your piece of the country. Sure if I didn't read a poem that puts your home in mind.

> *Away with us he's going,*
> *The solemn-eyed:*
> *He'll hear no more the lowing*
> *Of the calves on the warm hillside*
> *Or the kettle on the hob*
> *Sing peace into his breast,*
> *Or see the brown mice bob*
> *Round and round the oatmeal-chest . . .*

The words filled Paddy with a melancholy longing for his home. He thought of his mother and their very last conversation. 'Remember, Paddy,' she had said, 'the greatest person in all the world is the priest, the only one who can bring God to men, like the angels. May the Lord kindle the flame in your heart and fill you with his goodness, darling boy.'

'Don't worry, Mam. From now on, I'll be as good as the blessed angels themselves.'

It was dark by the time they turned in through the gates of St Columcille's College.

'There you go, young Paddy. Over there's the little seminary where you'll be stopping. And over that way, past the chapel, that's where the great seminary lies, where the young men become priests.'

The college was set in the middle of a park, with a winding driveway. It was more imposing than Paddy had imagined. Through the spread of leaves and branches, the long, four-storey building was lit up like a palace. Further away, beyond the chapel, was an even grander building that folded around a central quadrangle and had more windows than Paddy had ever seen. Suddenly, his chest felt tight and his breath short. He wished he was driving through the winding roads of the Burren with only the small light of his home before them and not the great college.

Paddy couldn't believe this place would be his home for years to come. He counted them up on his fingers – six years at the junior school, the place John Doherty called the little seminary, and then at least six more years at the great seminary. That was the same length of time that he'd been alive; a whole lifetime. It was like looking into a long, dark tunnel and praying that there truly would be a light at the end.

3

Small temptations

Paddy stood outside the refectory with Father O'Keefe as the boys filed into the hallway. Paddy watched their faces, wondering how long it would take for him to feel he belonged with them.

'Fitzgerald,' called Father O'Keefe. 'Over here.'

A tall, red-headed boy ducked out of the column of students.

'This is Patrick Delaney. Master Delaney, this is Master Edward Fitzgerald. He is a prefect in the third line and a member of the Sodality of the Holy Angels. You will find he is in a number of your classes. Fitzgerald, take Delaney to the dormitories. He's to have the bed next to MacCrae.'

Paddy followed Fitzgerald up the stairs. From behind he looked powerfully built with wide shoulders, as though he might be a champion football player.

'You can call me Paddy.'

'Not likely,' said the other boy tersely. 'And don't you try calling me anything other than Fitzgerald.'

Fitzgerald showed Paddy where he could store his things and explained the evening routine. 'And you'd best be taking off that costume too,' he said, nodding at Paddy's soutane.

'Haven't your parents bought you the uniform yet?'

'Sure, I have it on underneath. But my mam thought I should wear the soutane, seeing as that's why I'm here.'

Fitzgerald raised one eyebrow. 'So your people want you to be a priest? A Jesuit?'

'Well, yes.' Paddy blushed and looked at his hands.

'You're no more than twelve. How can you know that you're worthy?'

Paddy put his hands on his hips. 'I'm thirteen. And priest or no priest, I reckon I'm worth two of you.'

They stood eyeing each other off, each trying to decide if the other was worth punching.

Somewhere outside a bell began to ring, echoing in the cold night air.

'That's the bell for prayers,' said Fitzgerald. 'Come along.'

Kneeling in the chapel, Paddy was glad that he'd taken off his soutane. None of the other boys wore one. The air in the chapel smelt sweet and cold. He bent his head in prayer and prayed that Christ would call out for him and prove Fitzgerald an idiot. He wished he could have told Fitzgerald outright that of course he had been called. If only he could be as sure of his vocation as Mam and Uncle Kevin seemed to be.

Next morning, Paddy woke feeling tense with excitement. The long dormitory with its high, arched ceilings buzzed with noise. Paddy dressed quickly, and followed the slim, pale boy who had the bed opposite, down the stairs and along the corridors to chapel again. The Rector delivered a spiritual lecture, and then mass was held before the day's classes began. Bells rang every hour, clanging loudly through the old building.

Paddy had studied at the little National School near his village and had even had extra lessons in Latin and Greek with the parish priest, but he was far behind the other boys at St Columcille's. By midday, his hands stung from the six sharp cuts that the master had dealt him in Latin class for giving the wrong answer and another six in Algebra for talking when he should have been working.

In Religious Education, he sat beside the small boy called MacCrae who slept next to him in the dormitory. Paddy had noticed him in other classes, working with his head down, while everyone else shifted restlessly on the wooden benches. MacCrae's concentration never flickered. While Father O'Keefe wrote out a biblical quote on the blackboard with his back turned to the class, Fitzgerald reached over from the seat behind them and cuffed MacCrae hard across the head. Even then, MacCrae didn't respond but went on patiently writing, making sure each letter was beautifully formed. Every time the master turned his back on the class, Fitzgerald reached forward and cuffed MacCrae again. Still the boy did nothing. Paddy stared at him, wondering why he didn't at least say something. When Fitzgerald hit MacCrae for a third time, Paddy grew exasperated.

'Leave him alone,' he said in a low voice.

'Shut up, Delaney,' whispered Fitzgerald, right into Paddy's ear. 'You don't know anything yet. MacCrae's a girl. Someone's got to knock some of the stuffing out of him. He thinks he's holier than the lot of us.'

Paddy hated the hot feeling of Fitzgerald's breath in his ear. 'It wouldn't be hard to be holier than you,' he said. He turned in his seat and pushed Fitzgerald so forcefully that the big boy fell off the bench and sprawled on the wooden floor.

The master came sweeping down the length of the classroom, the wings of his soutane flying out behind him. The shiny black leather belt he kept for flogging the boys flashed at his side. Paddy shrank back, expecting to be hauled from his seat, but Father O'Keefe didn't look at him.

'Fitzgerald! You deserved that and worse. I am neither blind nor a fool, and you will live to regret ever assuming I am such. Hold out your hand.'

Paddy flinched as each blow fell on Fitzgerald's outstretched palm. Then Father O'Keefe turned to Paddy.

'Delaney, no doubt you thought it noble to intervene on MacCrae's account, but it is very presumptuous of you to sit in judgment of others when you cannot even keep your own copybook clean. You will kneel beside Fitzgerald for the remainder of the class.'

Paddy stepped out into the aisle and knelt on the hard wooden floorboards, relieved that he was to be spared. MacCrae glanced down at him and nodded before turning back to his work.

When the bell rang for recess, the boys swarmed out to the open playing field behind the college.

As Fitzgerald ran past Paddy and into the yard, he punched him lightly on the shoulder. 'No hard feelings, Delaney. You're game, even if you are an idiot,' he said.

Paddy rubbed his shoulder and smiled to himself. He wandered over to the playing field, watching the other boys chasing a football. Paddy was contemplating joining the footballers when MacCrae approached him.

'Thank you,' said MacCrae, pushing his glasses up

his nose, 'but there's no need for you to be sinning on my account. Sure, Fitzgerald makes my blood boil when he baits me. But if I hit him back, then I'll know he's beaten me.'

'It's no sin to give Fitzgerald what he deserves,' said Paddy.

'*For with what judgment you judge, you shall be judged; and with what measure you mete, it shall be measured to you again.* Matthew 7:2,' said MacCrae seriously.

'Look here, MacCrae, you can't be a saint every minute of the day.'

'It's different for me. I have to try. I want to be a man of God. I want to be a priest.'

'Well, most of the priests would as soon strap you as look at you!'

'They're chastising us to make us better men. It's not the same.'

Paddy stared at MacCrae, perplexed. As the tangled mass of footballers came racing past, Paddy dived into the fray, relieved to end the conversation. But MacCrae's words stayed with him.

That night when the Prefect of Studies said goodnight and switched out the light in the dormitory, Paddy lay thinking. The flickering gas lamp in the corridor shed a tunnel of light into the room and he could faintly make out MacCrae's profile silhouetted in the half-darkness.

'MacCrae,' he said.

'We're not meant to talk,' whispered MacCrae in reply. 'There's no talking allowed in the dormitories.'

'MacCrae, what do your family want you to do when you grow up?'

MacCrae sighed. 'We shouldn't be talking,' he said again.

'But have they said what's to become of you?' asked Paddy. 'You're clever enough to be anything.'

There was a short silence and then MacCrae relented. 'My father's a doctor, so I think he'd like it if I followed him into medicine. But I don't want to. I want to be a Jesuit. I know Father will say I'm too young to be sure if I have a vocation. But I am sure.'

'Why do you think you have a vocation?' asked Paddy.

'I was walking home from mass of a Sunday morning last year, and the sun cut through the low cloud and it was more than the clouds parting in the sky, it was like a light filling me up inside. I knew.'

'So you heard his voice? You heard God speak to you?'

'Not exactly,' said MacCrae. 'But that's when I knew.'

Paddy slipped out of bed and knelt on the cold floor. He folded his hands and began to pray. Even though he had already said his nightly prayers, he repeated them and then prayed the acts of faith, hope and charity. All around him, the other boys drifted off to sleep. Paddy felt he was pouring all of himself into the prayer but no lightness came to him. The words swam around and around in his mind. It was as if a fog rose up inside his head and the words simply moved aimlessly through the mist. Even when he was trying his hardest to concentrate on God, his thoughts began to drift, he lost his place and suddenly he was thinking about conjugating a Latin verb, or how much he'd disliked the watery cabbage at dinner. How would he ever be able to save the heathens in Africa if he couldn't see the light himself? He pulled Uncle Patrick's beads from under his pillow and tolled through the Rosary, finding some comfort in the smoothness of the glass and the simplicity of the prayers. Perhaps he'd see the light another day.

Mr Maloney was neither priest nor brother. He wore a small white flower in his lapel and his smile was gentle. Every Thursday, he came up from Dublin to teach the boys elocution. He entered the classroom on crutches, swinging his limp, wizened legs ahead of him. When he was settled behind the rostrum, he opened a small green book.

> '*Come away, O human child! To the*
> *waters and the wild*
> *With a faery, hand in hand,*
> *For the world's more full of weeping*
> *than you can understand.*'

The classroom fell absolutely silent as he read. His voice had a warmth and resonance that stilled even the least attentive boy.

'Can anyone tell me something about that poem?'

Paddy put his hand up. 'It's by Mr Yeats, sir. I believe it's called *The Stolen Child*.'

MacCrae glanced across at Paddy with a look of surprise on his face. He was usually the first one to put his hand up to answer a question.

'Very good. Delaney, isn't it? I didn't think any of you boys would be familiar with it,' said Mr Maloney. 'But to business, gentleman. I should like you all to consider the salutary sound of the letter "O", as in *O human child*. Not the nasty little gargle in the back of your throat that is so often heard in the school yard, but a full-bodied, beautifully rounded vowel that conveys beauty and longing.'

One of the boys snickered, but Mr Maloney only smiled and nodded. Then the whole class practised pronouncing a beautiful 'O'. Fitzgerald looked like a fish as he grunted out the sounds. MacCrae's 'O' was a tiny little note of surprise but Paddy found it easy to imitate Mr Maloney's perfectly formed vowels.

When they'd finished working their way through the warm-up sounds, the boys took turns reciting poems before the class. Some of them looked as if they'd be happier getting strapped. Paddy watched with interest, noting each boy's strength or weakness.

They were all assigned a different poem to learn for the following class. Paddy flipped open his book and found the one Mr Maloney had picked for him. It took him only a minute to memorise it. The words seemed to pour into his head like warm, sweet honey.

'Sir,' he said, putting up his hand. 'I've already memorised mine. Could I recite it now or shall I save it for next week?'

Mr Maloney looked at him appraisingly. 'I should very much like to hear it, Delaney. But I shan't be impressed if you are simply bragging. Give me your book, and step up before the class.'

The boys were very still as Paddy smoothly recited the poem. When he had finished, he glanced across at Mr Maloney. 'Was that all right, sir?'

Mr Maloney smiled, his face alight with pleasure. 'You have a remarkable facility, Delaney. I believe I will have to assign you extra lines to test this gift of yours.'

Fitzgerald rolled his eyes and sneered, with a 'serves you right, you show-off' expression but Paddy laughed as he sat down again. Learning poetry was not the sort of work he minded. It was a relief to do something easy, something that might earn him some credit with the masters. It wasn't like that in the other classes. Even Fitzgerald didn't spend as much time on his knees as Paddy.

On Saturday morning, as the boys poured out of the dormitories for morning sport, Paddy spotted Fitzgerald, cornered by Father O'Keefe in the stairwell. The long folds of the priest's soutane fell behind him, brushing against the banister railing. The Jesuits' soutanes were of a special kind with long black 'wings' of material that fell gracefully from the elbows. When they moved quickly through the corridors of the college, the black fabric would fly out behind them, as if the holy men were about to take flight.

As Paddy climbed the stairs, he became aware of the perfect, tempting alignment between the 'wings' of Father O'Keefe's soutane and the banister. It was impossible to resist. Fitzgerald glanced across, lifting his eyebrows in alarm when he realised what Paddy was about to attempt. Paddy winked. It took only a moment for him to tether the edge of Father O'Keefe's soutane to the balustrade, and bound up to the next landing.

He laughed to himself, but too soon.

'Delaney!' roared the priest.

His heart sinking, Paddy gripped the banister and cursed under his breath. He'd done it again – landed himself in trouble for no good reason. Why couldn't he resist even small temptations? He'd never manage to keep his promise to Mam at this rate. He sighed and turned to face his punishment.

4

Sanctuary dove

On Sunday morning, after mass, Paddy stood at the dormitory windows and saw the long, gaunt figure of John Doherty sitting on his cart at the college gates. Paddy ran down the winding driveway, kicking the falling autumn leaves ahead of him.

'So, little priest,' said John Doherty. 'Tell me what you learned during your week. Sure, but it's a grand college. Why, you might turn out to be like the blessed St Columcille himself, a sanctuary dove.'

Paddy laughed and climbed up on the bench beside John. 'Praying and studying hard, that's all I've been doing,' answered Paddy. 'Mass every day, the Angelus every morning, noon and evening, and every class or study beginning with a prayer. And the catechism too, I'm studying that every day.'

He was careful to keep his hands folded in his lap so that John couldn't see the cuts that criss-crossed his palms from yesterday's caning. 'I was hoping you'd have a poem to tell me on the ride. I've learnt some fine poems in our elocution class. Mr Maloney says if I keep up with my reciting, I'm sure to win a part in the Christmas play.'

John Doherty grinned. He smelt faintly of Guinness, even though it was still early in the day. 'Ah, the Christmas play – the theatre – that's a world of magic. Sure, if I didn't see the Rose of the World in the streets of Dublin last night, 'tis Miss Laura Dane, the famous singer. She came out of her theatre and the young men who'd been at the show, they leapt in front of her carriage and pulled her through the streets of Dublin, cheering. Sure if it's not the grandest thing, to make people happy the way Miss Dane does. I followed them too, all of us shouting her name, and then she sang from the balcony of her hotel while we was watching. I'd give my eyes to have heard her sing all the long night.' He glanced across at Paddy.

''Tis not the sort of conversation I should be having with a young priest.'

'Don't be worrying yourself, John Doherty. I'm not one yet,' said Paddy. 'Besides, when I do take the vows, I'll have to hear confession from murderers and thieves and heathens, so there's nothing for you to concern yourself with in telling me about you and Miss Dane.'

John Doherty laughed. 'Sure, you'll make a fine priest, Paddy, being quick to forgive an old sinner like me.'

It started to rain as John Doherty dropped Paddy off outside Cassidy's Tobacconist. Paddy rang the bell, and Aunt Lil let him in. 'You must be quick now,' she said, wiping her hands on her apron as she hurried up the stairs. 'The others will be here any moment and I'm late with your uncle's dinner.'

'Shall I help you in the kitchen?' asked Paddy.

Aunt Lil stopped on the step above and turned to gaze down at him.

'How can you be having the heart of an angel as well as

the face of one? Fancy wanting to help your old Aunt Lil! But the kitchen is no place for a boy, all the same.'

'I miss helping Mam with the supper so it would be a treat you'd be giving me.'

In the kitchen, Paddy rolled up his sleeves and set to work slicing and buttering the brown bread Aunt Lil set before him and then opening the oysters. He cut the small, firm muscle that held the shells shut, slipped a knife in to ease them open and then arranged the oysters on a big blue-and-white platter. Aunt Lil scurried around the table, directing the maid to tend to this and that and exclaiming anxiously as she lifted the lids of the pots. She reminded Paddy of one of the frightened rabbits that he used to snare on the Burren. Kathleen, the maid, quickly grew exasperated with Aunt Lil's fussing. When Aunt Lil's back was turned, she winked at Paddy and then rolled her eyes.

Paddy heard the sound of the shop door opening and a heavy footfall on the stairs.

'Oh my goodness!' cried Aunt Lil. 'There's your Uncle Kevin and Mr Coogan already. They've been taking their constitutional and they'll be hungry as lions but there's still Miss Eileen Ryan to come.' She bustled out of the kitchen.

'So you're the nephew,' said Kathleen, smiling at Paddy. 'You surely don't take after your Uncle Kevin.'

'No, I take after my father,' said Paddy.

'Well, he must have been a handsome devil. Pity to waste such a pretty face on a priest.'

She reached over to pinch his cheek, and laughed at Paddy's embarrassment as he wiped away a smudge of flour. Uncle Kevin shouted from the dining room, wanting to know where his Sunday dinner and Paddy were. Aunt

23 ⤙

Lil reappeared in the kitchen full of anxious frenzy, hands fluttering and then hurried Paddy out.

The dining room table was set with the best gilt-edged china, crisp linen napkins and polished silverware. Paddy took his seat between Mr Coogan and Uncle Kevin, suddenly feeling like a little boy again between the two big men.

Uncle Kevin asked Paddy to say grace. Paddy kept his eyes shut a moment longer than everyone else and added an extra silent prayer that the dinner wouldn't go on too long.

Kathleen came in with the platter of oysters and Uncle Kevin set upon them with gusto.

'The best oysters in the world come from Galway Bay,' announced Uncle Kevin. 'You know that, don't you, Patrick?' He tipped his head back and sucked an oyster off its shell.

'At home, Mam fries them or puts them in a pie.'

'There's a lot you'll be having to learn now you're here, in Dublin, away from your mammy's apron strings. And the first thing I'm to teach you is how to savour an oyster. Eat up, boy!' Uncle Kevin nodded at Paddy's plate.

Paddy stared at the silvery-grey mollusc in front of him and then took a deep breath before tipping it into his mouth. He didn't chew it. The shorter the length of time it was in his throat, the better. It was like swallowing a big lump of snot. Uncle Kevin looked at Paddy's expression and laughed.

'This boy,' said Uncle Kevin to Mr Coogan and Miss Ryan, slapping Paddy on the back, 'this nephew of mine, he's bound for great things. Bound for the priesthood. My sister's lad. His mother, poor soul, has not a penny to her name, and her husband long dead and all her hopes tied up with the child. So I brought the boy to Dublin. A fine education he's getting, thanks to our pennies and the Jesuits. And one day he'll be one of God's chosen, won't you, Patrick?'

'I hope so, Uncle Kevin,' said Paddy, feeling faintly uneasy. 'I'm to be a missionary and save the souls of the heathens in Africa.'

Uncle Kevin coughed. 'Or maybe you'll be a great man, here in Ireland, a bishop, an archbishop even. They may keep us Catholics down as hard as they like, but no one can keep a good Jesuit down.'

'Mam says the Africans need saving,' said Paddy. 'If I'm to be a priest, I'd like to go to Africa.'

Uncle Kevin looked at Paddy as if he'd turned into a strange species of animal.

'It's a long way off yet,' said Aunt Lil, soothingly. 'Patrick's got many years of study before he takes his vows. I'm sure he'll make the right decisions when the time comes.'

Miss Ryan leant a little towards Aunt Lil. 'Surely he would have been better off in the junior seminary of St Colman's at Fermoy, if you're sure it's the priesthood for him. The Jesuits will want him for so many years of study and they're much more particular about who they accept into the order. I'll wager not many of their boys are country lads from the Burren. And the cost of St Columcille's, well . . .'

'Time and cost be damned,' interrupted Uncle Kevin. 'I've worked hard for this. My brother, it was a Jesuit he wanted to be, learned and wise, a trained soldier of Christ. And young Patrick is to be the same.' Paddy squirmed uncomfortably in his seat.

Miss Ryan and Uncle Kevin began arguing about the different strengths of St Colman's versus St Columcille's.

Mr Coogan was staring at his plate. Paddy couldn't read his expression at all. Uncle Kevin noticed his friend's silence.

'What is it, Mr Coogan, that robs you of your speech?'

'Is it more priests the country is needing?' said Mr Coogan. 'Sure the way they're still speaking of Parnell, this country will never be free while they rule the hearts and minds of the people.'

'The priests speak the truth. The man was not a patriot.'

Mr Coogan laid his spoon by his plate and his expression clouded.

'My nephew will be a true patriot,' said Uncle Kevin in a steely voice. 'He will be a priest and speak the truth. Parnell was a disgrace to his country and his family. Patrick will make this family proud.'

A heavy silence fell on the table and all eyes turned on Paddy. Paddy froze, with his spoon halfway to his mouth. He knew he was expected to offer some sort of confirmation, but he simply lowered his spoon and stared miserably at his plate. Under the table, he rubbed his hands together and felt the sting of swollen flesh.

The afternoon dragged on and the light outside the window faded. Mr Coogan left early and Paddy was made to sit with Uncle Kevin while he smoked his pipe in a fug of bad temper. When Kathleen finally announced that John Doherty was waiting in the street, he grabbed his jacket from the hall stand, kissed Aunt Lil on the cheek, and shouted a hurried goodbye to Uncle Kevin. He took the stairs two at a time.

'Sure, you were quick with your farewells. I've never seen a boy so mad to get back to his studying,' exclaimed John Doherty as Paddy jumped up onto the cart beside him.

Paddy laughed grimly. 'How else will I become a sanctuary dove?'

As the cart trundled out of Dublin, Paddy shut his eyes and wished he really was a dove with wings that could lift him to the sky and take him far away from the weight of everyone's hopes and expectations.

5

Wise men and fools

Paddy was dreading the midwinter examinations. He tried hard to concentrate in study hall but when Fitzgerald came and sat beside him, he couldn't help being distracted and they spent most of the study time surreptitiously passing notes back and forth. And then there was the school play. Paddy was cast as the court jester. It was much more interesting practising his jokes than studying algebra and Latin.

The evening of the performance, a crowd of parents and relatives arrived outside the chapel, their breath steamy on the crisp night air. Inside the vestry, the boys swarmed around Brother Francis as he applied make-up to their faces, exaggerating their features with dark sticks of waxy pencil and pots of face powder.

Paddy looked in the mirror and laughed at the high, pointed eyebrows Brother Francis had drawn. His hair had started to grow back and a single wayward curl stuck out from under the jester's cap. Mam would be pleased to see that.

'Delaney,' said Brother Francis, 'stop preening. You'll be on in a moment!'

The band struck up and Paddy cartwheeled onto the

stage. The audience erupted with laughter at the sight of him and Paddy swept low in a bow.

'*The snow pities neither wise men nor fools,*
Yet grace and a cod-piece,
Brave all for good Christian faith
Heigh-ho kind folk, for the story unfolds . . .'

His head felt light, almost like a fever, and every inch of his skin tingled. The senior student who was playing King Wenceslas strode onto the stage and Paddy bowed low. Every scene went smoothly and Paddy didn't miss a single cue. He even managed to help the King, whispering the first words of the older boy's speech when he faltered. When the curtain fell at the end, the audience burst into applause. Paddy shut his eyes and drank in the sound, wanting the moment to last forever. He didn't want to go back to being just another ordinary schoolboy.

There was a light supper for the students and their families in the refectory. It was strange how ordinary everyone looked to him now that they were no longer part of the audience or the play.

Paddy was scanning the crowd in search of Uncle Kevin and Aunt Lil when he overhead someone mention his name. It was an elegant-looking woman talking to Father O'Keefe.

'But Father! Imagine how I felt when I discovered that young Delaney's uncle is my husband's tobacconist! Edward has been talking about this boy rather a lot in his letters home, and I am most concerned that no undue intimacy should arise between them. The Fitzgerald family, as you know, is a family of gentlemen. It simply wouldn't do for that boy to be latching onto Edward.'

Paddy blushed with anger and waited for Father O'Keefe's response.

'Put your mind at rest, dear Mrs Fitzgerald,' said the priest. 'I'm sure their association will be brief. Young Delaney is a gifted young actor, as you may have noted from his performance tonight. I am sure your Edward will quickly lose interest in the friendship when he realises Delaney is destined to outshine him in so many things.'

Paddy bit his lip to stop himself from laughing. He wondered ruefully if Father O'Keefe would have defended him if he had seen his exam results. Then Paddy spotted Uncle Kevin and Aunt Lil, standing at the end of the long supper table. Aunt Lil looked as nervous as always, clutching a small, old-fashioned evening purse and blinking like a startled animal. Uncle Kevin looked even redder in the face than usual and the top of his bald head seemed extra shiny.

Aunt Lil's eyes grew teary when Paddy approached.

'Oh Patrick,' she exclaimed, patting him on the arm. 'How I cried when you made your speech at the end, about King Wenceslas and the fate of the good in this cruel world. And then I realised, I was sitting next to Lady Fitzgerald! Fancy that! Sure, I dried my eyes and made sure I didn't shame you.'

Uncle Kevin shook his hand stiffly.

'No harm in a bit of Christmas fun, I suppose,' he said. 'Your Uncle Patrick would have been surprised to know this sort of thing goes on in a Jesuit school, but I'm sure your masters know best.'

Paddy felt deflated. If only Mam had been there, she

would have hugged him and told him how wonderful he was. And as to Lady Fitzgerald, Mam wouldn't have even noticed or cared if she was sitting next to her. Mam would have had eyes only for him.

The next Sunday, Uncle Kevin said, 'Now, I know you might have been imagining that you'd be going home to see your mam in the holidays. But I've decided we'll have you here with us for Christmas dinner and the evening. And then it will be back to school for you on Boxing Day.'

'But Uncle Kevin,' protested Paddy hotly, 'Mam can't want that. She said in her last letter that it's all she's looking forward to, me coming home.'

'Of course she'll be telling you that. But she's not well, lad. You can't be getting her excited and expecting her to tend to you when she's not in full health.'

'I can look after her if she's not well.'

Uncle Kevin thumped his hand on the dining table. 'Don't question my judgement on this, boy. She has your sister to look after her now and there are matters here you can't fathom. What of the expense of sending you across the country on nothing more than a lark? Do you think I'm made of money? First there's your schooling and now this blasted wedding.'

'Wedding?'

'That sister of yours is to be marrying Liam O'Flaherty within the month.'

Paddy's mouth fell open. 'Liam O'Flaherty! She'd not say yes to the likes of him! I'll tell her she can't marry him, and then you won't have to help with the wedding and I can go home for Christmas.'

'You'll do no such thing!' shouted Uncle Kevin, little

beads of sweat breaking out on his forehead. 'You'll not see your sister, nor your mother, and you will be here on Christmas Day and you will be grateful. Do you hear me! Grateful!'

Paddy looked down at his plate. He folded his napkin into a small square and laid it on the tablecloth.

'Thank you for the lovely food, Aunt Lil,' he said turning to his aunt. 'I think I'll wait in the shop for John Doherty to come and collect me, if you don't mind.'

Paddy made his way downstairs with anger in every step. Outside, winter dark was settling on the city streets and the lamplighter was beginning his rounds, while inside the shop the air was still and heavy with the scent of tobacco. His heart was pounding and he clenched his fists as he heard the dull rumble of Uncle Kevin's voice above him.

Beside the cash register was a box of cheroots with a picture of an American Indian on the lid. On an impulse, Paddy picked two cheroots out of the box and slipped them into his jacket pocket. He could hear his uncle's heavy footfall on the stairs. The back of his neck prickled as Uncle Kevin stepped into the shop.

'Don't keep John Doherty waiting, boy. Run out and get his tobacco tin. Do you think he fetches you back and forth for the pleasure of your company?'

When Paddy returned, Uncle Kevin pulled open one of the drawers in the wall. He drew out a wad of dark, pungent, chewing tobacco, and packed it into the tin.

'He's a good man, that John Doherty,' said Uncle Kevin. 'Mind you say a prayer for him.'

'Yes, Uncle Kevin,' said Paddy.

As Paddy turned to leave, Uncle Kevin called him back to the counter. Paddy felt the blood drain from his face.

'I'm no fool, Patrick,' he said. 'I know exactly what's going on in your head. But you have to understand that everything I do is for your own good. One day, you'll thank me.'

Paddy nodded and tried to smile, as if he understood, as if he was already grateful, as if he wasn't still burning with rage. The two cheroots felt heavy against his chest as he turned away from his uncle.

6

Crazed moon at Christmas

Paddy made his hands into a stirrup to boost MacCrae up. Once MacCrae was astride the high brick wall, Paddy took a running leap and scrambled up to join him, skinning his knuckles on the cold, rough stone.

'I can't believe you talked me into this,' said MacCrae, as he jumped across into the big pine tree and joined Paddy in a fork that was wide enough for the two of them to sit safely out of view of the seminary.

'There's nothing sinful about smoking baccy. Why, the Rector himself has a pipe, doesn't he?'

'Why didn't you ask Fitzgerald? Why me?'

'For God's sake, man,' said Paddy, 'you didn't have to come. I only wanted you to have some fun.'

MacCrae hung his head. 'You've been a good friend to me, Delaney. You always stick up for me. I just don't want us to get into trouble. Are you sure this is a good idea?'

'I told you, this is a rare treat.'

Paddy patted his jacket pocket where he'd been keeping the two cheroots. He took one out and rolled it between his fingers the way he'd seen Uncle Kevin do, then held it under his nose and sniffed knowingly. He held out the other one to MacCrae. Paddy struck a match and lit first MacCrae's and then his own. They sucked until the end glowed orange and then puffed furiously to keep the cheroots alight.

The first puff burnt Paddy's throat. He took a deep breath of sharp winter air, and then he inhaled again more carefully. MacCrae was sucking hard on his cheroot with a serious expression. Suddenly, he hung over the side of the branch and threw up. It would have been funny but for the shout of outrage that echoed from the base of the tree. Paddy glanced over MacCrae's shoulder and groaned. Standing at the base of the tree, his face distorted with rage, and his soutane streaked with vomit, was Father O'Keefe.

When Father O'Keefe had changed into a fresh soutane, both boys were ushered into his office. It wouldn't have been so bad for Paddy if he'd been caned alone. He knew how to brace himself for the blows. But watching MacCrae take his punishment, seeing his round glasses steamed up with tears and his tormented expression, was worse than any flogging.

After the caning, Father O'Keefe ordered them to stay standing as he sat down behind his desk and opened a book.

'Now boys, listen closely to this, especially you, MacCrae. These are the words of our own St Ignatius Loyola when speaking to a young man named Bartolomeo Romano. Bartolomeo was spiritually troubled, disobedient and a trial to his brothers. Ignatius wrote this to him: "This disquiet comes from within and not from without. I mean from your lack of humility, obedience, prayer, and your slight mortification, in a word, your little fervour in advancing in the way of perfection. You could change residence, superiors, and brethren, but if you do not change the interior man, you will *never do good.*" '

He said the last three words emphatically, gazing directly at MacCrae. MacCrae began to weep. Father O'Keefe shut the book and turned his gaze on Paddy.

'Delaney, you have a prodigious memory. Do you recall what our Lord said in Matthew 18, verse 6?'

Paddy shifted uncomfortably from one foot to the other.

'But he that shall scandalize one of these little ones that believe in me, it were better for him that a millstone should be hanged about his neck, and that he should be drowned in the depth of the sea,' he offered.

'I would like you, Delaney, to take those words to heart,' said Father O'Keefe. 'The world is full of temptation, boys. By mortifying the soul, the religious man empties out a resonant chamber within, where the voice of the divine might be heard. I know that both of you are listening for that voice. MacCrae, I know that you strive hard to advance yourself. Delaney, I have been told by your uncle that you too have hopes of one day finding a vocation within the church. These are great and noble things to aspire to, but to be called to Christ is not an easy path. You must not allow things of the world to distract you from your purpose and lead you into temptation.'

In the dormitory that night, the two boys undressed with care, nursing their tender hands. Paddy tried to catch MacCrae's eye, but MacCrae wouldn't look at him. Paddy pulled his nightshirt on over his head and slipped into the cold bed. When the lights were turned down, he whispered into the darkness, 'MacCrae, I'm sorry, I'm ever so sorry.

I never meant for you, for us, to be caught.'

MacCrae sighed. 'It's better that we were caught,' he said. 'Otherwise we might never have seen the error and never repented.'

Paddy didn't feel repentant. He knew he had broken the school rules, but he didn't feel ashamed or wicked. Then he thought of the look on MacCrae's face as the cane slashed into his hand. That, Paddy was deeply ashamed of. He put his hands together and prayed the Acts of Contrition, five Our Fathers and thirty Hail Marys, but when he had finished there was no resonance in the chamber of his soul, and no voice broke the silence of his unhappiness.

On Christmas morning, Paddy's hands were still pink and tender, with raised welts across the palms. He wouldn't be able to open any oysters today. But worse than the pain was the idea of having to face Uncle Kevin. He knew Uncle Kevin had received not only his exam results but also a letter from Father O'Keefe.

After mass finished, Paddy walked down the long drive, head bowed and hands thrust deep into his pockets. There were other boys waiting to be taken away for Christmas dinner as well, but their faces were full of bright anticipation.

John Doherty was waiting at the gates.

''Tis a lovely day to be celebrating our precious Lord's birthday,' he said, nodding at the snowy fields as Paddy climbed onto the bench beside him. Paddy was so enveloped in gloom, he found it hard to do anything other than nod.

'You're grim today, little priest. That's not right on a day like this. Is it that you're missing your own mam? I can understand that. I wouldn't want to miss having Christmas with Mam and my sister Eileen's little ones.'

'I wish I was having Christmas with you,' said Paddy gloomily.

'Well, that would be an honour, to have the little priest to bless us on such a day. Perhaps when you're finished at your uncle's you could come and join us for some supper.'

Paddy didn't like to tell John about the trouble with the cheroots nor any of the other punishments he'd received at St Columcille's. John Doherty believed Paddy was a perfect student; a saintly, well-behaved young scholar, and Paddy didn't have the heart to disillusion him.

Uncle Kevin was waiting in the street when they arrived at the shop. He was holding a wrapped gift and for a brief, impossible moment, Paddy thought it might have been a welcoming present for him.

'Merry Christmas, John,' said Uncle Kevin, not even looking at Paddy. 'A small gift to thank you for bringing the boy to us. We'll keep him with us this evening and make other arrangements to send him back to school tomorrow.'

'Now, I was just saying it would be grand, if you don't mind sir, if the lad joined us for supper this evening. I'll be staying up in town myself so I could bring him here again when we're done,' said John. 'And I'll be happy to collect the lad tomorrow.'

'I don't think that would be wise. The boy has things to answer to this evening.'

Uncle Kevin's hand was heavy on Paddy's shoulder as they walked upstairs to the rooms above the shop. Aunt Lil dived at Paddy and gave him a quick and anxious pat on his arm. The look of fear and pity in her eyes made his heart beat faster. She said 'But it's Christmas, spare the boy until tomorrow, Kevin, dear.'

Uncle Kevin didn't turn to look at her. He spoke through gritted teeth, 'Best to deal with this first. Once the boy's been punished, we can all enjoy our Christmas dinner.'

'They punished me at school,' said Paddy, holding up his hands to show the swollen welts.

Uncle Kevin ignored his gesture and steered Paddy into the office, shutting Aunt Lil out.

'I — ' began Paddy.

'Be quiet, boy!' shouted Uncle Kevin, 'and pray for forgiveness. How can you hope to find a place at the seminary if you're a thief and a liar? Your mortal soul is in jeopardy, boy. And the only way you'll understand that is if we thrash the devil out of you. Take your trousers off.'

Paddy was trembling as he undid the buttons. Uncle Kevin took off his belt and folded it in two and then he roughly grabbed Paddy by the collar and forced him to bend over, across the desk. Paddy braced himself for the first lash. It was harder than he'd anticipated, and his knees buckled. He bit his lip to stop from crying out. Blow after blow rained down, each one more savage than the one before.

On the desk in front of him stood the framed photograph of Uncle Patrick and Uncle Kevin on the day of their first communion. Their blank, indifferent faces stared out at Paddy. He hated them both. Beside the photo was a silver inkwell, and some of the ink slopped onto the desk with each reverberating blow. As Uncle Kevin drew his arm back for the next strike, Paddy closed his hand around the inkwell, spun around and threw it straight into his uncle's face. Uncle Kevin roared and dropped the belt, while Paddy darted around to the other side of the desk to grab his trousers. He bolted downstairs and through the shop, yanking on his trousers before running into the snowy street in his bare feet. He heard Aunt Lil calling, but he ran on, his feet slipping on the icy cobbles. He ran until his chest ached from gasping the freezing air. At the end of the next street, he stumbled in the slushy grey snow and fell on his hands and knees, panting. Suddenly, Aunt Lil was beside him, helping him to his feet. She smelt of oranges and warm bread. He pressed his face against her shoulder and then, all at once, tears ran down his face.

'Don't make me come back, Aunt Lil. I can't come back, not today,' he sobbed.

'Patrick, darling, he doesn't mean to be so hard. He wants you to be a fine priest one day. He has such hopes for you. We all do,' she murmured, stroking Paddy's hair.

'I can't come back. I can't. I'll walk back to school, Aunt Lil. I won't be bothering you. I'll walk back to school and never mind about Christmas.'

Aunt Lil touched his cheek with her cool hand and then looked down the length of the silent street in the direction of the tobacconist's.

'Wait here. I'll come back to you.'

Ten minutes later, she came hurrying around the corner. She brought Paddy his boots and a fresh pair of socks and a thick knitted scarf that she wrapped around his neck. She'd even brought his overcoat. When he had stopped shivering, she handed him a net bag with oranges in it, a bag of nuts and a folded piece of paper with an address scrawled on it.

'You go to John Doherty's and wait with him. I've drawn you a little map. He's just across the river. You can't be walking all the way back to the school in this freezing weather. You tell him how I sent you, and John will take you back to St Columcille's. God bless you, child, and now run, before your uncle realises what I've done.'

The streets were quiet, the snow fell like grace, the Liffey was grey and still. It was as if the city was dead, for all were inside with their families except for Paddy Delaney.

The street that John Doherty's family lived in had once been grand, with tall terraces all the length of it, but now the paintwork was worn and peeling around the doorways.

Paddy knocked on the first door off the hallway and a man directed him to a room upstairs.

'Why, it's the little priest!' exclaimed John Doherty as he opened the door. 'Your good uncle has sent you to us after all, has he?'

Paddy simply nodded and held out Aunt Lil's gifts. He was afraid that if he spoke he would burst into tears again. John seemed to sense something was wrong. He put his arm around Paddy and guided him into the room.

There was not much furniture, just a single chair by the fire, a small table and three beds. A woman was cooking bacon on the fire and the room smelt warm and smoky. There was a crowd of small children and they squealed when they saw the bag of oranges Paddy was carrying. John introduced him, and in a moment, all of them were crowding around him, exclaiming as if he was the most exciting person they'd ever met.

'I'm going to make a Christmas wish,' announced

Peggie, the littlest girl. She glanced across at Paddy. 'I'm going to wish that when I grow up, I'll marry that boy.' She pointed at Paddy and all the Dohertys laughed.

'You can't be marrying him, stupid,' said Moira, the eldest child. 'He's going to be a priest. Uncle John says so.'

Peggie pouted and put her thumb in her mouth, and everyone laughed again. Paddy looked down at the little girl, and for the first time that day he smiled. He took the oranges out of the net bag and even though his hands were sore, he started to juggle them. The little ones whooped with delight. Then Moira set about peeling the oranges and breaking them into segments for everyone to share. As soon as Paddy sat down on the end of one of the rickety beds, Peggie climbed onto his lap and put her arms around his neck.

Paddy felt sorry for the scant Christmas meal the Dohertys spread out before him. There was no goose, chicken or turkey. The sausages and bacon and black pudding were warm and filling but there was barely enough to go around. Someone from St Vincent de Paul's had brought the family a hamper with a rich, sweet Christmas cake and some little bags of boiled sweets for the children. There was also a big red candle that Moira lit with solemn excitement and set on the windowsill as the December afternoon folded into evening.

Mammy Doherty and Eileen served tea and there was a big plate of broken biscuits from the Jacob's factory. By the time he had finished eating, even though Paddy was sore in his body, he felt warm inside. The little boys bounced on the bed, their faces sticky with sugar and dirt. John pulled out a mouth organ and began to play and the whole family sang Christmas songs. When the candle grew low, and the small children sleepy, John turned to Paddy and gently touched his shoulder.

'Now, Paddy, it's too late to be taking you anywhere, my boy. I think you had best be stopping with the Dohertys for the night. I'm going out to check the nag, down in the stable yard, but you make yourself at home. They won't be missing you at school until tomorrow and, from what you've told me, your uncle won't be missing you neither.'

Paddy tried to hide his grimace. 'No, nobody will be missing me. Thank you kindly, John.'

Paddy couldn't see how eleven people were going to pile into three beds, but he had nowhere else to go. Mammy Doherty and Eileen set a pot of water to boil on the fire and then scrubbed the children's hands and faces so they looked shiny and clean again, and then in no time the three little boys were organised to get into one bed with Paddy. The two elder girls climbed into bed with their mother and the two smallest with their grandmother. John Doherty would sleep in the big chair by the fire.

Paddy was almost asleep when John Doherty returned, smelling of Guinness. He could hear the sound of men's drunken singing out in the street. John reached over and snuffed out the candle and then settled himself in the chair.

Outside the window, high above Dublin, a full moon rose up, its white face like a crazed marble through the frosted glass of the tenement window. Paddy shut his eyes and let the darkness take him.

7

The faithful departed

John Doherty no longer came to take Paddy into Dublin on Sunday afternoons. Uncle Kevin wrote to the Prefect of Studies saying he didn't want Paddy to visit until he had redeemed himself. MacCrae was wary of Paddy now, and even though Fitzgerald still punched him cheerfully whenever they passed each other on the stairs, Paddy could tell from his manner that his mother had told him to avoid the tobacconist's nephew. It was as if a black cloud lingered over Paddy and everyone could see it.

Paddy hated January, the deep, dark, cold month when the sky was always grey and hovering close to the ground, while mist lay heavy in the hollows. He longed for the brisk winds that blew off the sea and the high blue skies of the coast. On a particularly still and bleak January day, a letter arrived from his sister, Honor. He opened it as he walked across the grounds of St Columcille's and as soon as he read the first few sentences, he wished a strong wind would blow the letter from his hand and sweep it away.

Mam is too ill to pen this letter to you so I am
writing what I believe she would say to you and

*that is that you must try to do better. How could
you think so little of our Mam, to bring her grief
when you know she hasn't been well all this long
winter? How could you be so thoughtless?*

Each sentence was more cutting than a blow from
Father O'Keefe's cane.

Paddy crumpled Honor's letter and stuffed it into his
pocket, but the words continued to spin round and round
inside his head. Some boys were playing football in the
quadrangle. Paddy didn't want to join them. He felt tired
and heavy in his limbs as he made his way to the college
library. Since Christmas, it had been the only place he felt at
ease. It was a long room with high windows that the winter
sun cut through in the morning and was warm and bright
with gaslight in the afternoon. With a book open before
him, he could disappear into the words on the page and blot
out all the harsh things Honor had written. He pulled out
a small brown leather book that was wedged tight between
two fat ones and took it over to the study table.

It was a book of poems in Latin. He read them slowly,
savouring each word, playing with it until he had found just
the right way to translate it into English. It was the only
part of studying Latin that Paddy found easy. Sometimes
Father O'Keefe would seem almost annoyed and suspect
Paddy of cheating, so quickly did he find his way through
a Latin poem and yet stumble endlessly when conjugating
a simple verb. The little book of poems quickly absorbed
him. They were poems about St Patrick, St Brendan and
St Columcille. He especially liked one stanza from an
Invocation from the Blessed Bishop Patrick. Some of the

lines in it made his heart feel less heavy.

> Pelle merorem . . .
> *Cast out sorrow*
> *and sing with joy*
> *through night and day*
> *with your sweet voice*
> *from the rising sun*
> *to the highest stars.*

That night, he dreamt of a bright, open landscape where the wind swept off the sea and he ran free across the wilderness. He woke the next morning with the words of the poem ringing in his head, and as clear as a revelation, he suddenly knew what he needed to do to win back everyone's confidence, to give his mother hope, to make everyone proud.

Every Easter, St Columcille's College offered a poetry prize for the best translation from Latin of a holy work. Paddy knew that he could translate the poem that he'd read the day before. The words sang out to him, even as he broke the ice in his washbasin and scrubbed his face and neck before morning mass.

Every free moment that Paddy had, he scurried to the library and studied the invocation. It was a long poem and far more difficult than anything his class was studying. He had to be careful to make sure he got all the tenses right, that every part of the poem was true to the original but that it didn't lose any of its sweetness. When he had translated the first three stanzas, he showed them to Father O'Keefe.

The old priest frowned as he read through Paddy's careful lettering.

'And this is your own work, with no help from one of the older boys?' asked Father O'Keefe.

Paddy nodded. Father O'Keefe looked back at the page and Paddy could see he was impressed.

'This reads very well, Delaney. But you realise the Easter prize requires you translate the entire poem, not merely a few stanzas? And that it is grammatically correct. There are a few small mistakes here.'

'I understand, Father. But the other boys also told me that it has never been won by a boy in first year. That it's usually the senior boys who take the prize.'

Father O'Keefe sat back in his chair and looked out the window at the mist.

'This is true. But on the strength of this work, I think you should attempt it. And I think perhaps you and I should spend a little more time together, working on your grammar.'

Paddy tried not to grin from ear to ear.

That afternoon, as he worked on the poem, he imagined how good it would be to win the medal and take it home to the Burren in the summer. Honor had written that the one thing that might rouse Mam from her illness was to know that Paddy was becoming the scholar she had always dreamt he would be.

Every spare moment he could find, Paddy sat in the library or in the study hall, working on the poem. Until the last minute before they turned the lights down, Paddy would sit on his bed, reading his way through the thick Latin grammar books, working his way through all the extra exercises that Father O'Keefe had set him. As the dark settled, Paddy found light shining out of the pages of the books. The words swam behind his eyes even when he lay in bed at night.

On Palm Sunday, the boys shuffled in for mass. Thin winter sunlight cut through the high stained-glass windows of the chapel. Paddy knew that tomorrow the Prefect of Studies would announce the winner of the poetry prize. He got down on his knees and prayed as hard as he could, pouring his heart into a prayer that God would allow him to win. In his imagination, he played out the scene when he burst into the kitchen at home with the silver medal in his hand and saw the look of pleasure on his mother's face when he gave it to her. She would be well again because the happiness brought with him would heal her. When he prayed with the thought of his mam before him there were no clouds in his mind. God could see into his heart and knew that Paddy wanted the prize only for his mam.

The next morning, at Monday assembly, Father Gerard stood up before the whole school and read out the names of the entrants for the poetry prize. He spoke at length about the traditions of St Columcille's and why this prize was of special significance. Paddy watched his mouth moving and could hardly hear what he was saying. He just wanted the announcement to be over. To know if he'd won or if all that work had been a waste of time.

'This year, the poetry prize is awarded to the youngest student ever to receive it, Master Patrick Delaney.'

Paddy felt as if he was dreaming. Some of the junior boys were reaching over and patting him on the back and shoulders, but he sat frozen to the pew. Suddenly, Fitzgerald pushed Paddy to his feet.

'Go on, they're waiting.'

The Prefect of Studies pinned the silver medal on Paddy's breast pocket and then shook his hand. Paddy ran his hand over the medal, feeling the freshly engraved inscription. It was cold and smooth to touch.

On Maundy Thursday, even though the mass was so bleak and the altar boys worked to strip the chapel of all its ornaments, Paddy's heart sang. He tried to feel the grief of Christ's suffering on this terrible day, the day before he was crucified, but all he could focus on was the pleasure his mother would get when she received his letter telling her of the prize.

The next morning was Good Friday. Paddy was sent to see the Rector, Father Gerard. Father O'Keefe was there as well, his face very solemn as he opened the door to the Rector's office. The room was flooded with spring sunshine and outside on the lawn, the first daffodils shone gold against the green. Paddy raised one hand for a moment to shield his eyes from the bright rush of light after the gloomy hallway.

'Patrick, I have very sad news for you,' said the Rector. 'But I want you to know that if you lay your suffering before Jesus, he can heal any pain you feel.'

Paddy wanted him to stop talking right then. He wanted to cover his ears so that he wouldn't hear the next thing that Father Gerard was about to say. Instead he sat very still and stared out at the daffodils.

'Yesterday, a letter arrived from your uncle. I'm sorry to have to tell you that your good mother has passed away. I understand you knew she was poorly. I am sorry that arrangements weren't made for you to see her, but it seems no one knew how quickly her health would fail.'

Paddy felt as if all the brightness drained out of him as the priest spoke. When Father Gerard said they should pray for Mam's soul, Paddy knelt down beside Father O'Keefe and shut his eyes, but when he did, it was as if all the darkness of the world came to suck him down, down through the floorboards of the priest's office, down into darkness. He could faintly hear the sound of Father Gerard's voice chanting Psalm 129 and Paddy mouthed the words but no sound came from between his lips.

8

Falling from grace

That night in the dormitory, Paddy lay staring into the shadows. His mind was churning with questions. Father Gerard had given him a short letter from Honor explaining how Mam had died on a Thursday night and they had buried her alongside the lost brothers on the following Sunday afternoon. She also wrote that she had married Liam O'Flaherty.

Paddy had turned the letter over in his hands, as if there was something written on the blank pieces of paper between the lines, that perhaps there was some other message that he hadn't yet found. His mam had been dead for two weeks. Dead and buried in the ground. They hadn't even let him come home for the funeral and the wake. All this time he had been studying, trying to show himself worthy to his family, and they weren't even thinking of him. Was this his reward for trying so hard to be good?

He swung out of bed and knelt on the cold boards. He prayed, silently and fiercely, but in less than a minute, the black clouds started to roll into his mind and then dozens of questions filled his head, like echoing taunts. Why had God taken his mam? Why hadn't anyone come for Paddy?

Why wasn't there any comfort in prayer? Why couldn't he hear God if MacCrae could? Why didn't he know what he was meant to do?

'Delaney,' came a small voice in the darkness. 'I'm sorry for your news.'

Paddy looked across at MacCrae.

'It doesn't make any sense,' said Paddy.

MacCrae was silent for a while. Finally, he spoke in a low whisper.

'It's God's will. St Ignatius said that God has a plan for you. You have to believe that. If you surrender yourself into God's hands, he'll show you the way.'

Paddy lay his head down on the bed and let his hands hang limply by his side.

'I'm not like you, MacCrae.'

'No, but you have your own path to follow.'

Paddy's mind was full of dark thoughts and he couldn't see any path. At that moment, the only action he could envision was throttling MacCrae. If God bothered to look inside Paddy's dark soul, he'd probably damn him to hell. He got up off his knees, climbed back beneath the blankets and lay rigid, listening to the sounds of the other boys' breathing. Finally, when everyone was asleep, Paddy slipped out of bed. He dressed quietly, putting on extra layers and stuffing the rest of his clothes into his satchel. He pulled his cap low over his face and then, carrying his boots in one hand and satchel in the other, he tiptoed to the dormitory doorway.

The gas lamp in the hallway sent a golden glow across the stairs. Paddy held his breath and clutched his boots against his chest. Any moment, someone might come out, one of the brothers or priests on patrol. What would he say to them? How would he explain himself? He wasn't sure. He only knew he had to get away from St Columcille's. With Mam dead, there was no reason to stay.

Paddy made it out into the entrance without anyone raising the alarm. He ran across the grounds, the grass wet beneath his feet. Under one of the bare-leafed oak trees, he sat and wrung the moisture from his socks before putting them back on and his boots as well.

All the way along the dark road that led to Dublin, Paddy's mind whirled with thoughts and images. He thought of his mam, of the last time she had hugged him, of her standing at Gort waving the train goodbye, and how he would never see her again. All the things she had wanted for him didn't seem to count for anything. He thought of Honor, her cruel letters and her impossible marriage. And over and over again, MacCrae's words came back to him about the plan that God had made for him. Was all this pain and confusion a part of God's plan for him?

By the time he reached the shop, Paddy was shivering uncontrollably. He rang the bell. An upstairs window opened and Aunt Lil peered down at him.

'Oh sweet Jesus!' she exclaimed.

Uncle Kevin's face emerged beside her for a moment and then they both disappeared. Uncle Kevin was still in his dressing gown when he pulled the door open.

'What are you doing here?' he exclaimed. 'It's the middle of the night, boy!'

Paddy stared at his red-faced uncle. In the background hovered Aunt Lil, her face full of anguish. She was holding a lamp and standing at the foot of the stairs, one hand to her chin and her blues eyes brimming with tears.

Uncle Kevin followed his gaze.

'Lil, you get back upstairs to bed. I'll deal with this.' Then he turned to Paddy.

'My mammy is dead,' said Paddy.

Uncle Kevin sighed. 'I told the Prefect of Studies that you would come to us in the summer but that it was best not to interrupt your studies. Your studies, boy. It's what your mam would have wanted.'

'But you had the funeral without me!' shouted Paddy.

Uncle Kevin flushed even redder and then looked up and down the street. In that instant, Paddy knew he felt guilty.

'You shouldn't have come here, boy. But now that you have, you'd better be coming inside. I'll take you back to school myself in the morning.' He stepped aside, gesturing for Paddy to cross the threshold. Paddy took a step back into the street.

'I can't go back to St Columcille's.'

Uncle Kevin stared at him. 'Don't be a fool, boy. You've got your studies to tend to, your vocation. Now come in out of the cold.'

It was hard for Paddy to get the next words out. All the way to Dublin, the one clear thing that he had seen was the impossibility of what his uncle planned for him.

'Uncle, I don't have a vocation. I don't have the calling. The other boys, some of them, they know they can be priests because they know that they've been called. Maybe another boy wouldn't mind. But it's not like that for me. I don't feel anything in my heart. It would be wrong. It wouldn't be the truth, to be a priest if God isn't in your heart. If he hasn't spoken to you.'

'Ah, he'll speak to you yet, boyo. You'll hear it if you keep to your studies. You can't be doubting yourself. It's what your mother wanted, and I promised her I'd see you through.'

'But Mam's dead now.'

'That doesn't change anything. You're promised. Promised from when you were a baby.'

'I won't go back,' said Paddy, clenching his fists. 'I want to go home to the Burren.'

Uncle Kevin grew redder in the face. He grabbed Paddy by both shoulders and shook him roughly.

'Now you listen to me. There's nothing to go back for, boy. Your mam is dead and buried. Your sister's husband won't be wanting you underfoot. You're promised to the church.'

'I can't and I won't and you can't make me,' shouted Paddy.

'Mark my words, boy, if you dishonour this family, if you turn away from your vocation and disgrace your poor dead mother, there'll be no place for you in this house – no place for you in this family. You'll go the way of your father. He was the devil himself, the selfish lout. And you're the image of him, right down to your selfish, useless ways. You and your sister, there's no Cassidy in you – you're all Delaney.'

'Don't you talk about my mother or my father. If you'd given him an ounce of kindness, he wouldn't have had to go to England and leave us behind. And you never even came yourself to tell me of Mam's death. You kept me from my mam and now you want to keep me from my sister.'

'Your sister!' shouted Uncle Kevin. 'I should wash my hands of the pair of you. She didn't want to see you, did she now? In the family way, she is, and no husband in sight. Mother of God, I don't know what to do with the pair of you. I told Liam O'Flaherty he could have the house and her with it if he'd give the child a name, and thank God he said yes. It was the two of you that killed your poor mother, drove her to her grave. You damned Delaneys!'

Paddy stared down at the ground. The whole world was changing shape around him.

'I've done more than most men,' shouted Uncle Kevin. 'I've brought you to Dublin, paid for your schooling, put up with watching your ugly face across from me on enough Sundays. You've eaten my food, taken my kindness!'

'Kindness!' flung back Paddy. 'Taken your beatings, you mean.' He was crying with rage now. He hit out wildly and punched his uncle in the belly. Uncle Kevin gasped, then slapped Paddy hard across the face. The blow sent him reeling into the street.

'Get out of my sight. I'm finished with you Delaneys. Get yourself back to school. Either you go back to St Columcille's or you take yourself into the world and never darken my door again. Never again! Do you hear me?'

Paddy ran, his heart thumping and blood pounding at his temples. He could hear Uncle Kevin shouting after him. But if there was nothing else he was sure of, he was sure there was no turning back.

9

Come back early or never come

Paddy headed to Tyrone Street, counting his way along the houses, trying to remember which was the one he'd visited at Christmas. There were no lights on anywhere in the house and the hall smelt sour as he pushed the front door open and peered into the darkness. He felt his way up the stairs, counting the doorways along the hall by touch. Shyly, he scratched on Mammy Doherty's door. There was no answer and so he tapped again, this time more loudly. He heard anxious whispering on the other side and then the door opened a crack and a thin wedge of light slipped out into the hall. Mammy Doherty held up her candle and looked out anxiously.

'Mercy, child. What are you doin' here at this hour, banging on our door?'

'I'm looking for John Doherty, ma'am.'

'Why, it's the little priest,' she said, holding the candle closer. 'Did someone tell you about our John? You've come to pray for him, have you?' She peered into Paddy's face. 'Are you in trouble, child? Come in from the cold.'

The big shutters on the outside of the window had been pulled shut against the night, and the room was dark but for the candlelight. Paddy could see the outline of the children's small bodies on one bed, cuddled together. On the other side of the window lay the shadowy shape of a man lying like a king on his tomb, very still in the darkness. Paddy could hear the rattle of his breath. He stared in disbelief. Was this shell of a man the same person who had shared so many poems and stories with Paddy?

'He'd found work in the country, but he's come home to us for the end,' said Mammy Doherty. She took the candle over to the bed and stood there, stroking the hair away from John's face.

Paddy took off his cap and sat on a little stool between the bed and the fireplace. There was a small piece of turf and the remnants of an old shoe in the fire grate, smoking.

'Will you pray for him, Patrick?' asked Mammy Doherty.

Paddy wanted to tell her he couldn't pray for anyone. He wanted to explain that his prayers were useless, that they hadn't saved his mam and they wouldn't save John Doherty either. But there was so much need and longing on the old woman's face that he knelt beside the bed and put his hands together. 'Thy servant John for whom I implore thy mercy, health of mind and body, that loving thee with all his strength . . .'

'No, no, Patrick. You can't be praying for his strength, you have to be praying for a happy death,' she said, her voice cracking. 'There's no cure for him but to rest in the arms of Jesus. You pray to sweet Mary or Joseph or to St Barbara. They'll see to him.'

Paddy nodded mutely. 'St Barbara, patron saint of the dying, obtain for John Doherty the grace to die, like thee, in the arms of Jesus and Mary. Amen.'

But even as the words left his mouth, Paddy felt empty. He stayed kneeling, his hands clasped together but his mind was full of roiling blackness. He knelt until his body was aching. Mammy Doherty put a hand on his shoulder.

'You're shivering, child. Come.' She guided him over to the bed on the other side of the window, helped him off with his boots, and hung his wet socks on the smoky grate before sitting down in her chair again. Paddy curled up against the cluster of small children in the other bed. They smelt sour and unwashed tonight, but their breathing was soft.

When Paddy woke, thin rays of dawn light were seeping through the shutters. The small children slept on and Mammy Doherty snored in her chair by the fire. Paddy untangled himself from the children and went to stand by John Doherty's bed. John's breath moved in and out like the rattle of old bellows.

'*For he comes, the human child, To the waters and the wild, With a faery, hand in hand, From a world more full of weeping than he can understand,*' whispered Paddy.

John Doherty's lids fluttered and for a moment, Paddy thought he would come to consciousness, but then the cold grip of his illness drew the man down again. His body shuddered and the rattle of his breath resumed.

Paddy rested his forehead on the edge of the bed frame. He tried to make a prayer in his head – not to God but to his mother, so that she would know John Doherty when he crossed over – but the words wouldn't form.

Suddenly, Paddy couldn't think why he'd come. There was no place for him here. Without a word, he slipped out the door and downstairs into the street. It was still early, with the first grey light settling over the city. The milkman was out in his rattling cart, heading across town to deliver milk, and down the street a lamplighter was snuffing out the lamps.

It started to rain in thin, icy needles. Paddy stood under the statue of Dan O'Connell at the bottom of Sackville Street, sheltering from the rain. Across the road, raindrops pocked the surface of the Liffey. Paddy looked up at the sculpture, dark against the morning sky. He felt very small. For some reason, he thought of MacCrae. MacCrae would be a great man one day. Fitzgerald would be a gentleman. But what would become of him? Perhaps he'd be a carter, like John Doherty and fill his life with poetry and Guinness. But even John had a mother to nurse him at his death.

Paddy crossed the road and stared down at the Liffey's dark surface. He could faintly see the wavering outline of himself hanging over the edge of the bridge. He imagined himself sinking into the black water, imagined all the darkness of the river swirling around him as he disappeared beneath the surface. The river would draw him to it, down into the depths, and the black water would fill his dark heart. He leant further over the parapet and felt the medal in his pocket press against the stonework. He pulled it out and stared at it glinting on the palm of his hand. He'd worked so hard for the useless thing. He closed his hands around it tightly, so tightly that the edges of the medal cut into his palm. Then he drew his hand back and flung the medal as far as he could into the Liffey. It made a tiny plink as it hit the water. A Guinness barge was floating past, its deck stacked with barrels, blocking Paddy's view. The prize was sinking in the mud at the bottom of the river, with silt and slime closing over it, and Paddy knew it was lost forever.

IO

The Lapwing

Paddy followed the barge as it headed down river towards the docks, past the Custom House with its high dome and columns, down to Dublin Bay. The rain had stopped and the quay was alive with activity. As Paddy drew closer to where the great ocean-going ships were moored, the noise of the docks intensified. Iron steamships with anchors twice the size of a man were being loaded with cargo while crowds of small barefoot children played along the quay. Boys of all ages were working alongside the men. A sandy-headed boy stood crying out warnings in a shrill voice as the great loads of cargo swung on board. Men with their faces black from shovelling coal wiped their streaming eyes on their shirtsleeves, while smartly dressed gentlemen carrying fine leather bags alighted from carriages and strolled up the gangplanks of ships bound for ports all over the world. Paddy wandered up a side alleyway, dazed by all the noise and motion.

An old woman sitting in a doorway called out to Paddy. 'Here, boy, I'll give you a penny if you'll fetch me a pint.'

'Of milk?' asked Paddy.

'No, boy, porter. Here's a jug for you to put it in and

there'll be a penny for you to keep when you get back.'

She gave him directions and Paddy pushed his way through the crowd and handed the woman's jug across the counter of the pub.

'Getting ale for your mam?' asked a man who was standing at the counter, drinking.

Paddy felt a lump in his throat at the thought of his mother. He shook his head.

The man turned back to his friends and laughed.

'See, I was no more than a sprat, smaller than this lad here when I left Cardiff for the sea. And mind you, no one forced me to it. I stowed away on my first ship when I couldn't find a skipper who'd take me. I'd rather be sailing around the coast of Africa than stuck in the coal mines back home in Wales.'

Paddy wondered if the man had happily left his family behind or if perhaps grief and loss had driven him to sea. He took the jug back to the woman and watched as she held a hot poker in the porter to warm it. Then she reached into the folds of her skirt and drew out a penny from her purse. Paddy walked away, staring at the penny in his hand. Fetching porter for old ladies was not going to earn him a living, and if he wasn't returning to St Columcille's, he'd have to do something to earn his keep.

He stopped at a canteen next to one of the coal merchants and bought a cup of sweet tea and a rasher of hot, greasy bacon. As he sipped the tea, he watched ships setting out across the bay. The clippers were towed out of the harbour by steamers to where the sea breezes would send them across the world. In the distance, some were unfurling their sails, white against the dark grey sky. Paddy thought of the poem that had won him the Easter prize:

Run swiftly, O ship,
through the hollow sea,
breaking the waves
of the sea's pale swell.

If he had stayed at St Columcille's and become a missionary, one day he would have sailed across the world. Paddy watched the last clipper become a tiny speck and then disappear over the horizon, his heart full of longing. If only he could be away from the grey skies and the graves of Ireland, in a place where no one would know of his disgrace and his grief. Suddenly, like an arrow of bright hope in the darkness, Paddy realised he didn't have to be a missionary to sail to Africa.

The first ship he tried was the largest ocean liner he could find. He asked an officer in a white uniform with gold braid who he should speak to, but the officer simply looked at him as if he was an annoying insect.

'Where's your ticket?'

'I don't have a ticket. I want to be a sailor,' he said.

'I mean your seaman's ticket,' said the officer.

At the next ship he was asked even more questions.

'Where's your discharge book? Who were you with last?'

Paddy was bewildered and it showed.

'What? You never been to sea? We don't want first-trippers here.'

Other sailors laughed at him. 'You're just a babby, go home to your mammy, little schoolboy.' Paddy felt furious.

Most of them weren't much older than him anyway. Before he boarded the next ship, he tore off the jacket pocket that bore the St Columcille's emblem.

By the time he'd got to the tenth ship, he felt heavy with despair. A whistle blew for the ten o'clock break and the dockworkers headed towards the pubs and canteens. Paddy trudged up the gangplank of an iron barque called the *Lapwing*. It looked sleek and fast, just the sort of clipper to take him away from Ireland, away from the cold and the damp and the misery of the place.

'We're sailing this morning and we don't take first-timers,' said the first mate.

Paddy sighed with frustration. 'Everyone has said they won't have me because I've never been to sea, but they'd never been to sea before they'd been to sea either!'

The man laughed. 'There'll be a place for you, if you keep trying, but we've only got a crew of twenty-eight here and we won't be needing a cabin boy. You try one of the big fellas. They could use an extra sprat like yourself.'

Paddy looked at him again and realised he was the Welshman from the pub, the one who'd run away to sea and been a stowaway on his first boat. The man turned away and went below. Paddy noticed a door set at an odd angle into a wall on the deck. He glanced around. There were two sailors working nearby with their backs to him. Quickly he edged the hatch open and looked in. It was just a cupboard with a few ropes coiled inside. Heart in mouth, he slipped in and pulled the door shut tight above him. At least, if the first mate found him, reasoned Paddy, he might have some sympathy, as an ex-stowaway himself.

Paddy pushed the ropes to one side, tucked his satchel

down beside him and curled himself into a comfortable position. It was warm and dark in the hatch with the sun shining down on the metal door and only a thin strip of light around the edge.

Before too long, Paddy heard the shouts of the sailors casting off and the grating sound of the gangway being pulled aboard. The ship lurched away from the dock and Paddy gripped the pile of ropes to stop being pitched against the door. He mouthed some lines from Bishop Patrick's invocation: *An angel be with you, through the wide sea . . .*

Paddy woke to the sound of the wind. Instinctively, he braced his feet against the edges of the hatch to hold himself from being thrown sideways. There was no light shining through the cracks any more, and no sound from on deck. Paddy pushed up the lid of the hatch and peered out. It was night-time and the sky was black and starless. Stiffly, his numb legs tingling, he stepped out.

Inside ten minutes, Paddy had a fair idea of the lie of the upper deck. He even discovered where the galley was and snatched the end of a loaf of bread from the bread bin before tiptoeing back to his hiding place.

The second day seemed insufferably long. At one stage he had to climb out in broad daylight and pee over the side of the boat, all the while terrified that someone would see him before he could run back to his hiding place. The hatch grew hot and stuffy and Paddy felt sick with hunger, but he was too scared to go on deck during daylight hours, though he longed to be out in the fresh air. He thought of all the stories he'd heard of jungles and diamonds and gold and adventure and the cities and wide deserts. Perhaps soon they'd be somewhere in Africa. He fell into an uneasy sleep where dreams came and went, flitting across his mind like seabirds winging above the ocean.

As the days wore on, Paddy took to telling himself stories about what his life in Africa would be like. When he couldn't think up anything new, he recited poetry to himself under his breath. He didn't want to pray. It was as if his faith lay at the bottom of the Liffey along with his silver medal, and the thought of prayer was like inviting in the darkness.

At night, when it wasn't too rough, he would slip out for a quick visit to the galley and then scurry back into his hiding place. On one of his nocturnal explorations, he found a loose piece of canvas, which he took back to use as a blanket. He never managed to steal enough food to assuage his hunger and by the fifth day he was starting to feel ill.

He dreamt strange dreams. He imagined he could hear Honor and Aunt Lil whispering about him outside the hatch, and Aunt Lil telling Honor what a bad and wicked boy he'd been. He dreamt Uncle Kevin came on board, dragged him from his hiding place and thrashed him senseless on the deck. Sometimes, when a sailor shouted, it sounded exactly like Uncle Kevin, and Paddy would shudder. Even the wind had a voice, sometimes like MacCrae in prayer, or the monotonous tone of Father O'Keefe as he read to the boys in Latin.

And then, during a cold, dark night, Paddy dreamt of his mother and John Doherty, lying pale and listless on narrow beds – but the beds were at sea, just over the prow of the *Lapwing*. In his dream he leapt over the side of the ship to rescue them, but he was sinking, sinking deep below the pitching waves, calling out for help, crying out to his mother and John.

A rush of light filled his eyes. He raised one hand to protect himself from the dazzling brilliance. The shadow of a man loomed above him, and two powerful hands reached down and pulled him out onto the deck. Paddy tried to pull away but the man held him firmly by one shoulder and took Paddy's chin in his hand. A pair of brown eyes stared down at Paddy from a wide and ruddy face.

'Would you believe it?' said the man. 'Would you credit it! He must have been in here since Dublin, and he's shaking like a leaf. C'mon, boy. Poor little drowned rat, c'mon now, we'll not hurt you.'

Paddy was shivering uncontrollably. The big man scooped him up as if he was a tiny child, and carried him down to the galley.

'So this is our little thief?' said the cook, looking Paddy up and down. 'The captain won't be happy.'

'You never mind about the captain for now. I'm first mate here and I say the boy needs something warm to eat, don't you, lad?'

The big man wrapped a rough ship's blanket around Paddy and sat him down by the stove.

'I know you, don't I?' asked the first mate. 'You're the lad who came looking for work.'

Paddy nodded mutely and took the steaming cup that the man offered him. It was as if all the life flowed back into him when he felt the warmth of the tea slip down his throat. And then, to his humiliation, he started to cry, and the tears coursed down his cheeks and dripped into his mug.

'Here now,' said the first mate. 'You're all right now.' His voice was so full of warmth and comfort that Paddy only cried harder. He hadn't cried when they told him his mother had died. He hadn't cried when Uncle Kevin had thrown him into the street, nor when he'd sat beside the dying John Doherty. He couldn't remember the last time he had cried. And yet here he was, weeping like a baby, and the tears wouldn't stop. His shoulders shook with the force of his grief, and he put his head in his hands and tried to stem the tears. Then the first mate put one arm around him, so his warmth and strength flowed into Paddy.

'There, there, everything will be all right. You'll come to no harm while you're on board the *Lapwing*. Dai Llewellyn will see to that.'

Paddy swallowed and choked back his sobs. 'Who's th-th-at?' he asked.

'Why, that's me,' laughed the first mate. 'And who might you be that I'm making all these promises to?'

It took a moment for Paddy to steady his voice. 'Patrick Brendan Delaney of County Clare.'

'And what were you doing in Dublin, then, if you're a Clare boy?'

Suddenly, the whole story spilt out – his mother's hopes for him, his uncle's ambitions, the long months of study at St Columcille's, not knowing where to turn, John Doherty's death, throwing his medal in the river, and then stowing away on the *Lapwing*.

'I suppose you think I'm a bad sort. You were right not to give me a job.'

'If that's the worst you can come up with, lad, you're

all right – a saint compared with most of the boys on board this ship,' said Dai.

Cook laughed and put a bowl of steaming hot broth before Paddy while Dai cut him a piece of bread.

'You stay here in the galley with Cook until I've had a word with the captain,' said Dai.

Once word had spread of Dai's discovery, the crew crowded into the galley and stared at Paddy with disbelief. When Cook told them how he'd been stowed away for nearly a week in a cupboard, they laughed in amazement.

The captain wasn't as good-humoured as the crew. He slammed his hand down on the table and shouted so loudly that Paddy jumped back in alarm.

'Damn you! I should have you thrown overboard!'

The first mate coughed loudly and the Captain lowered his voice a little but his furious expression didn't alter. 'If we were stopping anywhere I'd put you off, but there's no port of rest until we reach Australia so you've a long voyage ahead of you yet.'

'Australia!' said Paddy, his eyes wide. 'But I thought – aren't we going to Africa?'

'You'll go where we can be bothered taking you, and you'll get off when we deem you've earned your fare,' said the captain angrily. 'Stowaways! They're nothing but trouble!'

Dai Llewellyn put his hand on Paddy's shoulder and the weight of it felt like a steadying force. He looked up at the big Welshman and Dai looked back at him with a sombre face, but for a moment, Paddy could swear he had winked.

11

The gift of a knife

Paddy quickly found his place among the *Lapwing*'s crew. He was up on deck in first light, helping scrub and swab the decks. He would fill the scuttlebutt with fresh water and help coil the rigging. Some days he worked with the ship's carpenter on repairs, sometimes he was in the galley helping Cook with the meals. He soon discovered that the *Lapwing* had a full load of cargo, mostly fine paper and crates of the best Irish whiskey, but there were no passengers on board.

Paddy's favourite time of day was the dogwatch, in the twilight hours between six and eight when all the men were on deck. Even Cook came up and smoked his pipe with the rest of the sailors. When the sea was still, Paddy would sit on the forecastle and watch Dai carving his collection of wooden spoons. They reminded Paddy of his mother's Claddagh ring which she'd always kept in a little box beside her bed. In the handle of Dai's spoons were carved intricate patterns, and caught in the middle of the ornate knotwork was a heart held fast by a pair of hands, just as in his mother's ring.

While Dai pared and whittled with his knife, Paddy

talked. He liked to dream aloud, about all the adventures that lay ahead of him in ports all over the world.

'Sure, I reckon I'll be a sailor, Dai Lwellyn. I'll have my own ship one day, a ship with sails like beaten gold, and she'll be the swiftest barque on the seas. You can be one of my crew, if you like. And we'll sail all the length and breadth of the world. We'll sail to China and India and Africa, and we'll be famous in every seaport in the world.'

Dai looked up from his work and grinned.

'A sailor, is it? Strikes me you'd make a better bard. A right little Taliesin, you are.'

'Little who?' asked Paddy, thinking it made him sound like some sort of tadpole.

'You not heard of him? The great Celtic bard? What were they teaching you in that school of yours?'

'Latin and algebra mostly.'

'Well, I'm sure there's plenty of books about Taliesin of the White Brow. See, he had the gift of the gab too. Taliesin brought good luck to his master, same as you've brought us all this fair sailing weather. Look at that hair of yours, if that isn't a symbol of good luck, what else could it be?'

'I don't feel very lucky,' said Paddy, touching his curls. They were just about at his collar now. Paddy reeled off all the unlucky things that had happened to him from losing his dad and mam to being caned at school, flogged by Uncle Kevin and then not being able to find a place on a ship.

'Well, you are lucky. Lucky we didn't throw you overboard for a start. If I'd known you were never going to stop jawing, maybe I would have.'

Paddy folded his arms, determined to be silent, but after a few minutes of watching Dai whittle, he said, 'Aren't you going to tell me the story? About Taliesin?'

Dai laughed. 'I knew you couldn't be quiet for long. All right then, there was this fine young Welsh prince, his name was Elphin, and on May-eve, his dad sent him down the weir to find what he would find. The prince was thinking he'd find gold, but all he found was a white-browed baby in a sack, hanging on the weir. "Behold a radiant brow!" cried Elphin when he set eyes upon the boy. And I was thinking just that myself when I opened the hatch and saw you curled up inside.'

'I bet you wish I had been a sack of gold!'

'Sure, if Elphin didn't think the same, but he took the child home and all the ride back, the babe sang tales in his master's ear, and Elphin knew he'd found a great bard of his own. And ever since I hauled you out of the hatch, why, you've never stopped talking. For sure, you'll be someone's bard.'

'What if I decide I'm a sailor instead?'

Dai laughed. 'Well, you'd best be finding yourself a hobby other than talking the hind leg off a donkey.'

He reached into his pocket and pulled out a small knife which he threw towards Paddy. Paddy caught it mid-flight and cradled it in his hands. It had a strong steel blade and a wooden handle that the blade folded into. When the blade was extended, he could turn a little ring on the handle to lock it into place.

'Now here's a treat for you, boy.' Dai pulled a piece of pale timber from the small black bag in which he carried his carving tools. It was about as thick as Paddy's wrist at one end and tapered to a point at the other.

'That's limewood. Beautiful white timber. Not the usual

sort for a love spoon, but when you're finished with it, it could be the finest spoon that ever a girl possessed.'

'But I don't know any girls.'

'You don't be wanting to wait until you do. It may take you years to make a perfect spoon. One day there'll be a girl you'll be wanting for your own, and a love spoon is a sure way of wooing her. A flower, that's a sign of affection, and a cross is for faith and a diamond for riches, but the chains, they're important because they show how you and your girl will be bound together forever, no matter how long you're at sea.'

Paddy traced his finger across the smooth white lime-wood. He couldn't imagine that any girl would ever love him for long, no matter how many love spoons he carved for her. He'd be bound to disappoint her. For the first time that evening, he fell completely silent. The eight o'clock bells rang, echoing across the still waters. The captain set the watch for the dark hours, the sailor at the wheel was relieved, and the galley was shut. Paddy slipped his knife into his pocket and followed Dai below decks.

As they sailed further south, the weather grew wild. When Paddy was sent to help with the rigging, his hands were too numb to work. Everyone wore oilskins and sou'-westers on deck, but nothing could stop the piercing cold. On the roughest days, Dai sent Paddy below to help Cook. It was a relief to be in the warm and steamy galley.

One morning, Paddy came on deck to find a sheer wall of ice rising up in front of the ship. Paddy gripped the rails with a mixture of terror and awe. The iceberg was so close, he could almost reach out and touch it. Only the rebound of a heavy swell against the steep side of the berg kept them from impact. The *Lapwing* surged alongside the glassy walls and Paddy held his breath. Water cascaded down the side of the iceberg, into the bluish-green depths beneath. At night, as he lay in his hammock, he could hear the sound of the ice-cracking echoing across the water.

Finally, they headed into the Indian Ocean, and the whole crew seemed to breathe a sigh of relief. Even though it had only taken a week to sail around the Cape of Good Hope, Paddy felt as if he'd been cold forever.

'I think the next job we sign on for should be on a steamer,' he said to Dai as they sat on the forecastle on a warm bright Sunday afternoon, whittling away at the love spoons. 'We could sail through the Suez Canal and see Africa.'

'A steamer, with black soot settling on you and the smell of coal all the long day? Not for me. There's nothing sweeter than the smell of land when you've been weeks at sea, nor nothing as clean as ocean air. You'll miss all that if you hitch yourself to a steamer.'

'But don't you get scared sometimes when the clipper gets tossed about?'

'I was born with the caul over my head – don't you know that means I can never drown?'

'Well, I could drown,' said Paddy. 'I don't even know how to swim. If I got washed overboard, that would be the end of me, even in calm water.'

'We'll have to remedy that,' said Dai, shaking his head. 'It would be just your luck to go tumbling, and mine to have to dive in and save you. Come here, boy.' He yanked at Paddy's shirt. 'Now get your boots off, and your trousers.'

'Can't we do this some other time?' said Paddy, squirming. 'Plenty of the other men can't swim. Why pick on me?'

'You can't teach an old dog new tricks, but a whelp like yourself, that's another matter. Get your clothes off. Orders, boy,' said Dai.

Sighing, Paddy did as he was told.

'Now see if you can keep your mouth shut or you'll be drowning before I can save you,' said Dai, gathering up a coil of rope.

Dai tied the rope firmly around Paddy's waist, then picked him up and threw him over the side. Paddy shouted as he hit the cold green water and sank deep. Opening his eyes, he saw the coil of rope black against the brightness above him. Then the rope pulled taut and scratchy against his bare chest and he was yanked spluttering to the surface.

Dai shouted down, 'Now, you have to get those legs kicking, boy. Roll onto your back and see if you can float. There's so little fat on you, I don't know if you can, but you must learn.'

Half the crew hung over the side of the clipper to watch him. Realising he had an audience, Paddy started clowning around, flapping his arms up and down like a drowning seabird.

'Stop your larking about, you show-off,' roared Dai. 'Now get your arms working!'

Dai made the rope go slack and Paddy felt himself sink again. He gasped and swallowed a mouthful of brine. Panicking, he flailed his arms and kicked his legs, bringing his head above the surface.

'Now you lie still again for a moment, lad,' called Dai.

'Get on your back, spread your arms and your legs wide and feel the power of the water. That's the trick to swimming in the sea. To know she's wiser than you and to go with her, not always fight against her.' Paddy turned onto his back and felt the gentle swell of the waves beneath him.

When Paddy had thrashed his way along half the length of the *Lapwing*, Dai hauled him back on deck. Paddy stood shivering and grinning while the water streamed off him.

'There's hope for you, lad,' said Dai, throwing him his clothes. 'We might make a sailor of you yet!'

12

Jonah

They sailed right around the edge of Australia, sometimes drawing so near to land that they could smell the scent of warm earth. They reached the entrance to Port Phillip Bay late one evening. The captain didn't want to tackle the narrow, treacherous stretch of water without a pilot ship to guide him, so they anchored in Bass Strait and waited for the morning.

All night the wind blew hard. Waves swept across the deck and the men came down below complaining what a dirty night's work it was. The roar of the waves and the creaking lurch of the ship made Paddy feel uneasy. The *Lapwing* had sailed through storms on the voyage south, but this one felt different. An extra sailor was sent to the wheel, and both men were lashed to it so they wouldn't be swept overboard. At eight bells, all hands were called to shorten sail. The inky sky flashed bright as lightning struck the coast, and Paddy shuddered. It was as if they were at the edge of the world and they would find no welcome on this dark shore.

Shortly before dawn, all hands were called again. Everything was chaos. Great walls of water towered above the ship and slammed across the deck. The *Lapwing* was drifting closer to shore by the minute. The wheel had been swept overboard, along with the sailors who manned it. Dai was trying to haul them back on board, and his hands were bloody from where the rope cut deep into his flesh. Paddy staggered towards the stern to help. He was only an arm's length from Dai when a sea mountain loomed above the rigging and then the *Lapwing* keeled over. The first lifeboat was sucked into the blackness, disappearing beneath the waves before anyone had a chance to board it. Another lifeboat was lowered and some of the sailors scrambled over the side.

Paddy looked frantically up and down the length of the foundering ship, searching for Dai, but he had disappeared. The whole of the deck was under water and what was left of the crew clustered around the last lifeboat. The air and sea swirled around them, full of screams and howling wind and the sheer black malevolent force of the ocean. Paddy scrambled aft, clinging hand over hand to the rail, screaming Dai's name until his throat was raw and hoarse. Suddenly, Cook was behind him, pulling him towards the lifeboat.

'But Dai —' shouted Paddy.

'There's nothing you can do for him,' yelled Cook above the wind. 'Get in the boat.'

The instant he spoke there was a deafening roar and the *Lapwing* plunged downwards, sucked into a deep ocean trough. Paddy screamed as he was propelled through the air and into the black swelling ocean. He thrashed against the first press of icy water and when a wave lifted him high, he saw the *Lapwing*, like a bird crushed in a storm, breaking up. Paddy couldn't believe it. All this way, all these miles he'd sailed, to drown on his first voyage. Anger and despair raged through him. He caught a fleeting glimpse of other men tossed like flotsam on the great waves. But even as he thought the sea would swallow him whole, he could hear the voice of Dai, telling him how it is a boy learns to swim. Paddy found himself letting the waves take him, and then riding them.

Suddenly, his feet touched sand. The surf still tugged against his legs but he managed to stagger up the beach. The ground felt unsteady beneath him, as if the whole world was pitching. Sinking to his knees, he crawled away from the wash of the ocean, up onto the shore of the new land. With a shudder of exhaustion, he collapsed.

Paddy woke, alone on a long expanse of white sand. When he rolled over and sat up, he found he was in a hollow at the crest of a dune. Every muscle in his body ached. He dragged himself to the top and surveyed the beach. Timber and canvas, tangled ropes and cloth were all piled high in a wall of wreckage and cargo that stretched for hundreds of metres along the shore. Swollen bales of yellowish paper looked twice the size they had in the hold, crates of whiskey were piled up pell-mell like badly constructed toy castles, and there were bodies too, strewn amid the wreckage. Paddy could tell by the angle of their limbs that there was no life in them. He climbed down the dune and approached the first body. It was bloated and blue. He could tell by the clothes that it wasn't Dai, but the face was so swollen and distorted that Paddy couldn't recognise the man. He turned away from the corpse, sick with horror.

Paddy was halfway along the length of the wreckage when he came across Dai's coat. He pulled the sodden, dark wool over his shoulders and trudged on. He tried not to look at the other dead bodies. If Dai was one of them, he didn't want to see. He kept his gaze on the sand beneath his feet. It was the glitter of sunlight on glass that made him stop. Lying half covered with sand were his coloured glass rosary beads. He scooped them up and dropped them into his breast pocket.

Half an hour later he found the other survivors crouched around a beached lifeboat. There were only four of them, Cook and three other sailors that Paddy had never got to know well. They had a crate of whiskey from the cargo beside them and had opened several bottles. Cook offered Paddy some, to warm him. Paddy took a mouthful but the whiskey burnt his throat and he huddled down under Dai's coat, staring numbly out to sea, imagining that any moment he would see Dai's dark hair coming up through the waves.

The five of them sat waiting, watching the brooding sea, bewildered that they were alive when so many had been lost. For all its malice, the sea seemed less threatening than the huge and empty landscape. The beach stretched for miles without a living soul in sight. From the top of the dunes, Paddy could see nothing but an endless expanse of grey-green scrub.

They spent the night on the beach. The next day, Cook laid out his flint and matches to dry, and on the second evening they managed to put together enough dryish kindling to make a small fire. Paddy tried to tell himself that perhaps the fire would draw Dai's attention and he would find them, but in his heart he knew Dai was dead.

That evening, when the other sailors thought Paddy was asleep, he overheard them talking.

'That little bugger's turned out to be a right Jonah, ain't he?'

'Aye,' chipped in another seaman. 'Who'd have believed it? Twenty-four men lost and Dai Llewellyn amongst them and the arseworm still alive.'

'Shut up, the pair of you,' grumbled Cook, screwing the cork out of another bottle of whiskey. 'It's nothing to do with the lad.'

'Dai reckoned he couldn't be drowned, born with the caul on his head and all,' said the other sailor. 'That sprat brought him bad luck. We should make him pay for it.'

'Better sailors than Dai Llewellyn have been lost at sea,' said Cook. 'The boy's nothing to do with it. You lay a hand on him and you'll have me to answer to.' He smashed the whiskey bottle against a piece of driftwood and brandished the neck at the other sailors. They grunted but no one spoke again.

Paddy shut his eyes tight and drew Dai's coat up a little higher over his shoulders. Maybe it was true. He was a nothing, a nobody. Not a priest, nor a sailor, nobody's son, nobody's kin – nothing but a Jonah.

Next day dozens of looters arrived and began combing through the wreckage. Paddy wanted to fly at them, beat them off, but his muscles refused to act. It was as if there was an imaginary Paddy that was shouting and bold and the other Paddy who was numb and defeated and simply watched the looters at work. The looters even ignored the rescue boat that beached on the shore near the huddle of shipwrecked sailors.

The rescue boat took Paddy and the other men to Queenscliff. After a doctor had checked each of them and declared them uninjured, they were given a fresh change of clothes and put on board a steamer to take them in to Port Melbourne. Paddy stayed below deck for the whole of the journey.

'Here,' said Cook, coming down to find him. 'Aren't you going ashore?'

Paddy shrugged and leant his head against the cabin wall.

'Look, son,' said Cook, turning Paddy around forcibly. 'You can't stay here moping. You can come and bunk up at the Seamen's Home. They'll feed you well and you'll get a change of view. It's what you need. There's plenty of ships you can sign on here. Big steady barques full of wool and bound for America.'

Paddy shrugged again and then blurted out. 'No one's going to want me. They'll all know I'm a Jonah.'

'You wait and see. You're not the first sailor accused of being a Jonah,' Cook responded. 'Too many men with more superstition than sense. Ships go down. It's a fact of the sea.'

He unhooked Dai's big coat and hung it across Paddy's shoulders.

'I'm glad you've got his coat. I know he would have wanted you to have something to remember him by.'

Paddy thrust his hands deep into the pockets of the greatcoat. There was a drizzle of sand inside, and wedged deep in the bottom, Paddy felt something else. He pulled it out. It was Dai's knife, the wooden handle now paler for the salt that marred its surface.

Paddy clutched the knife and trudged down the gang-plank with Dai's coat wrapped tight around him, into the harsh light of an Australian winter afternoon.

The Seamen's Home looked like the sort of building a group of gnomes might live in. It was made of red brick and stood not far from the port, at the edge of the city. Downstairs in the yard, men were pacing up and down as if they were still on deck.

There were men from all over the world – some had skin so black and shiny that Paddy found it hard not to stare at them. At dinner, an American man refused to sit at the same table as the black and yellow men and threw his knife down on the table in disgust. Paddy took his seat. He felt as different from the other sailors as the men of all colours.

The runner who showed him to his room was a young sailor, a Swedish boy. Key in hand, he led Paddy up to the fourth storey and into a tiny, darkened room. The only light shone through the fanlight above the door.

Paddy stretched out on the iron bed. In the opposite bed, a sailor reeking strongly of whiskey talked in some incomprehensible tongue, laughing and shouting as his moods took him. Paddy pulled Dai's coat up over his head and for the first time since leaving Ireland, he tried to pray. He pulled the glass rosary beads out of his pocket and tried to mouth the words of a prayer for all the faithful departed. It seemed wrong not to at least try. He tried to conjure an image of Dai along with the words of the psalm for the dead, but the only thing that formed in his mind was a wall of black water. He saw the storm again, and the sea raging over the decks of the *Lapwing*.

He swung his legs over the side of the lumpy mattress and sat up. The drunken sailor groaned and pulled his thin blanket higher on his shoulder. Suddenly, more than anything, Paddy wanted to go home. He thought of his mam standing at the kitchen table, of the windswept granite fields behind their house and his small, cosy bedroom at the top of stairs. But there would be no welcome for him in that house any more. Uncle Kevin's last words echoed inside his head and he knew he had no home in Ireland. Dai had said the sea was a sailor's true home but how could Paddy sign on to another ship with the curse of a Jonah hanging over his head?

Whenever Paddy lay down, the bed seemed to pitch and visions of the storm kept him from sleep. The night seemed to go on forever. By the time the dawn light began to seep into the room, Paddy knew he never wanted to sail again.

13

The bones of a man

The next day, Paddy wandered the streets of the city. There was a chill in the air that made him glad of Dai's coat. Melbourne's buildings were tall and elegant and there were crowds of people everywhere. He took a tram from the Seamen's Home and alighted outside a cathedral made of pale gold stone, with a pair of flat, square towers on either side. He bought a pie from a street vendor on the corner and scalded his mouth on the hot sauce that the man had made by pouring boiling water through a hole in the crust. Further along the street he bought two currant buns with the coins that Cook had given him.

In one of the big wide streets, a small crowd gathered outside a shopfront with a banner proclaiming 'Jim Crilly's Living Skeleton'. Black fabric swathed the window and a man stood outside, beckoning to the crowd.

'Only sixpence! Sixpence for this once-in-a-lifetime opportunity to see the amazing, the stupendous, the unbelievable Living Skeleton! Is he alive or is this the face of the living dead? See for yourself! Bear witness to the incredible! A man or a ghost? Judge for yourself. Only sixpence, roll up, roll up!'

Paddy handed over sixpence and went inside. The room, like the window, was draped in heavy black fabric. There were a few people standing by a small stage and in the centre of the stage was an upright coffin. Standing inside the coffin, his torso loosely wrapped in a piece of white fabric, was the living skeleton. His limbs were matchstick-thin and his hands like strange white spiders. But it was his hollow, sunken face that was most frightening to look at. The man was almost bald and Paddy could see the ridges of his cranium. The man's lips and cheeks were blue, and his breath rattled in and out of his open mouth. Paddy stood transfixed. He knew at once that the man was consumptive, and remembered John Doherty's face on that last night in Dublin. It made Paddy's chest feel tight with pity. He thrust his hands deep into the pockets of his coat and there he felt the second bun that he'd bought. 'Here, man. You're starving,' he said and without a second thought he stepped up onto the stage. The skeleton stared at him uncomprehendingly as Paddy took his hand, turned it over and placed the currant bun in it.

The showman called out from the doorway, 'Here, you, get off the stage!'

Someone grabbed Paddy by the collar.

'You shouldn't be making money from a man's suffering!' shouted Paddy. 'It's not Christian. He's a human being, a poor starving wreck of a man!'

The crowd murmured as the showman flushed red and hauled Paddy over to the door.

'The skeleton gets paid good money, you're robbing him of his livelihood,' he hissed in Paddy's ear.

'You're robbing him of his dignity. Can't you see he's dying!'

The showman's reply was to throw Paddy bodily into the street, all the while cursing under his breath. 'Reckon I oughta put a sign up – "No dogs, no Irish",' he said. 'Now clear off, you bloody larrikin.'

Paddy stood up. Looking down the street, he noticed a pair of boys watching him and sniggering behind their hands. Paddy broke into a run, the folds of Dai's coat flapping around him like wings.

All day, Paddy wandered the city. By evening, he had started to worry about where he was going to spend the night. He'd already determined not to go back to the Seamen's Home, but as the dark came down he found himself down at the wharves with nowhere to go. There was a slick on the water that was sour and unpleasant, not like the fresh, briny scent of the open sea. Paddy sat down, his legs dangling over the side of the wharf, and leant against a bollard. He looked down at the black water and then across at the docks and the pinpricks of light that illuminated the wharves. He pulled the coat tighter around him and thought of Dai lying somewhere out there, amongst the coral and the fishes.

'Blimey, there he is, that's the dumb Mick what was blueing with Jim Crilly,' came a voice from behind him.

'So? He's no use to us. May as well chuck him in the bay,' said another voice in disgust.

'Garn. Leave him alone. He's got guts, even if he's got no brains.'

Paddy couldn't help grinning to himself. It felt like the first time he'd smiled since the shipwreck. He looked over his shoulder. They were just a pair of boys and even in this light he could see their clothes were ragged. One of them held a cane in one hand and was leaning on it, his head tilted to one side.

'Oi, he's looking at us, Nugget,' said the surly one.

'Nugget' took a step closer to Paddy and nudged him with his worn boot.

'You're lucky me and Tiddler came along when we did. You looked like you was about to jump and do yourself in. And ain't that a mortal sin?'

'What would you know about it?'

They ignored the question. Tiddler leant closer and stared at Paddy. 'I reckon he looks like a right sinner. You know, Jim Crilly took the skeleton over to Prahran this arvo and the bugger dropped dead on stage! That would have been a sight worth sixpence. I heard Jim reckons it was indigestion from the bun this bugger gave away what killed the skeleton. His last supper from a right Judas, that's what Jim Crilly reckoned.'

Paddy got to his feet angrily.

'Sure, but I'm grateful for the news,' he said. 'If you'd like me to serve you the same dish, come a little closer.'

'Strike me fat, he's dumber than he looks!' laughed Tiddler, but he took one step back.

'Shut up, Tiddler,' said Nugget. He pulled a pipe out of his pocket and lit up. 'Look, Goldilocks, we're just heading downriver for a bit of a lark. There's a circus down on the river flats. You can tag along if you fancy.'

'We don't want him along,' said Tiddler, disgusted.

'I reckon any bloke that takes your measure and calls your bluff, Tiddler, is a man worth knowing.'

Paddy laughed. He decided to join them, if for no other

reason than to annoy Tiddler.

'So what brings you to old Melbourne town?' asked Nugget.

'Shipwreck. My boat went down at Point Nepean.'

'Oi, you wasn't on that *Lapwing*, was you?' asked Tiddler, suddenly impressed.

'To be sure. There were twenty-nine of us on board but only five survived.'

'So youse a sailor?' asked Tiddler.

'Not any more,' said Paddy.

It was almost dark by the time they reached the circus. A huge tent stood glowing on the banks of the river.

'How much will it cost?' asked Paddy. 'I don't have much money left.'

'Don't worry about it, cobber. Nugget Malloy don't pay for nothing.'

Paddy followed the other boys as they slipped under the ropes of the big top and wriggled under the canvas. They lay shoulder to shoulder beneath the bleachers. Peering out between the rows of seats, Paddy caught a glimpse of a man in a bright red coat and top hat. He whirled a huge stockwhip around his head and brought it down in the sawdust with a crack like a rifle going off. Paddy flinched, but a shiver of excitement ran down his spine.

A tribe of small acrobats cartwheeled into the ring and then out again. A trumpet sounded and two white horses cantered into the big top with a dark-haired acrobat astride their backs. He balanced with a foot on each horse, a purple and white satin cape flowing out behind him. Paddy caught his breath. The bareback rider raised his arms above his head and then threw his cape into the audience. He leapt from one animal to the other, twisting his body in mid-air and then landing sure-footed on the galloping horses. An attendant on a high platform held out silver hoops and the audience gasped each time the acrobat dived through them with effortless grace. When he galloped from the ring, a storm of applause and stamping feet thundered through the tent.

Suddenly, someone grabbed Paddy by the ankles and hauled him backwards. Beside him, Nugget cursed as he too was dragged under the bleachers. Outside the big top, Tiddler and Nugget wrenched themselves free from their captors and bolted across the river flat, disappearing into the darkness. Paddy stayed put. Three burly tent hands towered over him.

'Sorry, sirs. I hadn't the money for a ticket,' said Paddy, 'but I'd sell the shirt off my back for the chance to see that bareback rider again.'

One of the other men laughed. 'Cor, he's earnest.'

'I'll tell you what,' said one of the tent hands, 'if you're that keen on seeing the show, hang on to your shirt but come back tomorrow morning. You put in a few hours work around the place and the boss'll likely give you a ticket for tomorrow's matinee.'

'I'll be here, sir. First thing.'

That night, Paddy didn't go back to the Seamen's Home. He lay down beneath a tree, a stone's throw from the circus, and drew Dai's coat up over his head to keep the cold at bay. Despite the chill air, Paddy felt none of the bleak despair of the night before. The bright vision of the bareback rider rode through his dreams like a promise of things to come.

14

Daring Jack Ace

Before dawn, Paddy was waiting outside the big top. The first person to appear from the circus wagons was a small, golden-skinned, black-haired man with dark, almond-shaped eyes. He unrolled a rug on the damp grass and started stretching in the morning sunlight, then began to twist his body into amazing shapes. His limbs seemed to be made of licorice. Paddy's joints ached just watching. Suddenly the contortionist looked out from under a knot of limbs and grinned at Paddy.

'You can make like this? You come to circus for job?' he asked.

'Last night, a gentleman said I might be able to see the show if I worked today,' said Paddy.

'You, boy, you here work for Mr Sears' Circus then? We need boy. You hard-working boy?'

'Very hard-working,' said Paddy, nodding seriously.

The contortionist untangled his limbs and laughed. 'Mr Sears make very good deal. He smart. You be smart too. You tell him you want job, not only ticket. We need boy to help with horses, help with work. Too much work this damn circus.' He rolled up his rug and tucked it under his arm.

'You look like smart boy,' he said, tapping his forehead. 'You no let Harry Sears make you work for nothing.'

Harry Sears, the ringmaster, had a chest as big as a barrel of Guinness and long powerful arms. Even without his costume, he radiated authority. All morning, Paddy worked hard, following the ringmaster's directions. He raked the sawdust in the ring, fed and watered the horses, shovelled manure and emptied the slop buckets into the river. Even after Mr Sears told him he'd earned himself a ticket, he kept on working until the matinee began.

From the first blast of the horns, Paddy sat on the edge of the bleachers, every muscle in his body taut with excitement. Harry Sears' sons tumbled in the ring, diving over and over each other until Paddy wasn't sure where one boy began and the other ended. The exotic contortionist, Coo-Chee, twisted his body into such complicated shapes that he seemed more serpent than man. A sword-swallower pushed a long shining blade down his throat and Paddy pressed his fist against his chest, as if he could feel the blade against his own ribs. Each act presented itself as a small miracle but the most miraculous of all was the flying bareback rider, Jack Ace. He cantered into the ring on his team of white horses, risking his life each time he leapt fearlessly from one horse to the other. At the height of his performance, he reached up, took hold of a bar in the rigging and swung high into the roof of the big top. Paddy watched the white-clad figure flying above the audience and held his breath. In a single, swift movement, the man performed a somersault in the air and then landed gracefully on the back of one of the white horses. The audience cheered and Paddy cheered louder than any single one of them.

At the end of the show, Paddy went in search of Harry Sears. He found him sitting at the back of the big top drinking out of a tin mug.

'Mr Sears, I hear you've been looking for someone to sign on as a hand. I'd like the job, please, sir.'

'How old are you boy?

'I'm nearly fifteen,' said Paddy, adding a few months to his age.

'You're a big fella for fifteen.'

Paddy tried not to smile too broadly.

'Too big to train up for the circus. And too small for the sort of work a general hand has to do.' Harry emptied his mug and stood up.

'I'm fit for anything. I worked on a clipper doing plenty of hard work,' said Paddy urgently, following Harry. 'I used to help my ma on the farm back in Ireland. I'm not shy of work, sir.'

'You're keen enough, that's for sure. You know we're a travelling concern. We're taking to the road tomorrow, heading north to Sydney. Your old man give you permission to sign on?'

'I'm an orphan, sir, so I'm not needing anyone's permission,' said Paddy.

'All right then. You be here before dawn tomorrow to help load up and I'll take you on as a general hand. Two shillings a week and your fare.'

Paddy grinned. He walked away whistling. He slept under a bridge that night but as soon as the dawn rays crept over the city, he was back at the circus site, where the men were already at work loading up. There were eight wagons of gear and fourteen men and boys including Paddy, plus Ma

Sears, her sister and a confusing array of small children.

They took the road north out of Melbourne towards Warburton, past blossoming orchards. Paddy took a deep breath of the sweet, crisp air. He was glad to turn his back on the sea and see the horizon broken by forest and farmland. Beyond the orchards, flat golden fields folded out on either side of the road. Everything in Australia seemed to sit at strange angles to the world – the wild and the tame, the ordinary and the extraordinary. One day he was shipwrecked on a white beach, the next he was lost on the streets of a city and now he was travelling an endless open road.

They stopped in the late afternoon, at the edge of a village called Box Hill. There were no box trees and no hill that Paddy could make out, only a small dusty township. The men set to work raising the big top in an open field on the edge of town. Everyone helped unload the wagons, the smallest children staggering under the weight of ropes and canvas.

Harry Sears came over and thrust a big bass drum at Paddy. 'Here you are, time to drum up a crowd for this evening's show.'

'But I've never played a drum before,' said Paddy, holding the instrument at arm's length, as if it might explode.

'Ain't nothing to it, boy. Go and see Ma Sears and get her to give you an outfit, then strap this thing on and whack the billyo out of it. Everyone has to play in the band. It's the only way we're going to bring Box Hill to the show.'

Half an hour later, Paddy was marching through the village, banging on the drum with half a dozen of the other men squawking on battered brass trumpets, trombones and euphoniums. It didn't sound much like music, but the noise drew people out of their homes and into the street to watch. Paddy spun the padded drumsticks around and did a little dance step as he followed the other players. A small girl standing by her front gate waved at him and Paddy took off his hat and tossed it in the air, catching it on his head as he walked past. Paddy felt a satisfying glow at the sound of the girl's laughter.

That night, around sixty locals paid a shilling each to watch the show. After the crowds had left, the whole troupe gathered around a bonfire set well away from the flammable canvas. Ma Sears stirred a pot of mutton stew on the fire and ladled the dark meat onto tin plates.

'You were right flashy in the parade today,' said Ma Sears, as she dished up a plate for Paddy. 'You got a bit of showman's style, you have.'

She waved her ladle at Jack Ace. 'Here, Jack, you oughta teach that Paddy a few tricks and get him in the ring.'

Paddy was excited by the idea. 'That would be grand.'

Jack didn't answer. He was sitting off to one side of the fire on a fallen log, taking swigs from a small silver flask. Paddy sat down next to him to eat his dinner.

'You reckon you'd like to be an acrobat?' asked Jack Ace.

'I want to be a bareback rider, like you,' said Paddy, his eyes bright.

Jack Ace laughed and offered Paddy a swig from his whiskey flask but Paddy shook his head. The smell of it made him think of the wreck of the *Lapwing*, the drowned sailors, the dark and miserable past. Paddy couldn't bear to dwell on it, not even for a moment.

'First,' he said, 'I want to learn to do that trick where you do a handstand on the horse's back.'

'So you're good with the horses, then?' asked Jack.

'Maybe,' said Paddy.

Jack laughed. 'There's no maybes. You can't be afraid of hurting yourself. You can't be afraid of dying neither. You have to have guts to do what I do.'

'I'm not afraid.'

'All right then, I dare you to come along to a training session. I'll go easy on you, you being a beginner like. But if you're gonna stick at it, remember, you gotta be willing to take the dare. Every time.'

The next morning, as soon as he'd finished his chores, Paddy joined the Sears children for their training session in the big top. Jack was dressed in a close-fitting cotton singlet and leggings and his shoulder muscles gleamed with sweat as he worked through a series of chin-ups at a makeshift bar.

The smaller children had their own mats that they rolled out and practised tumbling on. Paddy was impressed by their daring and agility, but Jack Ace was hard to please. He prodded them roughly with his riding crop, and pulled them to their feet and shook them whenever they made the smallest mistake.

'Hopeless, the lot of you, look at those limbs sticking out. Elbows in!'

When he came to Paddy, he threw a mat towards him.

'Here, let's see you do a forward roll.'

Obediently, Paddy tucked his elbows in close to his body, kept his head down and rolled. Jack Ace watched, frowning.

'Not bad,' he said, reluctantly. 'For a first-timer. Now show me a handstand.'

Paddy flung himself at the mat but when his legs were in the air they just kept going and he landed hard on his back. Jack Ace caught his feet the next time he tried.

'Your arms are too wide. Keep your hands under your shoulders. And drop into it. Don't throw yourself at the ground,' he instructed.

Paddy tried again, and this time it worked perfectly. He kept himself upright until his head started to pound with blood, then slowly lowered his feet to the ground and stood up, grinning.

'You're not bad,' said Jack. 'Your back's a bit long, but you're not bad at all.'

Without warning, Jack spun around and lashed out at one of the smaller boys, knocking him to the ground. 'Here, I didn't say you could stop working. All right, you lot. Get over here,' he said, shouting at the tribe of small children who were scrambling over the bleachers.

'Time for my box of tricks,' he said, winking at Paddy. He set a jagged tin in the sawdust and then forced the smallest boy to do a handstand over the tin. Jack kept hold of the boy's ankles for a minute, keeping him clear of the sharp edges but as his grip loosened the boy began to whimper. 'You hold that for a count of ten,' said Jack, his voice hard.

Coo-Chee shook his head, rolled up his mat and walked out of the tent.

Within a second of Jack letting go, the boy fell onto the jagged tin and yelped in pain. Paddy helped him to his feet and wiped away the trickle of blood from the small boy's forehead but the cut was deep and the wound kept bleeding.

Jack grunted. 'Take him to Ma Sears. She'll clean him up,' he said dismissively.

Paddy stared at the man, suddenly revolted. 'What?' said Jack. 'Listen, boy, you have to have guts to be an acrobat. You have to take the dare, every time, risk your life. If you can't be daring, you'll be nothing.'

Paddy led the snivelling boy out of the big top and down to the creek where Ma Sears was drawing water.

'How was your first go?' asked Ma Sears, not looking up from her work.

'Bobby, he . . .' Paddy trailed off, not knowing how to explain what he had witnessed. Ma turned and took in everything instantly.

'You playing silly buggers again, Bobby?' she said.

'He wasn't doing anything,' said Paddy but Ma Sears held up her hand to silence him.

'Listen, Paddy. Jack's a hard man when it comes to the ring, but he gets results.' She picked up Bobby and thrust a pair of kerosene tins at Paddy. 'Here, bring us some fresh water and I'll get this one cleaned up.'

All morning Paddy went back and forth between the creek and the kitchen tent, filling the tins and brooding on the training session. Maybe Bobby did act up a lot. Ma Sears didn't seemed worried by it. Who was Paddy to judge? How was he to know if Jack was cruel or fair?

Paddy knew he could learn from Jack. And he was willing to work hard. He didn't want to be just an ordinary acrobat. He wanted to be something extraordinary. He wanted to ride into the big top and hear the audience gasp, to hear the sharp intake of their breath as he thrilled them with his skill and daring.

When he'd finished drawing water he crossed over to the paddock where the horses were grazing. He stood watching for a long time before a young dappled grey mare approached him. Paddy smiled. Keeping his gaze down, he cautiously stroked her neck and flank, imagining what it would be like to ride her. When she bent her head and nuzzled him, he whispered into her ear. 'One day soon, Tattoo, you and me, we'll show that Jack Ace just what daring really means.'

15

The wild child

They travelled into the Dandenong Ranges, where the tracks grew winding and narrow and giant tree ferns spread their fronds across the roadway. The air smelt damp and sweet and the forests echoed with strange bird cries. Paddy looked around him in wonder. Every twist in the road revealed a new vision of lush, damp rainforest. The sun filtered through the leaves of tall gums and dappled everything with shifting light. Flocks of coloured parrots darted in and out of the shadowy forest, swooping low over the caravan of wagons. Paddy could almost imagine fairy folk living in the folds of the gullies and beneath the spreading tree-ferns.

The circus never stopped for more than a night or two in any of the small mountain towns and at every stop, shearers and shepherds, farmers and timber-cutters emerged out of the forests to enquire about tickets for the evening show. Paddy was woken hours before dawn to help load up the wagons by torchlight, and the circus would take to the road again as soon as the day began to unfold. After Healesville, they travelled over the Black Spur and the air grew sharp and icy.

At a small town called Marysville, the circus set up camp on a wide field beside a swift-flowing river. Paddy was carting water up to the kitchen tent on the second morning of their stay when he noticed a ragged man dragging a small child towards the big top. The child was resisting every step, digging its heels into the mud to slow their progress. The child had a mane of long, tangled, black hair and its clothes were so raggedy it was hard to tell if it was a boy or a girl.

Paddy saw Harry Sears and Jack Ace look up from their mugs of billy tea as the man and child approached. The conversation between Harry and the man quickly grew heated. When the man flicked open the saddlebag he carried and pointed at its contents, Harry put down his mug and called out for Ma Sears to join them. Paddy followed, curious as to what the saddlebag held. He peered over Ma Sears' shoulder. Inside, nestled in the folds of a worn old blanket, lay a tiny, naked, newborn baby.

Ma Sears shook her head and drew the blanket over the baby, then turned to look at the older child, pushing the black hair away from its face. It glared back furiously with the deepest blue eyes that Paddy had ever seen.

'Underfed and filthy,' said Ma Sears, disapprovingly.

'Born wiry, that one,' said the father. 'Garn, Vi. Show the folk your monkey trick.'

He smacked the girl on the bottom and she scrambled up the nearest tree. Paddy couldn't figure out how she got a grip on the smooth, silvery bark, but in a minute she was at the first fork, twenty feet above them.

'See, she's limber enough. Only six years old and already she's a little monkey. The babby will be like her one day and you can have the pair for six pounds,' said the man.

'I'll give you four pound for the child but we can't take the baby,' said Harry Sears, after a hurried consultation with his wife.

The father looked stricken. 'But I can't keep the babby,' he cried. 'My wife, she died having this one. I can't keep either of them. I'm a timber-cutter away in the forest for days at a time. You can have 'em both for two quid.'

'Look, mate, I'll make it five pounds for the girl. You can give the money to someone and they might take the baby. We'll take the girl on as an apprentice. Train her well, give her a profession. But the baby's no good to us.'

The man flipped the saddlebag shut and sighed.

'Violet,' he called, looking up the tree. 'Get down here.'

At first the girl didn't move. She stayed in the fork of the tree, hugging the trunk.

'Violet!!' her father barked.

Reluctantly, the little girl shinnied down the tree and stood beside her father.

'This bloke and his lady, they run this circus, see. You're gunna stop with them now, learn how to do some more tricks. You'll be a good girl and do like you're told. Orright?'

The girl said nothing. She glared at everyone, including Paddy. He stepped back, startled by the ferocity of her gaze.

'Here, Paddy,' called Harry Sears. 'You reckon you've got some book-learning. You can draw up the papers.'

Ma Sears dictated the terms of the apprenticeship and Paddy wrote it down in his best hand. Then the father put his mark at the bottom of the paper and took the five-pound note. He didn't even turn to wave goodbye to his daughter. The little girl sat huddled in a corner of the tent, her arms wrapped around her knees.

'She's in a state,' said Ma Sears shaking her head. 'Crawling with nits. Her scalp's got infected too. Heat some water up, Paddy.'

The girl didn't resist as Ma Sears sat her on a bench and cut all her hair off, but a trail of tears ran down her face, leaving white streaks on her dirty grey cheeks. Paddy watched her out of the corner of his eye as he went back and forward from the fire with buckets of warm water.

The girl let out a blood-curdling scream as Ma Sears wrestled her into the tin washtub. She thrashed about like a wild thing, writhing in the sudsy water. Suddenly, Ma Sears lost her grip, the tub was upturned and the small girl bolted into the forest.

'Paddy, after her!' called Ma Sears.

Paddy ran after the naked child. He caught a fleeting glimpse of her burrowing into the dense undergrowth but when he reached the spot, she was nowhere to be found. He stopped, turned his head to one side and listened to the hushed bush.

It started to snow. Flakes fell like angel dust, landing on the spreading fronds of the tree-ferns. Paddy strained to see or hear any clue that would lead him to the girl. The snow started to fall thick and fast. A muffled sob caught his ear.

Paddy lifted a frond of giant tree-fern. The little girl was huddled against the hairy trunk, shivering. With her shaved head and her pale naked limbs, she looked like a lost elf. Paddy took off his coat and slipped it around her shoulders.

'C'mon now,' he said gently. 'C'mon out. It's not so bad.'

The little girl began to cry, her whole body shuddering as she wept.

'I want my mama,' she sobbed.

Paddy crouched down beside her under the tree-fern and watched the snow falling.

'I miss my mam too,' said Paddy. 'She's an angel in heaven, like your mama. Maybe they're up there right now, having a chat together and a nice cup of tea. Maybe your mama is saying to my mam how you ought to go back to the circus like your da wanted you to. And my mam is saying, sure that's a grand idea because her boy – that's me, Paddy – she's telling your mama how her boy will watch out for you.'

The little girl looked up at him and once again, Paddy was startled by the intensity of her blue eyes.

'Violet,' he said softly. 'C'mon back. I promise it will be all right.'

Without taking her eyes off his face, Violet slipped her hand into his and together they walked through the snowy forest.

'You were quick enough chasing the girl,' said Harry Sears that evening. 'Reckon you can take over from Jimmy, bringing up the rear of the caravan from here on in. If one of the horses wanders away from the cavalcade, you chase it as fast as you can, bring it back to the wagons.'

Next morning, as soon as the circus gear was loaded, Paddy climbed onto the back of the pole wagon, the last wagon in the procession. Violet scrambled up beside him. She wore a little red knitted cap that Ma Sears had given her to cover her bald head, and a baggy shift that one of the

Sears girls had outgrown. She settled herself down amongst the canvas and tent poles as if it was where she belonged.

Paddy didn't mind her company on the first day but after a few days, everyone in the troupe started calling Violet 'Paddy's shadow'. Every time he looked around she'd be somewhere close behind, watching him intently. Paddy couldn't even disappear for five minutes without her racing around the circus camp, shouting out his name.

When the circus set out again, Violet was settled in amongst the canvas and tent poles before dawn.

'Now, Violet, you don't want to be riding up alongside me every day.'

'Yes I do,' she said.

'No, you want to ride with May and Flora up the front. That's where the other little girls go.'

'No, I have to stay with you,' said Violet solemnly. 'Our mams want it.'

Paddy sighed and climbed into the wagon. Violet snuggled down beside him, frowning with concentration as they both watched the horses following behind. Before long, Tattoo, the dappled grey mare that was his favourite, began to lag behind. When they rounded a corner, she disappeared from view.

'Now, no mucking about while I'm gone,' he said to Violet, as he leapt down from the back of the moving wagon. Violet nodded obediently. When he glanced back over his shoulder, she was watching him earnestly. Paddy smiled. Even if she was annoying, it wasn't so bad having her along.

Paddy ran barefooted across the stubbly ground. It didn't take long to catch up with Tattoo but he didn't hurry to join the cavalcade. When he was sure they'd fallen a long way behind, he led her into a nearby field, grabbed a handful of mane, and swung himself up onto her back. They rode around the paddock and then back along the dusty yellow road at a slow trot. As soon as the circus came in sight, Paddy slid to the ground, took a short length of rope, threaded it through Tattoo's bridle and then jogged after the last wagon.

Violet was cross with Paddy for taking so long, and from then on she kept a sharp eye out for the horses, anxious that Paddy should catch them quickly.

The circus zigzagged across the colony, following a meandering path north to the border, and Harry Sears complained about the trade at every small town. Times were tough everywhere and Paddy could tell by the look of folk that they had nothing much to spare.

Between towns, Harry and the other men went out hunting. Paddy would help Ma Sears skin a brace of rabbits or however many possums they had managed to catch. The first time they brought back a wallaby, he turned the carcass over and stared at its belly, wondering where to sink the knife. Suddenly, he jumped back.

'Ma, I think it's still alive. Its belly, it's moving like.'

She ran her hand over the wallaby. 'There's a little surprise come with this one,' she said. She slipped her hand into the pouch of the wallaby and scooped out a tiny joey. 'Here, hold it close to you, Paddy. It needs the warmth. They make lovely little pets, these joeys.'

All the circus kids came crowding into the kitchen tent, as if they knew by instinct that there was something to see. They jostled each other, each demanding a turn at holding the animal, but Ma swatted them away like flies.

'It's Paddy what spotted it first.'

'But isn't it my turn to have a pet?' asked Joe, the eldest Sears. 'Besides, Paddy won't be able to take care of it. He's gotta chase the ponies. That wallaby needs to get carried around all day till it's bigger. Someone's gotta keep it warm and all.'

Ma Sears looked at Paddy and nodded her head. 'Sorry, Paddy. Joe's right. But you can't have it neither, Joe. We need one of the little kids who ain't so busy with other work to mind it.'

Paddy looked down at the little bundle. He wanted fiercely to keep it for his own. He glanced across at the crowd of smaller children. Standing at the edge of the group was Violet. Her hair was starting to grow back now, a dark fuzz of spiky black.

'How about Violet?' asked Paddy.

Ma Sears smiled. 'That's an idea. Come here, Vi.'

Paddy knelt down beside Violet and showed her the tiny creature.

'What do you want to call it?' asked Paddy. 'You can give it a name.'

'I fink I'll call it Sonny,' said Violet. 'My mama, she had a baby called Sonny.'

Ma Sears took a length of old pudding-cloth and made a sling which she tied around Violet's neck. She sent one of the other children to bring her a piece of woollen blanket and when the sling was lined with the wool, she gestured for Paddy to come close. Paddy slipped the baby wallaby into the sling and Violet's eyes grew wide. She giggled as the joey nuzzled against her chest until only one dark ear protruded from the sling.

Violet stopped complaining about how long it took Paddy to catch the horses. He could return after hours away to find her perfectly happy, chatting to the baby wallaby as if it understood all her prattle. It gave Paddy the chance to spend whole mornings alone with Tattoo without worrying about Violet fretting. He kept just out of view of the circus wagons, herding the other horses ahead as he trailed the rear of the troupe.

In the weeks that followed, Paddy and Tattoo formed a special bond. Of all the circus horses, Tattoo was the most patient and the quickest to respond to his instruction. It was almost as if she knew what he needed to learn. As the dry spring merged with the hot summer months, Paddy learnt to ride as if he and Tattoo were one and the same, a single creature, part-horse, part-boy.

One morning, as Paddy leapt down from the pole wagon, Violet called after him.

'What?' shouted Paddy. Violet was leaning out of the back of the wagon waving to him frantically. He ran back and jumped up on the step.

'Sonny says, you be careful. Sonny says we gotta watch out for each other, the way our mams said.'

Paddy groaned with annoyance. The horses were falling further behind. 'Vi, I have to run,' he said.

As he pulled away from her, Violet's sleeve slid up and Paddy noticed a long purple bruise on the inside of her arm. He almost stopped to ask how she had got it but Tattoo had already disappeared from sight and there was no time to lose.

''Member,' called Violet after him. 'Me and Sonny is watching out for you!'

With a flash of guilt, Paddy realised he hadn't been watching out for Violet. She had become exactly like his shadow, a familiar presence behind him that he paid no attention to. Why should he feel guilty? It wasn't as if Violet was the wild child he'd led out of the forest any more. She had Sonny to play with and Ma Sears to feed her. She was used to the ways of the circus. She didn't really need Paddy any more. Or did she?

16

Stealing Violet

Violet had a natural gift as an acrobat. Jack Ace or Coo-Chee could show her a trick, and inside three attempts she'd have perfected the move. Less than a fortnight after joining the circus, she could perform cartwheels, handstands and forward dives with ease. Harry Sears reckoned the money he'd handed over for Violet was the best five quid he'd ever spent.

Paddy didn't often make it to the morning training session, as the work of the camp kept him so busy. When he did, Jack Ace treated him with a grudging respect. Paddy was growing stronger by the day and since joining the circus had grown taller than Jack. Sometimes he would act as a base while the smaller children scrambled up his body and balanced on his shoulders.

One morning, when they were camped on the banks of a winding creek just over the border of New South Wales, Jack Ace called out to Paddy to help him rig some ropes and pulleys between two gum trees. Jack was never his best in the mornings, and this morning, after drinking late into the night, his eyes were puffy.

'We're gunna teach that shadow of yours a few new tricks,' said Jack.

Following Jack's instructions, Paddy climbed up the tree and tied a seaman's knot to ensure the contraption held fast.

Jack led Violet over to where the pulley was suspended and tied a rope tightly around her waist. Violet wriggled uncomfortably, tugging at the rope.

'Here, let me tie it again,' said Paddy, stepping forward.

'No,' barked Jack. 'She's right. You take the other end. I need you to keep it taut so she don't fall.'

In one swift move, he hoisted Violet into the air and onto his shoulders, then took firm hold of her ankles.

'Now, Vi,' said Jack, 'You gotta do just like you do on the mats. Just like you do for Coo-Chee. A forward roll but straight off my shoulders.'

Violet's face grew pale. 'Don't want to,' she said.

'C'mon now, you'd do it for Coo-Chee, so you can do it for me. Take my hands.'

He let go of her ankles and put his arms up for her to catch hold of his hands, but Violet was too quick for him. The moment he loosened his grip, she leapt forward into the air. Paddy braced himself and pulled hard on the rope to stop her falling. Violet dangled in mid-air, a look of surprise on her face.

'Bloody hell!' shouted Jack, slapping the back of her legs and taking hold of her ankles again. 'Now you see, Paddy has you, so you're not gunna hit the ground. Give her a bit of slack this time, so the rope goes with her when she turns.'

Violet looked at Paddy nervously. 'You can do it, Violet,' he said. 'I'm watching out for you.'

A moment later she dived forward, turning a perfect full

somersault in mid-air and then spreading her arms wide, as if she were a bird about to take flight. Jack grabbed her legs again and put her on his shoulders once more. Violet winced as he gripped her calves tightly.

'There's no call for you to be so rough with her,' said Paddy.

'You keep out of this. She won't learn no other way.'

'She'll learn faster if you don't bully her,' said Paddy.

Jack lifted Violet off his shoulders and set her on the ground. He walked over to Paddy and stood menacingly close.

'Don't you go telling me my business. You don't know bull about this caper,' he said, his voice thick with suppressed rage. 'Get Coo-chee. He can handle the mechanic. I don't want you near this kid while I'm training. You put her right off.'

Paddy dropped the rope and stepped away. 'And do yourself a favour, keep out of my sight,' shouted Jack.

'You hurt Vi, and you'll have me to answer to,' said Paddy.

Jack Ace looked Paddy up and down with undisguised contempt. Then he laughed. Paddy clenched his fists by his side.

'I mean it,' said Paddy. But Jack was already walking away from him, back to where Violet stood waiting.

Paddy was bucketing water out of the river when he heard Violet's screams echo across the campsite. He dropped the water can and ran to the big top. Violet was scrambling up the bleachers, trying to cover her head with her arms, as Jack Ace pursued her with his riding crop. Jack caught her by the ankle and pulled her towards him, beating her around the head and body, dragging her down the bleachers and throwing her into the sawdust. For a moment, everyone in the tent stood frozen as Jack Ace drew back his boot and kicked Violet hard in the stomach.

Paddy didn't stop to think. He was beside Violet in a moment and punched Jack Ace in the jaw with a powerful uppercut that sent the man sprawling.

Violet lay whimpering in the sawdust. Paddy knelt down beside her but she kept her eyes shut and folded her arms across her chest. There were long red welts swelling up across her arms where the riding crop had cut her flesh.

'Vi, are you all right?' he asked.

Before Violet could answer, Jack Ace staggered to his feet and grabbed Paddy by the back of his shirt. The sun-worn fabric tore in his rough grip and as Paddy spun around, Jack punched him hard in the face. The blow caught Paddy on the eyebrow and the skin instantly split open. Blood trickled into his eye and momentarily blinded him. A second blow in the side of his head nearly knocked him off his feet, but he caught his balance and charged, head down. This time, Jack was ready for him. Paddy might have grown taller than Jack, but the strength of the man astonished him. Jack caught Paddy by the throat and with his other hand started pummelling him, driving him into the sawdust. Suddenly, Harry Sears was there, pulling them apart and dragging Jack away.

The two men started arguing while Paddy sat with his head in his hands, trying to stem the flow of blood from his face wounds with a piece of torn shirt.

Harry Sears strode over to him. 'What the hell do you think you're doing, interfering with the training?' he shouted.

'He wasn't training her,' said Paddy angrily, his mouth full of blood. 'He was beating her! She's only a little girl.'

Jack Ace scowled at Paddy. He stepped towards him, fists clenched, but Harry Sears pushed him away.

'This is a circus, not a bloody boxing outfit. Leave it, Jack.'

He grabbed Paddy by the arm and hauled him to his feet. 'Get yourself over to Ma Sears and she'll fix up your wounds. And keep out of the tent while the little kids are working.' Then Harry picked up Violet. She was bleeding from the mouth and her eyes were half shut.

'Get on with it, Jack,' he called over his shoulder.

Paddy staggered to the tent opening. The ground swayed uneasily beneath him.

Ma Sears sat Paddy on an upturned crate and dabbed iodine on his split lip and brow.

'You're lucky you didn't lose your teeth,' she said, shaking her head with disapproval. 'You steer clear of that Jack. You've put him offside good and proper now.'

'I don't care,' said Paddy moodily. 'I should have punched him square in the nose.'

'Now you stop that talk. You forget about it. Jack will too. Give him a few weeks. You're a good boy, Paddy. And I've been watching how you've been with the horses. You'll be in the ring soon enough and Jack Ace will have some serious competition then, so don't you go making a rod for your own back. You'll be needing his help when you're ready for the ring.'

'But Violet . . .'

'Violet's none of your business. She's got to learn. I know, sometimes Jack can be a bit rough but he'll ease off when Violet starts working the way he knows she can. She'll be a fine little performer one day and we'll have Jack to thank for it.'

Paddy didn't respond. The thought of thanking Jack Ace for anything made him want to throw up.

That evening, while the others sat around the campfire telling ghost stories, Paddy wandered away and stood listening to the crack of dry timber falling in the nearby forest. A dusky red moon rose up over the bush. Paddy looked across to find Violet standing near him in the half-light.

'Oh, Violet. You all right now?' he asked.

She touched her belly with the tips of her fingers. 'Still sore,' she said.

Paddy knelt down beside her and rested one hand on her shoulder. 'You've got to mind Jack Ace. You've got to do as he says, mind what he tells you, so he doesn't go losing his temper with you.'

'But you'll save me if he does, won't you?'

Paddy ran one hand through his hair and took a deep breath. He had been dreading this conversation. 'I can't stay around to watch out for you every minute of the day, Vi. I can't be with you every time you have to train with Jack. Today was a bad day but if you work hard, it won't be like that all the time.'

Even as Paddy said it, he shivered at the thought of what Jack might do to Violet next time she drew his wrath.

'He hurts me all the time,' said Violet in a small, sad voice. She pulled up her sleeves and the hem of her skirt and pointed to the patterning of bruises on her arms and legs.

'Sweet Jesus,' he said, stricken. He led her back towards the fire and they sat together, a short distance away from the others, just outside the ring of firelight.

Violet put her thumb in her mouth and leant her head against Paddy's shoulder.

'I don't know what to do, Vi,' said Paddy.

Violet giggled. 'Don't be silly,' she said. 'You always know what to do.'

Every muscle in Paddy's body was aching from the pummelling Jack had given him. His lips felt fat and swollen and one eye was ringed with throbbing bruises. He felt utterly defeated. His dreams of being a circus daredevil were disintegrating around him and all the excitement of the circus had drained away, but when Violet smiled up at him, he understood what he had to do.

Later that night, when the campfires had burnt down and the last of the circus folk had either gone into the big tent to bed down on the bleachers or rolled up in their swag to sleep by the fire, Paddy tiptoed over to the wagon where the Sears children slept. Violet always lay on the edge, away from the other children. Paddy squatted under the big wheels, listening until he was certain the rhythms of the children's breathing were settled in sleep. Then he reached into the wagon and slipped a hand over Violet's mouth, to stop her squealing. Immediately, Violet grabbed his wrist and leapt out of the wagon, slipping her arms around his neck and clinging to him.

'Shhh, there you go,' he whispered in her ear. 'Don't you be making a fuss now. We've got to be like two possums, and scurry out of here quiet-like.'

Paddy pulled out what bedding of Violet's he could remove without waking the other children and wrapped it around her shoulders. Then he realised she had Sonny slung across her chest.

'You can't bring Sonny with you,' said Paddy. 'He's too big for you to carry.'

Violet stared at him in dismay.

'Oh all right,' he said, trying to mask his irritation. 'Give him to me.' He scooped up Sonny and tied the knot tight around his neck.

'Where are we going?' asked Violet.

'A safe place. I'm not sure where yet. But when I see it, I'll know we're there.'

The moon was high and white as they turned onto the road. Paddy hesitated for a moment. If they headed north, the circus would quickly overtake them. They headed south to Albury.

As the moon sank low in the sky and dawn drew closer, Violet began to drag her feet and complain that her tummy hurt. They hadn't covered much distance and Paddy dreaded the daylight. Harry was sure to send a rider to look for Violet. He wouldn't let go of his five-pound investment easily. Paddy led Violet off the road into some thick bush and they made a little nest for themselves amongst the roots of a giant gum. He eased the joey's sling off and handed it to Violet. She fell asleep almost immediately, curling herself around Sonny, but Paddy lay awake, his thoughts churning. He stared down at Violet, sleeping quietly beside him. What had he landed himself with? What was he going to do with a six-year-old girl? What would happen if Harry Sears and Jack Ace caught up with them?

In the morning, he woke to the sound of horses galloping south. He knew the sound of each of the circus animals. Someone was riding Tattoo and another rider was on the white mare, Elsie.

'Violet,' he said. 'Wake up. We have to go.'

'Where?' she asked sleepily, stretching like a cat. The raised welts on her arms were dark today, like tiger stripes across her fair skin. Paddy stared at the markings.

'A long, long way from here,' he replied.

Overhead, a flock of sulphur-crested cockatoos took flight. Paddy pulled Violet to her feet and led her deeper into the bush. They headed west, casting long shadows into the heart of the wilderness.

17

Keeping faith

They walked most of the day. Violet didn't complain, but every hour or so she would take Paddy's hand. Paddy didn't want to hold her hand. He was busy trying to clear a path through the bush, knowing they had to find their way back to a road before darkness fell, and he already had the burden of Sonny and the sling to contend with. The only consolation was that he didn't have to worry about Violet getting lost. She stayed so close to him that it was hard to get a good swing at the dense undergrowth without knocking her off her feet.

Late in the afternoon, they sat on a fallen branch and shared the last of the bread and salt beef that Paddy had taken from the kitchen tent. Sonny poked his head out from inside the sling and Violet fed him some crumbled bread from the tips of her fingers.

'Can I take him back, just for a little while?' she asked.

Paddy was glad to unburden himself of the wallaby.

When they'd finished the last of the water in Paddy's water bottle, she asked 'Are we lost?'

Paddy looked about him. 'Lost? No, we're just making sure that Jack Ace doesn't catch up with us.'

'Good,' said Violet. 'My dad told me never go walking in the bush alone, 'cause if you get lost you'll get dead real quick.'

Paddy stared down at Violet. She had taken off her red knitted cap and was turning it over and over in her hands. Her short, curly black hair was full of bits of twigs and leaves and there were scratches on her cheeks. He knew she was afraid, but he couldn't think of anything to say that would comfort her and not be a lie. He turned away and swung his stick harder at the long tangle of grass and bracken.

Suddenly, Violet let out a cry of alarm. 'Sonny!'

Paddy saw the small wallaby bounding into the scrub and groaned. Violet held up the empty sling. 'He jumped out. Quick! He's getting lost!' She bolted off in the direction the wallaby had taken, calling out to Sonny frantically. By the time Paddy caught up with her, she was lying on the ground weeping. The joey was nowhere in sight.

'Never mind, Violet,' he said, exasperated. 'Sonny will be all right. This is his home.'

Violet sat up.

'And we'll be home soon too. A new home,' she said, solemnly.

Paddy shivered. It was unnatural how much she trusted him.

They went on, clambering over fallen branches and when the bush grew too dense, crawling through a tangle of yellow grass and scrub. Violet lost her cap and started to cry again.

Paddy grimly dragged her onwards. If they could just get to the banks of the Murray before dark, then they'd have water to put in the billy.

Suddenly, Violet tugged her hand free and dashed into the bush.

'Violet!' shouted Paddy. But she was back in a moment, grinning. In her hand was the red knitted cap.

'It was just over there, on that branch,' she said. She pulled the little red cap on tightly. Paddy looked into the impenetrable bush, disbelievingly. They had come full circle.

The afternoon gold quickly turned to black and though the sky was bright with stars, there was still no moon to light their way. Finally, Paddy knew he had to stop. The thick trunk of a white gum stood out. He took Violet by the hand and led her over to the tree.

Paddy unrolled their swags and Violet pulled the ragged blue blanket up so it covered her completely. She was asleep in a moment. Paddy envied the ease with which she slipped into dreams.

The moon rose copper-red through the gums, and the stars faded. He watched the light play between the leaves, strange alien foliage that drooped downwards. He thought of the grey granite of the Burren, bleak and beautiful, and the summer afternoons when he had run wild across the landscape, eating his fill of blackberries, chewing on wild grass, and drinking from wells and streams. In the evenings, there were always the lights of the cottages to guide him home.

They had walked all day without seeing so much as a bark hut, and Paddy knew it was easy to travel for days in this vast landscape without seeing a living soul. He looked down at Violet. Her forehead shone white in the moonlight beneath a tangle of dark curls. He sighed and lay down on the ground beside her.

Paddy woke with Violet's arms wrapped tight around his neck. During the night, she'd nuzzled in close, like a baby possum. He pulled her arms away and sat up. It was early morning and a mist was drifting between the trees. They had to be near water. He shook Violet awake and set off into the mist. They didn't speak. Their mouths were dry with thirst. Paddy stood very still, one hand on Violet's shoulder, and listened. Very faintly, he heard the splash of a creature at the water's edge. With a whoop, they both ran towards the sound.

Paddy stepped down into the brown, muddy water and filled the billy from the surface layer. He offered the can to Violet and she drank thirstily.

Paddy smelt smoke well before he saw the fire. 'Violet, follow me!' he said. He scrambled across the twisting roots of the river gums, trying to see through the morning mist. He couldn't hear voices, but the smoke had the distinctive fragrance of damper mingling with the scent of burning gum leaves and the moist river air. Then he spotted a flicker of firelight on the riverbend ahead.

'Ahoy there!' called Paddy,

Violet cupped her hands around her mouth and cried out in a high, shrill voice, 'Coo-ee! Coo-ee!'

'That's what you call when you've been lost and then you're gunna be found,' she said importantly. 'You call coo-ee.'

Paddy laughed and cupped his hands too, to send cries echoing across the water.

A moment later, they heard an answering cry. A man stepped out from amidst the river gums and waved at them with both arms. Half an hour later, Paddy and Violet were sitting around a campfire, each with their hands cupped around a mug of sweet black tea. Jim and Tom listened to Paddy with interest as he told them how he and Violet had run away from the circus. Violet squatted beside him, drawing pictures in the dust with a stick.

'You shouldn't have taken the little girl with you, boy,' said Tom. 'It's hard times all over. At least she had a bed and some tucker and a woman to care for her.'

'But they weren't taking proper care of her!'

'And you reckon you can?'

Paddy fell silent.

'Our mams want us to stick together,' said Violet. 'I have to stay with Paddy.'

'You kiddies cousins or something?'

'Something like that,' answered Paddy darkly. 'C'mon, Violet,' he said, hauling Violet to her feet. 'We better be moving on.'

'Steady on there, boy,' said Jim. 'You don't want to go wandering off into the bush and get yourselves lost again. We're heading down to Gunyah Station. Why don't you two tag along? They're starting the shearing soon and they'll be needing a tarboy. You can have a word with old man Gordon, the station manager. He might have an idea of where the little tacker can find a home.'

Paddy opened his mouth to reply and then hesitated. 'You catching flies?' asked Jim, laughing at Paddy's expression.

Violet laughed too. Even though she had never questioned him, not even when Sonny ran away, Paddy could see the relief in her face now they were out of the bush and in the company of other people. Violet looked from the shearers to Paddy, waiting anxiously for his response.

'I'll be glad of the work,' said Paddy.

The men packed up camp, doused the coals of the fire and hitched their swags across their shoulders. The sun rose bright and hot as they followed the track south-west. Soon the scrub thinned and opened out into wide, flat paddocks. They rounded a bend in the road and everyone stopped, gazing at the wide paddock to their left.

'Blimey,' said Tom. 'What a bloody mess.'

The soil was dry and dusty, the ground riven with holes and every few feet, rabbit carcasses lay limp and twisted, their bodies shrunken in the sunlight.

Violet went up to the fence and stared at the carcasses with a blank expression.

'Here, come away from there, Vi,' said Paddy, taking her hand and drawing her back. 'Don't look.'

'The rabbits, the drought, the squatters, and those crooked bankers down Melbourne way. The whole bloody country's going to the dogs,' said Tom, shaking his head in disgust. 'It's buggered.'

'You should have gone off with old Bill Lane,' said Jim. 'Gone off to Paraguay and made a new Australia.'

'Shut up, will ya,' growled Tom. 'I would have gone with him, if the missus would have come.'

'Where's Paraguay?' asked Paddy.

'South America,' said Tom. 'William Lane, he was a great bloke. Fought real hard for the shearers' union up Queensland way. When the government and the pastoralists got together and broke the back of our strike, well, Lane reckoned the country was buggered. Got a shipload of shearers and their families and his mates and set off for South America.'

'Making a new Australia,' said Jim. 'Poor buggers. Some of them have come home and a sorry tale they're telling.'

'Some of them are still there, sticking it out,' argued Tom. 'Pack of pikers, the ones that gave up. Lane was right about this bloody country.'

'Don't listen to him, Paddy,' said Jim. 'Sure these are hard times but it's not such a bad place. Reckon I'd rather be here than back in Scotland where my old man came from.'

Then he started to whistle and before long, the whistle had turned into a song. Paddy was surprised when Violet joined in. She knew all the words.

You may sing of the Shamrock, the Thistle, the Rose,
Or the three in a bunch if you will;
But I know of a country that gathered all those,
I love the great land where the Waratah grows,
And the wattle blooms on a hill . . .

Reluctantly, Tom joined in too. Finally, Paddy picked up the chorus and sang along with them as they passed by the field of dead rabbits.

18

Gunyah Station

It took two days to reach Gunyah Station, a collection of stone and corrugated-iron buildings sprawled in the fold of a golden rise of hills. Apart from a small stand of gums near the buildings, there was not another tree for miles around.

A crowd of twenty men and boys were gathered in the dusty yard outside the station. Jim and Tom seemed to know half of them by name. Paddy edged closer as Jim argued with the boss.

'I reckon he'll make a good worker. You could use another boardboy, couldn't ya? He'd make a fine broomie or tarboy.'

'What about the girl? This isn't an orphanage, Jim,' said Mr Gordon, looking disapprovingly at Violet.

'Sir, she's no trouble, really,' said Paddy, interrupting. Mr Gordon ignored him.

'The Sisters of the Good Shepherd have an orphanage down in Bendigo,' said Mr Gordon. 'If we take her into the police or the hospital, they'll send her down there.'

Paddy blanched. He had to think fast. 'Please sir, it's

only till the shearing's finished. I'm taking her down to Melbourne, to our aunt.'

Mr Gordon grunted. 'But what is she meant to do in the meantime? We can't have her getting underfoot.'

'What about Mary?' asked Jim. 'She still the station cook? She's got a couple of piccaninnies, don't she? Couldn't the kid run around with her lot until we're done?'

Mr Gordon looked at Paddy sharply. 'A lot of folk wouldn't think it right, a white girl running around with a bunch of blacks.'

'It's only for a week or two, sir. And I'll watch out for her, when I'm not working.'

'All right then. Mind you, you'll be paying food rations for the girl as well. This is a working station, not a charity. We can use an extra boy, but if you're slack, mark my words, the pair of you will be straight to the police.'

'Yes sir,' said Paddy.

'Take the girl around to the kitchen. We can't be having a little girl in the shearers' quarters. There's a room out back where she can sleep, so long as she doesn't make any trouble.'

Paddy took Violet by the hand and led her round the back of the homestead. Through the flywire screen, he could see a woman inside the kitchen. When she came to the back door, Paddy was startled to realise she really was an Aborigine. Paddy had seen some native people before. At the circus, Harry Sears would make them sit away from the white folk, though they paid the same money.

'Mr Gordon said to ask, if you wouldn't mind, missus, could you keep an eye on Violet here while I'm helping with the shearing?'

Mary looked down at Violet and laughed. Violet was filthy. There'd been nowhere to wash her along the road. Her black hair stood out like a hedgehog's bristles. Mary sat her down at a bench in the kitchen and set a bowl of porridge before her. Violet ate it with alarming speed. She licked the bowl clean and sucked the remnants from her fingers. 'I like it here,' she said to Paddy. 'Is this our new home?'

'For a little while,' said Paddy.

The shearers' hut had bark walls and a tin roof. The floors were dirt and there was a long table down the centre of the shed. Three tiers of bunks ran all the way around each wall. Paddy dropped his bedroll onto one of the bunks. After sleeping on the ground for months, a hessian sack filled with chaff felt like heaven.

The next morning Paddy woke to find Violet curled up like a possum at the end of his bed. He leapt up and threw the blanket over her, hoping no one had seen, then he took her outside and dropped her, yawning, on a bale of hay.

'What do you think you're doing creeping into the bunkhouse in the middle of the night? Do you want to get us both in trouble?'

'I was lonesome.'

Paddy ran his hands through his hair and groaned. 'I reckon I'll be glad if the policeman came and took you away. I should tell the boss that the policeman can come and get you.'

'You wouldn't do that,' said Violet confidently. He could never shake her faith him, even when he tried.

'Violet! You go and wait in the kitchen with Mary.

I'll come and see you at the end of the day.'

'No,' she said, stamping her foot. 'We have to stick together. You said.'

He glared at her and when she sullenly turned her back on him, he whacked her hard on the bottom.

'Go on with you.'

Violet let out a little squeal and bolted.

The sun came up over the station and the shearers began to stir. Cook had a huge fire going under his camp oven and when he raised the lid, steam billowed into the cool morning air.

After breakfast, all the men and boys climbed into wagons and headed out to the shearing shed. Paddy was awestruck by the sea of sheep in the pens.

Jim was one of the fastest workers, a real gun shearer. As soon as a sheep came through from the catching pen, he'd have it on its back and his shears passed through the thick wool in one swift movement. With three cuts and a turn of his wrist, the whole of the fleece was off in a matter of minutes.

The activity in the shearing shed made the circus ring seem quiet in comparison. The air was thick with grease and dust. Paddy was assigned as a picker to five different shearers, and the work was hard and fast. When the shearers took off the fleeces, Paddy ran to gather them up and then threw them onto the skirting table where experienced wool-rollers would trim the fleeces and throw them in a bin for the classer to grade. Paddy then gathered up the remnant, the skirting, and took it to another table where the piece-pickers sorted it into grades. On top of all that, if one of the sheep was cut he had to run with the tar bucket so the shearer could daub the wound. Sometimes the shearer had to sew up the cut and Paddy would wait, holding the heavy tar bucket, while the needle curved in and out of the sheep's raw pink skin. The stench of tar seeped into him, until he felt as if he could taste nothing except tar and wool-fat in the back of his throat.

By mid-morning, Paddy's back and arms were aching and he was struggling to keep up. The fleeces were riddled with burrs and thorns that cut his hands. By the time the men stopped for smoko, the skin on his palms was raw and tender.

That evening, Paddy was so exhausted that he could barely eat the mutton stew that the cook served up for him. Even before the men had finished their meal, Paddy crawled into his bunk in clothes stiff with grease and dust, and instantly fell asleep.

An hour before dawn, Paddy woke with a start. His body was still sore but it wasn't the physical pain that woke him. He had forgotten to visit Violet. He looked to the end of the bed. She wasn't there. He wanted to feel relieved but instead he had a tight, sick feeling in the pit of his stomach. He shouldn't have been so cross with her. Moonlight was seeping in through the cracks in the hut wall. Paddy swung his legs over the side of his bunk, ready to pull his boots on and set out to search for Violet. There was a squeal as his feet made contact with a small body curled up on the floor.

Paddy felt a swirl of emotions: relief, anger, and a secret pride in Violet's devotion. She looked like a kitten curled up in the ragged strip of blue blanket that she'd dragged from the homestead. He pulled on his boots and then scooped her up, awkwardly carrying her out of the shearers' shed.

At the back door of the homestead he set her on her feet. The kitchen was in darkness. Paddy wondered what to do. He didn't want to disturb Mr Gordon. What if Gordon said they had to leave? He had no idea where they would go next.

As the sky began to lighten, Mary arrived.

'This little one giving you worry?' she said, reading Paddy's expression.

'She doesn't want to sleep in the homestead and if they catch her in the shearers' hut, I'll lose my job,' said Paddy.

Mary listened thoughtfully. 'You come along my place.'

Paddy followed her across the home paddock and over a small rise. On the other side of the hill, a small bark hut stood beneath a stand of gums. Inside, curled up on a pile of possum skin rugs, lay Mary's two children. In a minute, Violet was nestled down beside the other children.

Mary and Paddy walked back to the homestead together.

'That little one, she talk about you all day,' said Mary. 'You damn good brother, taking care of your sister.'

Paddy thought of Honor, his real sister. He hadn't even replied to the letter she'd written telling of their mother's death. He had barely thought of her since he'd set foot in Australia. But it was different with Violet. Even though she wasn't his sister, Violet needed him. And perhaps, in a way he couldn't explain, even to himself, he needed Violet.

19

Scribe

Sunday was a quiet day on Gunyah Station. A few of the shearers lay on their bunks with magazines or books. Others went rabbiting, or played cards and gambled away their future earnings with IOUs scribbled on scraps of paper.

In the morning, Paddy sat down beside Violet on a log outside the shearers' hut and wrote her name in the dusty soil with a stick.

'When we get you to a real school, you'll be able to say you know your letters.'

He placed the stick in her hand and made her follow the outline of each letter.

Suddenly he found one of the shearers, Mac, standing over him. 'You read and write, then?'

'Yes.'

Mac withdrew a crumpled letter from the inside pocket of his jacket. Paddy smoothed the page out and scanned the looping handwriting.

'Well, read it to me, boy,' said Mac.

Paddy frowned. The letter was very badly written with lots of words misspelt. Paddy read it out loud as best he could.

Dear Son,
It's two year and four months since last we heard
your news and we have received no money from
you. Your sister Elizabeth is not well. She can't
get out to chapel but the nuns come to her. I have
work at the mill but it is hard and we think of
you and your prosperous life and hope you cannot
forget your family here in Ireland. Your mam.

Mac slumped low and put his face in his hands. 'How can
I answer that? The thing is, you do forget, when you're
here and there's the sun and the work and the hope.'

'I could help you write a reply,' said Paddy.

They settled down in the shearers' quarters. Men were
playing cards at the other end of the table and they looked
up with interest as Mac and Paddy began to work. When
Paddy had finished, he read the letter back to Mac.

Dear Mother,
I received your welcome letter and write you these
few lines to let you know that all is well with my
wife Kate and myself and our little family.
  I hope it will be a consolation to you, Mother,
that I am happy out here away from tyrannical
landlords and Irish Bailiffs. Glorious it would
appear to us if you all in Ireland were possessed
of the same amount of freedom that we have
out here and without which no people can be
prosperous. I hope a change will take place
soon. Things cannot continue as they have done
and I pity the poor starving Children of Erin.

I enclose five pounds which is every penny I can
spare for the moment. Kate had another baby
boy last Christmas and we've named him Daniel
after Father. My youngsters are growing up well
with pure Irish blood running in their veins and
you'd be proud to see such sturdy-limbed boys.

If we all never again shall have the pleasure
of meeting here below, I hope we shall in the
Glorious Land of Promise. Remember me to
my sister Elizabeth and all inquiring friends,
I remain your loving son until death,
Seamus MacSwiney.

Paddy folded the letter neatly and handed it over to
Mac. Mac wiped his eyes with the back of his sleeve and
drew a deep breath.

'Sure the old woman will like that. A grand letter, it is.'

Paddy quickly discovered he was in demand. All
afternoon men came to him asking if he could write
letters to their wives, their mothers and their sweethearts.
Some of the shearers were so grateful that they gave him
sixpence for his trouble. Each time Paddy set pen to paper,
he thought of the letters he could be writing for himself to
Honor or Aunt Lil, but it made his heart feel tight in his
chest. The past was a dark place that he didn't want to
visit, not even in a letter.

Late that afternoon, while Violet was in the kitchen with
Mary and Paddy was sitting on the steps of the shearers'
hut, a policeman rode into the yard. Further behind him,
marching across the home paddock was another officer
leading a line of Aboriginal men. Around each man's neck

and wrists were heavy manacles through which loops of chain ran, so each man was chained to the man behind him. Paddy stared at them, bewildered.

'Here, Billy boy,' called Jim, looking directly at Paddy.

Feeling sick with anxiety, Paddy crossed the yard.

'Sergeant Smith here was passing by and thought he'd stop and ask us a few questions. He was wanting to know if I'd come across a boy and a little girl on the track in to Gunyah Station. Now I didn't but I was wondering if maybe you might have, seeing as you came from the other direction.' Jim winked and then waved his hand in front of his face, as if he were shooing away flies.

Paddy took his time before he answered thoughtfully. 'No, sir. Can't say that I did.'

'Don't see why the kids would turn up here,' said Jim.

'Me neither,' said Paddy.

'They're runaways,' said the policeman. 'A gent put in a missing persons report for them a couple of weeks back. I thought maybe one of you blokes might have crossed their path on the way in.'

'I'll go and ask the other shearers if they saw them,' offered Paddy helpfully.

Paddy ran into the shearers' hut and stood at the end of the table, staring silently at the men, his palms sweating, his heart pounding. He counted to fifty and then sauntered out into the yard again.

'No, sir,' he said, to the police officer. 'No one's seen hide nor hair of them.'

The police officer thanked them both, turned to walk away and then he stopped.

He turned back and looked straight at Paddy. 'Any of

the tarboys go by the name of Paddy Delaney?'

'There's a Jack and a Ted and two Jimmys but no Paddy.' Paddy smiled earnestly.

'I didn't think so,' said the officer, nodding. 'Thanks for your help, mates.'

He mounted his horse, called out to the other policeman and together they led the procession of chained men onto the road.

'Thanks, Jim,' said Paddy. 'I was lucky it was you he talked to first.'

'No worries. I've never been one for helping the traps. Lucky old man Gordon was out with his missus.'

Paddy stared after the dismal procession of chained men. 'Jim, why are all those men chained together? Is that what they'd do to me and Violet? Chain us up and take us in?'

Jim laughed. 'Nah, you're a white fella.'

'But what did they do?'

'Nothing, probably. They're witnesses. There's been trouble over at Eardisley Downs Station and they're being taken in for questioning.'

'Witnesses? But why are they treated like that?'

'I told you, they're blacks,' said Jim. 'You don't need to go worrying about them. It's yourself you gotta worry about. Call yourself Billy Smith or something if anyone goes asking, and get that Violet to lay low. You're lucky she wasn't about or she'd be back with them circus folk quick smart and you'd be in the lock-up. If I was you, I'd get right out of New South Wales as soon as the shearing's finished.'

Paddy nodded but he couldn't stop thinking about the chained men. If he had become a missionary, would he have been able to save their souls? Would he have been able to stop the police from treating them like that? Perhaps Violet was the only person he'd ever be able to save.

Later that afternoon, Paddy and Violet sat in the shearers' shed together. Paddy flipped through the *Bulletin* magazine, reading out articles to some of the men.

'Here,' said one shearer, handing him a newspaper. 'Read us a bit of the Melbourne news while you're at it.' Paddy scanned through the paper, looking for something of interest to share with the men.

A small advertisement on the entertainment page caught his eye. *'The Lilliputian Theatre Company seeks talented young performers aged 6 to 16 for New Zealand Tour. Auditions for parts in their production of The Pirates of Penzance will be held at the Haymarket Theatre, on Saturday 21st November, 2.00 p.m.'*

'Here, Jim,' said Paddy, 'You ever heard of this Lilliputian Theatre Company?'

Jim shook his head but another of the shearers piped up. 'I saw that mob in Sydney last year. Took my kiddies along for their Christmas pantomime. It was a swell show. All little tackers, dancing and singing as if they were a pack of midgets. You wouldn't credit what those kids can do.'

A whole troupe of kids, all working together. Paddy looked down at Violet. *New Zealand*, he thought. Jack Ace would never find them there. Paddy tore out the page with the advertisement, folded it up small and put it inside his swag. The auditions were being held on Saturday. Shearing would be finished by Thursday. Somehow, Paddy would have to find a way to get them both to Melbourne.

20

The Lilliputians

On the last day, the men sheared the rams, a slow and difficult task. Paddy was kept busy with the tar bucket and the smell of blood made his nose tingle. When the last ram was shorn and sent down the chute, the bell rang, the whistle blew and Gunyah Station was cut out.

In an hour, the sheds were deserted. The men took their pay and headed back onto the road. On horse, on foot, even one man on a bicycle, they set off in all directions. Tom, Jim and Mac all came and said goodbye to Paddy before hitching their swags onto their shoulders again and taking to the road. Jim pressed a pound note into Paddy's hand. 'For the kid,' he said. Paddy shook his hand and thanked him.

Paddy stood waiting with Violet while bales of pressed wool were secured on the bullock dray and then they scrambled onto the top of the load. Swirls of dust rose up behind them as Gunyah Station disappeared from view and the long road stretched out ahead. In the late afternoon the next day, they reached the banks of the Murray and crossed over the wide river into Echuca, from where they'd catch the night train to Melbourne.

Violet was asleep before the train left the station. Paddy tried to prop her up so that she slept in her seat but in the end he gave up and woke to find her curled up against him as usual.

When they reached Melbourne, Violet was overwhelmed by the sights and sounds of the city. She let out a little shriek as they stood on a busy street corner and a crowded tram trundled past. Paddy had to drag her away from the shop windows. If he loosened his grip for a moment, she'd run and press her face against the plate glass, staring in wonder at the displays.

Paddy took her straight into an emporium. The staff looked at him suspiciously but when he laid the pound notes on the table, one of the shop ladies took Violet away and brought her back in a simple cotton dress and a pair of shiny black boots. Even though Violet complained that the leather pinched, he could tell she was pleased. She stood on the pavement outside the emporium, staring down at the shiny black shoes and grinning from ear to ear. Delicately, she pointed one toe out in front and then the other, hopping from foot to foot in a little dance.

The city streets shimmered in the heat and the smell from the horse manure was pungent. Paddy felt too hot under the weight of Dai's coat but it was easier to wear it than carry it. They wandered up through the city, asking directions to the Haymarket Theatre.

When Paddy turned into the stage door, his heart started to thump so loudly that he worried Violet would hear it and be infected with his nervousness. If they didn't get work with the Lilliputians, he didn't know what they'd do next. He wished he'd had enough money to buy new clothes for himself as well as Violet. Self-consciously, he brushed the dust from his coat.

There were dozens of kids lined up to audition. Violet clung to Paddy's arm as they waited in the line for their names to be entered in a big leatherbound scrapbook. He shook her loose while he spoke to the man, trying to act more confident and grown-up than he really felt.

'We're casting for *The Pirates of Penzance*,' said the man. 'Taking the troupe to New Zealand on tour. Which one of you is auditioning?'

'We both are, sir. I'm fourteen, sir, and the little girl is six.'

'You're tall for fourteen,' said the man disapprovingly. 'We like our kiddies to be small for their age. What's your names, then?'

Paddy watched as the man wrote down Billy and Violet Smith.

They sat on a bench in the wings, watching each of the children walk out on stage to perform. Paddy could feel the sweat prickling on his forehead and the back of his neck.

Each of the children had to sing a song, make an attempt at a few dance steps and, if they could, demonstrate some other skill. When it came to Paddy's turn, he felt himself blushing nervously as he stepped out into the middle of the stage. He sang *Ave Maria*. His voice had grown deeper since the last time he had sung it, but the notes rang clear and true through the theatre.

'You have a fine voice. Can you show me anything else, boy?' asked Mr Pollard. He had a clipboard on his lap and wrote a few scratchy words on the sheet before him.

'I have a good memory. I can memorise anything, sir.

And I can recite, too. This one is by Mr Henry Lawson.'

Mr Pollard listened patiently as Paddy recited a poem Jim had taught him, *Freedom on the Wallaby*.

Mr Pollard nodded and sucked his cheeks in thoughtfully. 'Next,' he called.

Violet skipped confidently out onto the stage and grinned at the adults watching her.

'This song is my favourite. My mam taught it to me.'

She sang in a high, sweet voice *Believe me, if all those endearing young charms*. Paddy saw the expression of delight on Mr Pollard's face and shifted restlessly from one foot to the other, his fingers crossed. Violet did a couple of turns of the stage, skipping and tumbling, showing off the tricks that Jack Ace and Coo-chee had taught her, and then she bounded back to Paddy.

'We'll both be in the show! We'll both be in the show!' she crowed.

They sat on a long wooden bench beside the other auditioning children, who all seemed to have their parents with them. After the auditions had finished, a stout woman walked along the line, talking to the parents. When she came to Paddy, she stopped.

'Where are your parents, young man?'

'We don't have any.'

The woman looked at him sharply. 'No guardian? No grandparents?'

'No, ma'am. But we'll both work hard, if you take us. You won't be sorry.'

Mrs Pollard blushed.

'I'm sorry, sonny. You were very good but we can't take you. You're too old.'

'But it said from six to sixteen in the paper!' said Paddy.

'We already have a couple of lads your age. But your little sister here, she's another story. She'll be a real crowd-pleaser. Our audiences come to see the little ones. It's what our show's all about.'

'But Violet can't be in your show without me. She needs me to look after her. And she has to learn her letters. I've been teaching her to read.'

'We'll take good care of her and teach her a trade. We also employ a teacher and give all the children daily lessons. Your little sister will learn to read and write, don't you worry about that. This is a great opportunity for her. All these other families, they're more than happy to send their children off with the company. It can't be easy for you to be looking after your little sister on your own.'

Paddy was silent. He looked down at Violet and she slipped her hand into his and smiled, her face bright with trust. Paddy swallowed hard, the words catching in his throat. 'We have to stick together.'

'Listen, boy. I don't know what your story is and where you're living, but if the welfare catch onto you, they'll take your little sister away from you. She'll be a lot better off with us than in any orphan asylum.'

The woman reached into her pocket and took out a shiny new shilling.

'Here you go, you take this for now and have a think about it. Bring her back this evening and I'll give you five pounds. I promise you, you'll both be better off.'

Paddy grabbed Violet by the wrist and dragged her out into the harsh sunlight. He hadn't planned for this at all.

He hadn't considered what would happen if one or the other of them failed to win a part in the production.

They wandered aimlessly around the city streets while the afternoon shadows grew longer. Paddy bought two hot saveloys from a street vendor and when they'd finished eating, he counted the change. After paying for their fares to Melbourne, Violet's outfit and the saveloys, there wasn't a lot of money left over, despite the extra pound Jim had given him and Mrs Pollard's shilling. He'd have to come up with a new plan quickly.

He was re-counting a handful of pennies when someone shoved his shoulder and the coins went flying. Paddy looked up to see Nugget Malloy standing beside him, leaning on his cane.

'I remember you,' said Nugget. 'You're the crazy mick that we took to the circus and got sprung with, ain't ya?'

'Sure, and I remember you too. You and that other boy did a bunk.'

Nugget shrugged. 'Never did figure why you didn't make a run for it like me and Tiddler. What happened to you?'

'I joined the circus, didn't I?'

'So that's where you find the midget?'

Paddy looked at Violet, who was busily gathering up the pennies.

'It's a long story,' said Paddy. 'We need to find board and lodgings and I need a job. Got any suggestions?'

'Cor, that's a long list. I can't see many landladies taking the pair of youse. And a job, you reckon? What's the midget gunna do while you're working? The streets ain't no place for females. The welfare will take her off you quick smart.'

Paddy didn't reply. He didn't know the answer to any

of the questions. Nugget scratched his head thoughtfully.

''Course, you could dump the midget with the nuns. They took me sisters.'

'We have to stick together,' said Violet, stamping her foot and glaring at Nugget.

'Angry little ant, ain't she?' said Nugget, looking amused.

Paddy ignored them both. 'Do you know any place where we can get some lodgings for tonight?'

Nugget rubbed his chin thoughtfully. 'There's an old dame up Fitzroy way, Mum Whiteley. She might take you in for a night or two, if she's got room. But it'll cost you.'

'I don't want any favours,' said Paddy. 'I can take care of myself – and the midget.'

21

Mean streets

They walked through the city as the electric street lights flickered, sending an orange glow over the crowds. Violet wasn't excited at the prospect of tagging after Nugget and dragged her heels. On the far side of town they came to a suburb where narrow terraces lined both sides of the street.

'Do you live up around here?' asked Paddy.

'Nah, I'm a free man. I doss down wherever I fancy.'

'What about your mother and father?'

'What about them?' said Nugget, jutting his chin out.

'Never mind,' said Paddy. It was exactly the sort of answer he'd give himself.

As they approached the corner of the next laneway, the air was filled with a hum of angry activity. Paddy slowed his pace but Nugget hurried to the corner and gave a shout.

'Crikey! It's the Fitzroy Push taking on the Carlton mob,' he yelled, laughing with excitement as a crowd of men came charging up the laneway.

There seemed to be hundreds of them, with faces flushed in fury and breath reeking of beer. Nugget charged into the fray as if he knew exactly what to do, but Paddy grabbed Violet's hand and looked for a way out. Someone tore Paddy's swag from him and flung it into the crowd and when he tried to retrieve it, they were drawn into the thick of the riot.

Men were pulling palings off fences and hitting each other across the head, and some in heavy boots set to kicking their opponents as they fell. Bricks and sharp pieces of blue metal flew through the air. Paddy saw Nugget, armed with a paling, lashing out at a tall larrikin in heavy boots and a tight jacket. Suddenly the larrikin swung to the left and punched Paddy full in the face. Paddy's head jerked back and for a moment everything went white.

Violet screamed and threw herself at the larrikin's leg, sinking her teeth into his thigh. The larrikin looked down in amazement and tried to peel her off, but Violet hung on and bit him even harder. Then the man raised his fist. The punch never landed on Violet. Paddy grabbed her around the waist and pulled her free. The larrikin's fist caught Paddy hard on the cheek. He reeled away, trying to force his way out of the brawl.

The police came charging around the corner, some on horseback and others on foot, swinging their batons.

'Bloody hell!' shouted Nugget. He grabbed Paddy's sleeve as he pelted past. 'Run for it!'

Paddy's lip and nose were streaming blood and his head throbbed with pain but he hugged Violet to his chest and followed Nugget through the rioting crowd. If they kept their heads down, they could just avoid the swing of the officers' batons. Men and boys were running away from the fracas in all directions. Some of the larrikins were being herded into the back of a wagon. Just when Paddy thought they were free, someone grabbed the collar of his coat and wrenched him backwards. Paddy didn't look to see if it was a larrikin or a police officer. Letting go of Violet for a second, he wriggled free of the coat, grabbed her hand, and ran.

They rounded the corner just in time to see Nugget disappearing into a narrow laneway. By the time they caught up with him, Violet was gasping for breath. She crumpled in a heap on the bluestone.

'Is the midget all right?' asked Nugget.

Paddy knelt down beside her.

'Vi?' he asked. She stopped gasping and started spitting.

'He tasted horrible,' she said. She wiped her tongue on the sleeve of her dress and pulled a face. Paddy laughed with relief.

The three of them sat down with their back against the brick wall. Paddy could feel a bruise swelling on his cheekbone and his mouth kept filling with blood.

'Jesus, mate,' said Nugget, laughing. 'What a stoush! Bit of a lark, wasn't it?'

'No, it wasn't,' said Paddy. 'If those coppers had caught us, they would have taken Violet away for sure.'

'You're right there. The street's no place for little sheilas. Even a dumb mick like you should know that. I s'pose we oughta get you down to Mum Whiteley's, then.'

Paddy groaned. 'There's no point. I've lost all my money. I can't pay. I've lost everything. My swag, Dai's coat, my wages. Everything.'

Nugget looked from Violet to Paddy pityingly. 'I can show you a good spot to doss down for the night.' He led them to a deep set arched doorway at the end of the lane.

Inside the doorway was a pile of old newspapers. Paddy rustled the papers into a hollow and then laid extra sheets over Violet as a makeshift cover. He settled down beside her and looked up at Nugget. 'Are you staying?'

'There's a two-up game round the corner. Thought I'd see if I can pick up a shilling. I'd have asked you along but you've got the midget and . . .' Nugget shrugged.

'Never mind,' said Paddy.

'I'll come by and check on youse in the morning,' said Nugget, tipping his cap and disappearing into the night.

Next morning, Nugget was as good as his word. He laughed at Paddy's swollen, battered face and pinched Violet's cheek so she spat at him. Nugget took Paddy by the arm and dragged him a little away. He leant close to Paddy.

'Listen, mate. There's a convent down Albert Park way, right near Stubb's baths. I'm heading down that way meself, meeting some mates for a dip. Why don't you dump the kid with the nuns and join us? You can't go on sleeping rough with her. It ain't right. As I see it, you don't got no choice.'

Paddy looked back at Violet. Her new shoes were already scratched and scuffed, her new dress torn and soiled. He felt more lost in the big city with her than he had in the bush. Wearily, he nodded. 'Can you lend me the fare?'

The tram stopped right opposite the baths. Nugget led them past families picnicking on the beach road to a long, high wall. Through the gates of the convent was a treeless yard and an austere brick building.

'Here you go, you poor little blighter,' said Nugget, grinning at Violet.

Violet started to cry. 'Now look what you've done.

What do you mean, poor blighter?' said Paddy.

'I didn't mean no harm. Both me sisters used to be with the nuns. They hated the place. My sisters are Malloys, they couldn't keep their traps shut so they was always getting flogged for something, but your little mouse, she'll be right.'

Paddy knelt down in front of Violet. 'Don't worry, Vi. It won't be for long. When I've found a place for us to live and a job, I'll come back for you. You know I'll come back for you.'

Nugget laughed. 'They won't let you have her, you mug. They wouldn't let my ma have the girls back and she was their bloody mother. Flo, she turned fourteen last year and they finally let her go. She's down at the biscuit factory now, so I guess it turned out all right but I'm glad it was her and not me.'

Paddy grabbed Nugget by the front of his shirt and slammed him against the convent wall. 'Why are you telling me this now!'

'Easy does it, mate,' said Nugget. 'It's only the truth.'

Paddy groaned and let go of the other boy.

'I can't give her to the nuns, then. I'll think of something else. Something will turn up.'

'You're cracked,' said Nugget, straightening his shirt and jacket. 'Lost all your bloody marbles. I'm going in for a dip, mate. If you fancy joining me, you'd better be leaving the midget with the nuns 'cause you can't bring her in the baths. Lads only.' He sauntered across the beach road and disappeared into the crowd.

Paddy stared after him, enviously.

'C'mon, Violet,' he said taking her by the wrist and

dragging her across the road to the beach. They took off their shoes and paddled in the shallow, cool water. At the deep end of the baths, boys were jumping into the water, shouting with excitement. It seemed like an age since Paddy had played like that.

They spent the whole day on the beach. When the sun got too hot, they sat under the pier. Violet scraped a hole in the sand and then arranged a pattern of shells around it. Paddy sat watching her, brooding. Then Violet began adding other objects to the pattern and Paddy drew closer. Scattered among the shells were pennies. 'Where'd you find them?' he asked.

'You dropped them, yesterday. You let me put them in my pocket, 'member?

Paddy felt a sudden flash of hope as he gathered up the pennies and then his heart sank again. It wasn't enough. It wouldn't even buy them a proper meal. As he knelt beside her, counting up the coins, he noticed another part of the pattern she was weaving. Around the very edge of her castle lay a string of coloured glass beads.

'Violet,' he said, grabbing the small girl's wrist. 'What have you done?'

Violet stared up at him, confused. 'I don't know.'

'Those beads.'

This time Violet blushed scarlet. 'I found them. They were in your pocket. The pocket of the big coat. I found them. They're mine now.'

Paddy picked them up, shaking off the sand. Uncle Patrick's rosary beads.

'They're mine,' said Violet, pouting.

'Do you even know what they are?' said Paddy, furious.

'Do you know what this is?' he asked, holding the tiny crucifix on the end of the rosary in front of her face.

'He's my friend,' replied Violet.

Paddy groaned. 'Violet, these are special beads. They're for saying your prayers.'

'Is prayers a game?' she asked, curious, crawling through the sand towards Paddy and resting her elbow on his knee.

'You know, praying. Like when you say your prayers before you go to sleep. Like the prayers your mam taught you.'

'Mam didn't teach me no prayers. I don't know no prayers.'

The afternoon light cut through the pillars of the pier and lay warm on the sand. 'You make like this,' said Paddy, kneeling beside her. Then he took Violet's hands and pressed them together, wrapping the rosary beads around her fingers and thumb.

He taught her to say 'Hail Mary', feeling each line as a wound inside him and yet determined to teach her. She stumbled over the words to begin with, but soon caught the rhythm of the prayer. When she could recite it back to him, he crawled away from her, strangely exhausted. There was so much that she needed that Paddy couldn't give her.

The shadows grew longer and still they sat beneath the pier. Violet had put the rosary beads around her neck and gone back to making her castles in the sand. Paddy passed the pennies from one hand to the other, lost in thought. The tide moved up the beach and covered Violet's diggings, and the sun began to sink lower over the bay.

'I've got a plan now, Violet,' said Paddy, suddenly determined. 'C'mon.'

'Where are we going now?' she asked.

'You'll see.'

At an icecream cart in Bourke Street, just up from the Haymarket Theatre, Paddy bought a goblet of strawberry icecream with the last of the pennies. Violet's chin was quickly plastered with pink.

'You'll have to be a bit tidier with your food once you're with the Lilliputians,' said Paddy, wiping her face clean with the sleeve of his shirt.

'So will you,' said Violet, pointing to a smudge of icecream on Paddy's cheek.

Paddy looked away.

'I'm not going, Vi,' he said. 'They didn't want me.'

'Then I won't go either!' she said adamantly. Paddy knelt down beside her.

'No, Violet, you'll go. I've been thinking about it all day. You have to go. I can't take care of you any more and you wouldn't like it with the sisters at the convent. The theatre's the best place for you. You'll have a grand time of it. They'll take you to all sorts of beautiful places and you'll be the great star. When you come back to Melbourne, I'll be sitting right there in the front row and I'll be so proud. You want me to be proud of you, don't you?'

Her small face crumpled in distress. Tears streamed down her cheeks.

'Will you stop that malarkey!' he said crossly.

Violet flung her arms around his waist, clinging to him, refusing to be disentangled. 'You said our mams wanted us to be together!' she gasped through tears.

Paddy wrenched her arms free and held her wrists. He knelt down in front of her, staring hard into her tear-streaked face. 'We will see each other again, one day. I promise. But I *can't* keep you with me now, Vi. Sweet Jesus, don't you understand? I would if I could. But the police will catch you and me too. They'll take you away and lock me up. They might even give you back to Jack Ace. You don't want that, do you?'

Violet blinked and then hiccuped. She shook her head, her black curls bouncing against her cheeks.

'It's decided.' He took her hand and led her into the theatre.

22

Beggarman, thief

Paddy stood on the corner of a city street, staring aimlessly at the passing crowd. He knew he'd done the right thing. He wanted to feel relieved that he didn't have to worry about taking care of Violet any more. But a cloud of misery gathered around him like a stifling cloak. In his mind's eye, he could see Violet, turning to wave as Mrs Pollard led her away and as she disappeared from view, what little brightness was left in his life was sucked away. All his thoughts seemed black, as if they were coated in thick sticky tar. He had no idea what to do next, no idea in which direction hope lay.

He didn't even notice Nugget Malloy sauntering up the street towards him.

'You again,' said Nugget. 'Where's your midget? You ditch her?'

'The Pollards took her,' said Paddy flatly.

'Blimey, that was a smart move. They give you anything for her? I heard they gave old lady Waites twenty quid for her pair of girls.'

'I didn't want any blood money. They offered me five pounds but I didn't take it.'

Nugget laughed. 'Tiddler reckoned you was dumb but I didn't think you was that thick.'

'Well, maybe I'm not as smart as you, Nugget. What do you do to earn your keep?'

'This and that,' said Nugget evasively. 'It's been bad around Melbourne for years. I flog race cards, matches, get a bit of work here and there.'

'I need to find work,' said Paddy. 'Something, anything.'

Nugget shifted uncomfortably from foot to foot, as uneasy talking about employment as if it were an unsavoury disease.

'You can't be worrying about the future when it's Saturday night in town. Bourke Street, that's the place to be. Tiddler and some of me other mates should be working the street by now.'

'Do they sell matches too?' asked Paddy.

'They keep themselves busy,' said Nugget.

Bourke Street was crowded. The coffee palaces were full and long lines of cabs crowded the streets as people spilled out of the theatres. Nugget wove his way confidently through the throng with Paddy close behind.

At the top of the street, Paddy saw Nugget slip his hand into an elegant young man's coat pocket. The movement was so slight, so deft, that Paddy thought maybe he was mistaken until he saw Nugget tuck a wallet into the back of his trousers. He grabbed Nugget's arm.

'What are you doing?' he whispered angrily. He snatched at the wallet, determined to return it, when suddenly someone grabbed him by the back of his shirt, lifting him right off his feet.

'Damn pickpockets,' said the man, wresting the wallet

from Paddy. 'I'm sick to bloody death of you lot.'

'Wait, Eddie,' said a calm voice. 'I think you've caught the wrong one.'

The old woman who had spoken was holding Nugget by his ear. She obviously had a firm grip, because Nugget was wincing.

'Now then, Nugget Malloy, what do you think you were doing, having a blind stab at Eddie?'

Paddy was amazed to see Nugget blush.

'It wasn't me,' said Nugget. 'You got the wrong boy.'

The old woman glanced sharply at Paddy, taking the measure of him. Then she turned back to Nugget, took him by the collar and shook him like a cat.

'I don't reckon he looks like a ripperty man,' she said, 'though if he spends enough time with you, Nugget Malloy, he's bound to take to thieving.'

'He was the one holding the wallet, wasn't he?'

Paddy flushed with anger. 'I was going to give it back.'

The old woman laughed and gave Nugget one last shake. 'Now, don't you try your nonsense around me, Nugget Malloy. I know you too well. You understand? You're lucky Eddie didn't set the coppers on you.'

Eddie snorted and turned to the old woman.

'You're wasting your time talking to this pair of scoundrels, Mum.' Eddie lowered his voice. 'Can you stake me that few shillings?'

She opened a small black change purse and extracted the coins. As soon as he had the money, Eddie quickly disappeared into the theatre. The old woman turned back to Nugget.

'And here's two bob for you, too,' she said, handing the

coins to Nugget. 'You make sure you spend it on tucker and not smokes or two-up, understand? And you keep your paws off this innocent. I'd take his word above yours and if you try turning him to the bad, you'll have me to answer to.'

Nugget glanced sullenly at Paddy. 'I didn't know you was already a friend of Mum's,' he said, accusingly. Then he turned and ran off. Paddy fought down an urge to run after him.

'Thank you,' said Paddy. 'I appreciate your help but I can look after myself.'

'I wasn't doing it for you. Someone's got to talk sense to that Nugget. He's going to end up in jail if he's not careful, just like his father,' said the woman, watching Nugget disappear. Then she turned her attention back to Paddy.

'Mrs Bridie Whiteley,' she said. When she smiled, her green eyes were surrounded by a pattern of deep lines and Paddy noticed a long scar, like a lightning bolt, that ran the length of her face, but her expression was kindly.

'Billy Smith,' said Paddy.

'Smith? But there's no mistaking that accent. You're not from County Kerry, now are you?'

Paddy shook his head.

'And tell me then, who's been laying into you, Billy?' she asked, putting one hand gently under his chin and turning his face upwards.

'It's nothing,' said Paddy, embarrassed.

'Why aren't you at home? Are you frightened that your mum or dad will take you to task for scrapping?'

Paddy didn't answer.

'You're on your own, aren't you?'

Suddenly, Paddy felt misery wash over him like a great wave. He nodded wearily. As if she read his thoughts, the old lady hooked one arm under his and led him up the street.

'It's not far to my place, but the tram's a nicer ride,' she said.

She paid his fare and they sat in the open section of the carriage.

'Here we are, love,' she said, as the tram stopped alongside a bluestone cathedral. 'My house is around the corner from here.'

Paddy followed her into a narrow street lined with terrace houses. The name of each building was etched in fine lettering in the fanlights above the door: Constance, Alice, Emily. Finally they turned up the steps of the last house, Charity House. The old woman led Paddy upstairs to a small bedroom at the back of the building. A thick red rug covered the floorboards and every wall was lined with pictures. Beneath the window was a narrow cast-iron bed with a beautifully embroidered coverlet. Blossoms lay scattered across the windowsill of the room. For a moment, Paddy thought of Violet. If she'd been with him, she would have gathered them up in her hands. He wondered where she was sleeping tonight, if the Pollards had a nice bed for her or if they'd gone straight down to the wharves and slept on the boat that would take her to New Zealand.

'You look done in, lad,' the old lady said, pouring some water from a jug into a basin on the washstand. 'You clean yourself up a bit and then come downstairs for some tucker.'

The water was cold and the soap smelt sharply of lye.

Even so, Paddy had never imagined that washing his face and hands could feel so good. Though his bruises were tender, it was a relief to wash away the dirt, salt water and dried blood.

After the noise and bustle of the city streets, the quiet of this room was like a haven. He lay down on the bed and wondered where he would sleep the night. Wherever that was going to be, he knew one thing for sure. Tomorrow morning there would be no arms wrapped tight around his chest, no head on his shoulder. No Violet. He shut his eyes, trying to drive away the thought of her.

23

Fire and gold

Morning sun dappled the bedroom floor. Paddy sat up with a start and saw the old woman standing by the window, sweeping the blossoms from the sill.

'I'm sorry, ma'am, I only lay down for a minute and then . . .'

The old lady turned and smiled at him. 'You must call me Mum. All the young ones do. And never you mind about the bed. Often as not, I fall asleep in my chair when I'm stitching late at night, so I didn't miss it.' She scattered dry breadcrumbs in place of the blossoms. In a moment, there was a rush of wings as birds came fluttering in to land on the sill.

'Do you like birds?' asked Paddy.

'I cannot bear to see any living creature go hungry,' she said. 'So you must come and have some breakfast.'

Paddy splashed his face with fresh water and padded down the stairs in his bare feet. On the landing, he met a small elderly man in a striped suit. The man wore a blue silk cravat and had a stiffly waxed moustache.

'Are you another one of Bridie's street arabs?' he asked.

'I don't think so, sir,' answered Paddy.

'Good-o. That last one was a right little devil,' he said. He pinched the end of his moustache and stared disapprovingly at Paddy's bruises. Paddy smiled nervously and then hurried down the stairs.

A big black pot of porridge sat on a trivet in the centre of the dining table. The old lady was setting places around it for a number of people. A small fire burnt in the grate, even though the morning wasn't cold, and the room was bright with morning sunlight.

'Do you take in lots of street arabs?' asked Paddy.

'I help those I can when I can, but I have to earn my living. This place may be called Charity House but it's a fine lodgings for actors, not a boys' home.'

'A man on the stairs said something about the last boy being a devil.'

Bridie laughed. 'That was old Wybert Fox and you know the devil he was speaking of well enough. Nugget Malloy. I've a soft spot for the boy on account of his grandmother being my old friend. But he pinched Wybert's snuff and pawned his watch, so I had to have stern words with him. He's like his grandmother, bless her soul, and doesn't take kindly to playing by the rules.'

'I noticed that,' said Paddy. 'Do you have many guests?'

'There's always a passing parade of lodgers. Upstairs at the moment, I've got the Tallis twins, Lulu and Millie. They've got the balcony room. Lovely girls, used to dance with the Butterfly Brigade but they've got their own act now, fronting all the Bijou ballerinas. Wybert Fox has the other upstairs room. He's a grand old figure. Been here the longest, nearly a year now, but his show's doing so well he'll be off to Sydney for a season. Theatre folk are hard to keep in one place. Flash Bill Hurley's got the downstairs room. Have to put him at a bit of a distance from the girls, he's always after a bit of mischief, the rascal. They all like it here, only ten minutes walk down to the theatres and they know I keep a clean house with good fare.'

Paddy liked the warmth in the old lady's voice and the way she smiled as she spoke. He wished he had enough money to pay for a few nights lodging.

'Nugget, he was going to bring me up here when I first arrived in town, to see if you had a spare room. But that was before I lost all my money.'

'He didn't take you down to John Deary's two-up rooms, did he?' asked Bridie, crossly.

Paddy laughed. 'No, but I wish he had. I couldn't go because . . .' Paddy trailed off, thinking of Violet.

Bridie looked at him curiously and then poured them each a cup of tea.

'Billy?' she said, gently.

Paddy started, forgetting he had told her that was his name.

'It's not my real name,' said Paddy. He took a deep breath as he tried to think up an explanation but instead, the whole story came out, from leaving the Burren, running away from St Columcille's, the wreck of the *Lapwing*, to the circus, finding Violet and leaving Gunyah Station. When he told her of handing Violet over to the Pollards, his voice caught.

'Perhaps it's worked out for the best,' said Bridie, shaking her head.

'How can it be for the best?'

'A boy like you would be wasted in the Lilliputians. You

can already read and write. You could get yourself a position as a clerk, work your way up. A real job with steady pay. You don't want to get yourself mixed up with a bunch of ragbag actors. Maybe you could study in the evenings at the University, become a lawyer or a fine scholar.'

Paddy laughed. 'Studying? I've no money, no home, no work, no family – nothing! If only the Lilliputians had *let* me waste my time with them!'

Bridie shot him a curious look and Paddy was worried that she was offended. She pushed her chair away from the table and picked up the teapot.

'You bring your bowl out to the kitchen when you're finished,' she called over her shoulder.

Paddy licked the last of the porridge from the dish and followed her into the back yard. A corrugated iron lean-to stretched along one side, and inside it, Bridie was cooking bacon and eggs on a range.

Paddy put his bowl down beside the trough.

'Thank you kindly, ma'am. I'd best be getting on my way. I'm hoping to find some honest work today.'

Bridie turned to Paddy. 'Billy or Patrick? Which is it to be?'

'Billy,' said Paddy, decisively. 'I don't feel as if I'm Paddy Delaney any more. I need to start all over again.'

'Well, Billy, I've a lot of work on at the moment, getting everyone ready for the Christmas pantomimes. See, I work on costumes as well as running the boarding house. I have a girl to help with the cleaning but I could use an extra pair of hands, to do chores and run errands for me. I can't be paying you but I'll feed you well and keep you warm and dry and slip you the odd sixpence when I can spare it.'

'You're offering me work?'

Bridie laughed. 'Just your lodgings in exchange for this and that, until you find your feet.'

'I'm not like Nugget,' said Paddy. 'You won't be sorry.'

'I saw that the moment I set eyes on you,' she said.

She handed him a small axe and Paddy spent the morning splitting kindling for the range and stacking wood in the narrow yard. In the afternoon, Bridie sent him to the shops in Brunswick Street, to buy the newspaper and items that the lodgers had asked for – hair wax for Flash Bill, snuff for Wybert Fox and throat lozenges for the Misses Tallis.

That evening, Bridie made up a bed for him on a red chaise longue that stood under the window in the front parlour of the terrace house. It wasn't really used as a parlour at all. Bolts of fabric were piled up on shelves either side of the fireplace and a sewing table with a treadle machine was set against one wall. A long trestle table with lengths of cloth draped across it served as a work bench, and a wooden cabinet opened to reveal dozens of little drawers, each one full of haberdashery: ribbons and buttons, fasteners and lace.

'Now I've work to finish before you can turn in,' she said. 'There's some magazines, *Table Talk* and *The Lorgnette* over there. I buy them for my customers, to keep them busy when they come for a fitting. Or you can get the *Argus* from the dining room.'

'Ill read to you while you work, if you like,' said Paddy.

Paddy sat on the chaise longue reading out loud while Bridie busily finished off sequined outfits for the Christmas pageants. The costumes glittered as her hands moved swiftly across the fabric. For a moment, as Paddy read, he could almost imagine he was home again. If he kept his eyes on the page, he could pretend that the old woman quietly sewing wasn't Mrs Bridie Whiteley, but his own mother, grown old with missing him, and here he was, like a storybook hero, returned from years of adventuring. But when he looked up, everything was strange and unfamiliar.

'Billy, are you all right?' asked Bridie. She put her sewing aside and gazed at him intently with her sharp green eyes.

'I was thinking about home, about my mam,' he said softly. 'But I can't be thinking about everything that's lost. I can't be living in the past.'

'No, you're right there. But the past is always living in you and it's only lost if you won't remember it.'

'It hurts to remember.'

Bridie reached out and rested her hand on Paddy's arm. 'You can make a new life for yourself, Billy. Lord knows, to survive in this world, we all make our lives over again and again. But one day, when you've made your new life, those old memories will be precious. Precious as gold.'

'It doesn't feel like gold now. It feels like fire. Like everything's burnt and black.'

'When I was your age, I saw men risk everything in their search for riches. Some of them made fortunes and some of them lost everything. But what I found is that real gold, the most precious thing we truly have, runs like a deep seam in our hearts. One day, you'll understand that. There's pain in it now, but one day you'll see that out of the fire comes the purest gold.'

As the days at Charity House slipped by, Paddy's bruises healed and he started to feel stronger. Bridie kept him busy for much of the mornings but in the afternoon she would send him on errands around Fitzroy or into the city and then he was allowed to do as he pleased. Sometimes he'd bump into Nugget and they'd idle away an hour or two together in Bourke Street. It was easy to forgive Nugget, even if it was hard to trust him. Nugget claimed he preferred the street to living with Bridie, but as the weeks went by and Paddy became more settled in Fitzroy, he grew envious.

'Next thing you know, she'll be adopting you proper. Everyone reckons old Mum Whiteley's got a fortune tucked away somewhere. They reckon she owns Charity House outright and that she's got a secret stash of gold underneath the floorboards.'

'I don't see how she could be rich. She's always giving things away to anyone who asks.'

'You're right there. In '93, when the depression was worst, people starving all over the city, I reckon Mum Whiteley fed half of Fitzroy. My old lady, she never had any food in the cupboard, but we could count on Mum bringing bread and mutton. I don't know. Maybe it's all a dickon pitch to kid us, but the old lady is sweet on you, that's for sure, and your worries are over.'

Paddy felt he still had plenty to worry about. He had no money, no job and no idea of what he was going to do next. But he was starting to feel that maybe he'd found a home.

On a bright December morning, several weeks after Paddy had arrived at Charity House, Bridie handed him two baskets loaded with materials and announced that she needed a porter for her morning's work.

The theatres were empty and the foyers in darkness

as they walked along Bourke Street. Mum led Paddy into a lane and knocked on a stage door. Then they made their way along a labyrinth of narrow hallways. In a crowded, damp-smelling dressing room, three women were brushing each other's long hair. They all wore white leggings decorated with blue and silver beads and the tallest woman wore a long cape heavily embroidered with lions and unicorns. Each wore a vest with symbols of the British Empire embroidered across the front. Paddy recognised the Irish harp on one. When the actress saw Paddy staring at her chest, she winked at him. Paddy blushed and looked away while Mum set to work burrowing into her baskets to put the finishing touches on their costumes.

'Where'd you find this little helper? He's a handsome devil, Mum,' said one of them, pinching Paddy's cheek.

'Leave him alone, ladies,' said Bridie, bending low to adjust the hem of Scotland's cape.

The ladies of the Empire winked at Paddy. When Bridie tried to adjust the front of their costumes they angled their bottoms in Paddy's direction and wiggled them until Paddy was scarlet with embarrassment.

Outside in the street, Bridie glanced at Paddy and chuckled. 'Well, I should have known better than to take a boy your age near that lot. Mercy, what a palaver! I must remember to keep you away from the theatres!'

'Maybe I should get a proper job, Mum,' said Paddy.

'I've been thinking about that myself, Billy,' said Bridie. 'I've been thinking that perhaps in February, when the school year starts, you should be going back to your studies.'

'What!' said Paddy. 'I can't go back to school. I'm too

old. And besides, there's no money for the fees. You can't be paying for me to go to school.'

'I've had a word to Father Ryan and he said perhaps there's some help to be had from the Hibernian Catholic Benefit Societies for a boy with so much promise.'

Paddy laughed even though he was annoyed. There was nothing that would induce him to return to school, to floggings and long hours in a classroom.

In February, Paddy was relieved to discover that Father Ryan hadn't been able to help Bridie find a scholarship. As Paddy was nearly fifteen, he was too old for the state schools, so nothing was settled upon. Paddy kept helping around Charity House, running errands and spending his afternoons exploring the city streets with Nugget. Spending time with Nugget was an education all in itself. As the months slipped by, Nugget taught Paddy how to fight, how to play two-up and how to blow smoke rings.

On a night of unexpected rain, Paddy woke to the noise of someone slamming the iron gate and stumbling up the front steps, swearing. The brass knocker banged forcefully. Paddy pulled his trousers on and went out into the passage. Bridie was there before him. She looked older in her dressing gown with her silver hair hanging loose over her shoulder.

'Should we open the door?' asked Paddy, nervous at the ferocity of the knocking.

'Aye, it's sure to be Eddie,' she said undoing the bolt. 'It's about time he came home.'

The man on the doorstep pulled off his trilby and shook the rain from a thick mane of curly red-brown hair.

It was the same elegant dandy that Nugget had tried to pickpocket all those months before. He slouched over the threshold, muttering something incomprehensible, and fell flat on his face in the hallway. Bridie looked at Paddy and grimaced.

'Help me, will you, Billy, there's a good lad. I suppose I'll have to make up a bed for him on the floor.'

They each grabbed an arm and dragged the man down the hall. Bridie's face was lined with strain.

'I can manage him,' said Paddy, heaving one of the drunkard's arms over his shoulder. 'Where do you want him?'

Bridie led the way into the parlour. She rolled out a thin flock mattress before the fireplace and Paddy dropped the visitor onto the bedding. Mum covered him up, wiping the tangle of curls away from his face with a tender gesture.

'Is he your son?'

'Not exactly. But he is my responsibility,' she replied. For a moment she rested a hand on the sleeping man's shoulder and Paddy thought she looked more melancholy than anyone he'd ever seen.

After Bridie had gone back upstairs, Paddy settled down on the chaise longue. The air in the room was heavy with cigar smoke and whiskey, and the man was now snoring loudly. Paddy pulled his blanket up over his head and tried to pretend he was alone.

It took a long time for sleep to descend again and then his dreams were dark and troubled, as if a bitter new wind was blowing over the threshold of Charity House.

24

Ned Kelly by night

The next morning, Bridie sent Paddy down to the Princess Theatre with two hatboxes. By the time he returned, Eddie was sitting in the dining room hunched over a cup of muddy coffee.

Later, Paddy heard him arguing with Bridie in the front room, their voices rising and falling as if Eddie was angry and Bridie trying to placate him. Paddy thought he heard the chink of coins and then Eddie left the house, slamming the front door behind him. Paddy half-hoped that he wouldn't return but in the late afternoon he was back in the dining room, drinking whiskey from a tin cup.

'Boy,' he called, as Paddy tried to slip past him and out into the yard.

'My name is Billy.'

Eddie put his feet up on one of the chairs and pointed at them. 'These boots of mine need cleaning. Pull them off and give them a polish.'

Paddy glared at him. 'There seems to be a misunderstanding,' he said.

'My understanding is that you are meant to earn your keep.'

'I don't see what being your boot boy has to do with earning my keep.'

'You polish old man Fox's boots and Flash Bill's, you can polish mine. And you'll address me as Mr Whiteley when you speak to me. Now remove my boots.'

Paddy stuck his hands in his pockets. Even if the man was a Whiteley, he was a bludger. 'Take them off yourself,' he said.

For a moment they eyed each other angrily, and then Eddie laughed. He undid the buckles and threw his boots at Paddy.

'Have them back to me in fifteen minutes, no more,' said Eddie, taking another swig of his whiskey.

Resentfully, Paddy carried the muddy boots outside, slamming the door behind him.

That night, Paddy found Eddie asleep on the chaise longue. When Bridie saw Paddy standing in the parlour doorway, looking furious, she put a hand on his arm and gestured to the mattress on the floor.

'I'm sorry, Billy,' she said. 'But Eddie's a bigger man than you and he's needing his rest. He's starting in a new role tomorrow.'

Paddy stretched out on the floor before the fireplace. When Eddie started snoring, Paddy imagined smothering the man with his own pillow.

Paddy couldn't understand why Mum turned a blind eye to all Eddie's bad behaviour. Any other lodger would have been turned out on their ear if Mum had caught them drinking whiskey in the middle of the day, but not Eddie.

When Wybert Fox vacated his room, Eddie took it over immediately. Paddy was sure he wasn't paying any board but the only person he could discuss it with was Nugget.

'That sponger,' said Nugget. 'Sucks the old lady for all she's worth, though he's not a bad actor. I heard he's taken over the lead in *The Kelly Gang*. I reckon I'll have to see it again now he's playing Ned.'

Mum was going to see *The Kelly Gang* too. It seemed everyone in Melbourne had seen the show. Paddy tried not to feel interested but on the evening that Bridie was to attend, he sat at the dining-room table, pushing his food around disconsolately.

'It's the best play of the season,' said Bridie. 'I've heard they borrowed the iron armour that Kelly himself wore!'

'It sounds grand,' said Paddy.

'I'm glad you say that, Paddy. Because if you don't mind accompanying an old woman, I'd like you to come along. I've already bought you a ticket.'

Paddy looked at her in surprise, and then hesitated. If only Eddie wasn't in the play, the treat would be perfect.

'I'll get my cap,' he said, and ran up to the front parlour.

Folded up neatly on the end of the chaise longue was a crisp white shirt, a pair of trousers and a smart new jacket. 'I couldn't have you on my arm dressed like a street arab, could I?' said Bridie, brushing away Paddy's thanks.

The Princess Theatre glowed like a fairy palace. The foyer was thronged with people in fine clothes while outside was a rowdy crowd with tickets for the upper circle. Paddy and Bridie took their seats in the stalls and Paddy looked around him in wonder. The red velvet curtains were trimmed with gold braid, and on either side of the stage, water cascaded over two small waterfalls. Beautiful women sat fanning themselves in the boxes. Above them, the chandeliers glittered in a haze of cigar smoke.

Paddy watched with amazement. On stage, Eddie was clear-eyed and powerfully impressive, nothing like the drunken good-for-nothing that Paddy knew him as. The whole audience was riveted.

At the end of the show, everyone leapt to their feet, including Paddy, applauding and whistling until the whole cast came to the front of the stage and took three curtain calls. Paddy forgot his animosity towards Eddie and clapped until his hands ached.

Outside, Bridie bought two slabs of dark fruitcake, and a cup of coffee for each of them.

'One day, I'd like to be Ned Kelly,' said Paddy. 'I had a grandmother that was a Kelly, so I could call myself Patrick Kelly, or even Dan Kelly, because I'm Brendan too. And I could wear that armour and shoot the top off a bottle of whiskey, just like Eddie in the play.'

'They tell a lot of stories about the bushrangers that make the life sound grand. But it's never a grand thing to have to kill for your living. I remember the day they hanged Ned Kelly. There were people weeping on the streets, but no one's tears could save him.'

'Oh, I don't mean I want to be a bushranger, but I'd like to act at being one. Can you imagine anything grander? Eddie is so lucky.'

'I'm sorry he never got a proper education. He could have been anything he wanted.'

'Mum, why don't you like the theatre?'

Bridie laughed. 'Billy, I love the theatre, it's been my life, but it's an easy world to fall in love with and a cruel trade to live by. I've seen great men end their days with nothing to show for years of hard work. I'm one of the lucky ones. There's always work backstage but since the crash there hasn't been much money in the theatre.

'It's not like the old days. After the Star closed, that was our theatre in Ballarat, I came to Melbourne with the finest actress of her generation. Amaranta El'Orado, the Songbird of the South they called her. They were heady days. People had more money than sense! When we were at the Princess Theatre there'd be hundreds of miners throwing nuggets as big as walnuts onto the stage. I'd run out and gather them up and then Amy and I would put them in the safe. All that gold and all that splendour, all gone now.'

Bridie put her coffee cup back on the stall and gazed down Bourke Street with a faraway look in her eyes.

Paddy tried to imagine a stage littered with gold nuggets. But more exciting than the prospect of riches was the vision of a crowded theatre full of cheering people. He longed to be the person at centre stage. He had promised Violet that one day he'd be watching her from the front row of a theatre. How much better would it be if she returned to discover that Paddy had become Melbourne's idol, so that together they could bask in the limelight.

25

Where in the world

On a bright winter afternoon, Eddie came back early from the city and sat in the dining room with an open bottle of whiskey and a glass before him. Bridie loaded up a basket with jam and bread and tied her bonnet on.

'Are you coming along then, Eddie?'

'Not bloody likely. Don't think you can trick me into visiting that old witch again,' he said.

'She's been good to both of us, Eddie.'

'Get that little bludger Nugget to go with you, if you want company. She's his grandmother, not mine.'

'Never mind,' said Bridie. She hoisted the basket onto her arm.

'I'll come,' said Paddy.

'You don't even know where she's going!' snorted Eddie. 'Then again, I suppose you're the sort that would find a lunatic asylum amusing.'

'I like to help,' said Paddy, picking up her basket. 'Not like some.'

They took two trams, first the cable tram and then one drawn by horses to the Princess Street hill in Kew. The Metropolitan Asylum for the Insane was a huge, ornate building, like a palace, with a great tower at each end rising above the surrounding bush.

'It's so grand,' said Paddy, wonderingly.

'From the outside,' said Bridie, 'but God preserve us from ending up in such a place.'

The gatekeeper let them in, and they took the path up to the office. Paddy signed a leather-bound book with his own and Bridie's names, and they went through into an open quadrangle lined with long verandahs.

Bridie knocked on the door of one of the rooms before opening. Inside was dark and there were several beds along one wall. There was a constant drone from one of the patients, and Paddy felt his heart grow tight in his chest.

The woman in the bed was so withered and crone-like that Paddy could hardly believe that she was the same age as Bridie. Her pale blue eyes had a frost of white across the irises. She looked at Paddy, as he shifted the basket uncomfortably from one arm to the other.

'Who's that? Is that your Tom you've brought, or is it his boy? Who is it, Bridie?' she demanded.

'No, Biddy. He's an orphan lad. Patrick Delaney, from County Clare. But we call him Billy.'

'Handsome. You always have a handsome lad with you, Bridie.'

Just then, a nurse put her head around the door and gestured for Bridie to come and speak with her.

'Where's she gone now, Eddie?' said Biddy.

'I'm not Eddie,' said Paddy.

'No, that Eddie's a scoundrel. Born a scoundrel,' said Biddy, shaking her head knowingly. 'You're not Nugget. Too handsome to be a Malloy. Maybe you're Brandon.

Aye, that's who you must be, Brandon.'

Paddy laughed. 'I'm called Billy – not Brandon. But sure you're right about Eddie. A scoundrel and a lazy bugger.'

'Too much heart and not enough commonsense, that's our Bridie, especially when it comes to Eddie,' said Biddy. 'She was always a soft-hearted fool, that Bridie. Here she comes a-visiting me, after all these years. She watches out for old Biddy Ryan.'

Biddy laughed, a coarse high cackle like a wild bird. She strained to sit up and Paddy saw that she was strapped to her bed. He looked around helplessly, not knowing if he should do something, and was relieved to see Bridie come back into the room.

'You take yourself out, Billy. I'll join you shortly.'

Biddy was writhing, hitting out with her hands as if pushing away invisible assailants. Mum stepped forward and held her wrists, gently coaxing her to lie still.

Paddy stepped out into the quadrangle and realised he was trembling. He wished he hadn't come. An old man stood on the end of the verandah weeping, until a nurse came and took him inside. Another man strode back and forth across the green, pacing like a caged tiger and muttering to himself.

Paddy ran to where the grounds gave way to thick bush, to a high point overlooking the golden river. Through the trees, he could see the dome of a distant cathedral. It looked so out of place in this wild, pale gold landscape. The cry of a bird whipped through the air and echoed off the water. He lay back in the long grass and thought of the Burren, of the way the wind moved across that landscape, how the air was always full of rain, not like this dry, light wind full of sun.

He didn't hear Bridie approaching. She set her basket down in the grass and sat beside him.

'She's a mad old thing, you mustn't mind what she says, Billy.'

'Who was Brandon and why did she think I looked like him?'

Bridie looked startled. 'Brandon! Why, she never even met him, the silly old fool. When we were young, I talked of him often enough. Brandon was my truest, dearest brother that I left in Ireland many long years ago. I made a promise to him which I haven't been able to keep and it haunts me to this day.'

'Why don't you write him a letter and explain why you couldn't?' asked Paddy.

Mum sighed. 'I wouldn't know where in the world to send it.'

They walked in silence down the hill from the asylum. The horse-drawn tram moved slowly towards town. Paddy leant against the railing and stared at the silhouette of the city, dark against the winter sky. Where in the world was Violet? Would he ever be able to keep his promise to her?

Bridie had some shopping to do before she went back to Charity House, so Paddy went home alone. He was hoping that Eddie would have headed out for the evening. Ever since *The Kelly Gang* had finished, Eddie had had too much time on his hands. Before he'd even opened the gate, Paddy knew Eddie was still at home. He could hear the man roaring from out in the street. When he slipped through the front door, he heard the sounds of crashing crockery and furniture being overturned. Paddy pushed open the door to the dining room.

'What the hell do you think you're up to?' he said.

'Are you talking to me, runt?' shouted Eddie Whiteley. He was standing in the middle of the room amongst the mess, swaying.

'That's Mum's good china! You bloody drunken idiot!'

Eddie Whiteley snorted. 'Who are you, anyway? What right do you have to talk to me like that? A snivelling little charity brat.'

'I earn my keep, which is more than you do.'

'Shut up, useless little snot-rag. She keeps you busy with useless errands. Useless, useless little arse-worm,' he said, the words slurring together.

Paddy clenched his fists and was ready to take a swipe at Eddie when Mum came into the dining room. She took in the situation at a glance.

'Come with me, Eddie,' she said, taking his arm. 'You need a cup of coffee to settle you.' Grumpily, Eddie allowed her to lead him to the door.

'Billy, will you please set this room to order?' she said over her shoulder.

Paddy stared at her, wild with disbelief. 'No!' he shouted. 'Why doesn't he clean it up? It's his mess! Or better still, why don't you tell him to clear off? Why don't you make him go!'

'Billy, you know this house is always open to you, but this is Eddie's home.'

She turned and left the room with Eddie. Paddy stared after them for a moment, then wrenched open the door and ran down the stairs, away from Charity House.

26

Taking chances

For the next few days, Paddy slept on the streets, finding shelter in doorways or under bridges. Sometimes in the early morning there was a chill in the air that made Paddy dread another night sleeping rough. During the day, he scavenged for food and kept out of the way of the police. There were other boys and men living on the streets and sometimes the police arrested them for vagrancy but Paddy had picked up a thing or two from Nugget. He knew how to make himself scarce.

He was sitting on the steps outside the Public Library waiting for it to open when he spotted a familiar figure hawking newspapers on the corner. Nugget took the steps two at a time and sat down next to Paddy.

'I never thought I'd see you doing an honest day's work,' said Paddy.

Nugget laughed. 'No worries. Nothing honest about this caper. They're last week's news. Found 'em in a lane-way. Soon as anyone buys one, I do a bunk. Like you. I hear you done a bunk, or did you let that scumbag Eddie Whiteley throw you out?'

'Did he tell you he threw me out?' asked Paddy angrily.

'Nah, but it wouldn't be the first time. Mum's taken in strays before and Eddie likes to make it difficult for them. Didn't think you'd give up so easily. How long you been sleeping rough?'

'Five days now,' said Paddy, rubbing his back where the step had cut into him. 'And I haven't given up. I needed time to think.'

'Mum put the word out she's looking for you.'

Paddy put his head in his hands. 'I don't want to sponge off her the way Eddie does.'

'You was pulling your weight,' said Nugget.

'She got by fine before I turned up. I have to find a proper job and pay for my lodgings. I want to help her out like a man, not an errand boy.'

'I could have a word with me uncle and you could do some cockatoo work for him, running bets for the tote.'

Paddy laughed. 'That's your line of work, not mine. If I can't get work in a theatre, maybe I'll go bush.'

'That's not going to help old Mum Whiteley. Besides, you'll starve in the country just as quick as here. Beggars can't be choosers, mate. If it's the theatre you want, you oughta get back to Charity House. Someone around there could put you in the way of a job. No one's gunna take you on if you're living on the streets.'

Paddy sighed and took one of the newspapers from Nugget, smoothing the printed page out before him. 'But if I do go back, what am I going to do about Eddie? I can't stand being around the place with him out of work. Why does Mum put up with him?'

'Dunno. She was married to his old man once, but Eddie's ma was someone else, an actress. Mum never had any kids of her own. My ma used to reckon that's why she liked me, 'cause she didn't know what stinkers boys really are.' Nugget laughed. 'Mum don't have no blood kin. That's why she and my gran were cobbers. They came out on the boats together.'

'But she does have blood kin. She has a brother.'

'Get out! Where is he? Ireland?'

'I suppose he's still there. I wish he'd come and throw Eddie out on his ear. If Mum had a real relative, then she wouldn't put up with Eddie.'

Slowly, an idea started to form in Paddy's mind. He traced his finger along the columns of print. Whenever Paddy read the papers to Bridie she always liked him to read out the advertisements. She especially liked him to read the personal columns, the people who were looking for wayward husbands, old acquaintances, missing children.

'Nugget, will you stake me a shilling?'

'A whole deaner? What for?'

'I need to buy paper and ink and some stamps. I'm going to write to the newspapers in Ireland. I'm going to put an advertisement in to find Mum's brother.'

'What? Put a notice in? You have to pay for that too.'

'Maybe. I'll convince them it's for a good cause.'

'What a dreamer! Even if you did find him, he's not gunna come all the way across the world to turf Eddie out on his ear.'

'Well, I'm going to try,' said Paddy stubbornly. 'I want to do something for Mum.'

'He's probably six feet under. Waste of dosh, if you ask me,' said Nugget, but he reached inside his jacket pocket and pulled out two sixpences all the same.

Paddy spent the rest of the day sitting in the reading room of the big city library, carefully composing some letters. He finished the first one and copied it out twice, addressing the envelopes to newspapers in Dublin, Belfast and Cork. As he tipped the clutch of letters into the post box, he felt as if he was a spinner, having just tossed the pennies in a game of two-up. The coins were in the air and no one could know where they would land.

Bridie ladled a spoonful of thick soup into Paddy's bowl and set it down in front of him, along with a cup of sweet black tea.

'I'm glad you came back, Billy.'

'I'm sorry for causing you worry. I've done a lot of thinking. I like living with you, Mum, but I can't just be running errands for my keep. I have to do more.'

'You're right there, Billy. You need to be thinking about your future, and I know someone who can help you. I spoke to him on the telephone from the post office this morning. He wants to meet you.'

'Is it someone who can help me get a job in a theatre?'

Bridie looked away. 'No, Billy, not the theatre. We're going to see a gentlemen who can help you make a career for yourself, a powerful man in the Colony. Sir Gilbert De Quincey.'

Paddy stirred his soup, and let his hair fall across his face. Why wouldn't she accept that he wanted to be an actor? He wished he'd never told her about St Columcille's.

They travelled by tram across the city and past the Botanical Gardens to Toorak. Sir Gilbert's home was a mansion, decorated with cast-iron lacework all along its balconies and verandahs. A long gravel driveway winding through a garden full of soft, dark trees and clipped bushes led to the front door.

A maid ushered them into Sir Gilbert's study. An old man was sitting by the window, an open book in his lap. He stood up to greet them, taking Bridie's hand in his and smiling down at her with a familiarity that Paddy found bewildering. Paddy couldn't think how Bridie would be friends with someone like this.

'Mrs Whiteley's young protégé, I presume,' said Sir Gilbert turning to Paddy.

'Billy Smith, sir.'

Sir Gilbert nodded and ordered the maid to bring tea.

'So you'd like a position as a clerk in a law office, I believe?' said Sir Gilbert.

Paddy frowned and shot a look at Bridie.

'No sir, I'd like to be an actor.'

Sir Gilbert laughed and turned to Bridie. 'Another young thespian, Mrs Whiteley. I thought you said this boy was different?'

'He is different, Sir Gilbert. He has a fine hand, can read anything and has a quick mind.'

'Mrs Whiteley and I once knew another Billy. Billy Dare by name. An Irish lad, perhaps a bit like you. A wild reckless type. Good at pretending to be other people,' said Sir Gilbert. 'Shot a bushranger, wasn't afraid of anything. You would have liked him.'

Bridie laughed, but Paddy could see she was annoyed. Paddy had that strange feeling, as if he was on the outside looking in at the old people, as if the air was heavy with memories.

'I was thinking, Sir Gilbert, that this Billy could be a scholar, or a man of letters, given a chance.'

Sir Gilbert frowned. 'You're too sentimental, Mrs Whiteley. It's the great failing of the Irish. Sentimentality. You thought that rascal Eddie was a fine figure of a boy too.'

'Eddie never had any chances, Sir Gilbert. If you recall, he was obliged to leave school at fourteen. That was the year of the crash, the year that every penny of the small inheritance his father had left him was squandered by the Imperial Bank. The bank that you advised us to place our trust in.'

Sir Gilbert coloured and his blue eyes grew bright. 'Bridie, that is not just. You know the De Quinceys lost a great deal in the crash. You, of all people, should know what a burden Degraves placed on us all with his land deals.'

Bridie folded her hands in her lap and grew very still. The silence hung heavily in the room, and Paddy could hear the mantel clock ticking loudly in the seconds that followed.

Finally, Sir Gilbert sighed. 'We must be patient, Mrs Whiteley. The recovery has been slow but great things are afoot. I'm only recently returned from Adelaide. We approved a federal constitution. It is only a matter of time before the colonies unite. Do you have any idea what this could mean? A federal authority governing Australia!'

It was Bridie's turn to sigh. 'A grand prospect, I'm sure. But this is a very small thing that I'm asking of you, Gilbert.'

'I would dearly like to be able to assist this boy, but

185

I cannot magic a position as a clerk out of thin air.'

'Then you must try harder,' said Bridie.

Sir Gilbert threw up his hands. 'Mrs Whiteley, does your stubborn persistence know no bounds?' He turned to Paddy. 'Do you have any experience of horses? We have need of a good stable boy.'

Bridie's face fell. 'A stable hand?' she said.

'It's all I can offer, for the moment.'

'It's all right, Mum,' said Paddy. 'I don't mind. I'm good with horses.'

'I mind,' said Bridie.

There were forces at play in this argument that Paddy didn't understand. He wished the appointment was over and they were riding the tram back into the city.

Bridie stood up and curtseyed to Sir Gilbert and suddenly her voice was stiff and formal. 'Billy and I will discuss your offer. I appreciate you taking the time to see us, Sir Gilbert.' She gestured to Paddy and he knew it was their cue to leave.

'Bridie . . .' said Sir Gilbert, his expression full of apology.

But Paddy knew the interview was over.

27

The unexpected

Three days later, Paddy picked up the paper to read to Bridie as she worked.

'Sir Gilbert's dead,' he said, in a voice that shook with disbelief.

All the colour drained out of Bridie's face. The costume she was working on slid from her lap.

'Read it to me,' she said.

When he'd finished, Bridie bowed her head.

'He shouldn't have died before me,' she sobbed.

In the following days, Bridie was caught in a daze of grief. In the mornings, the lodgers came downstairs to a cold dining room and quietly grumbled to themselves before going out to find breakfast elsewhere. She even forgot the birds that gathered on her bedroom windowsill, pecking expectantly at the glass. Messengers arrived at Charity House asking why hadn't costumes been delivered. Paddy and Eddie formed an uneasy truce, each trying to deal with the lodgers and the enquiries as best they could.

The funeral was held in the big Anglican cathedral, St Paul's. Bridie wouldn't set foot inside a Protestant church, so Paddy and Eddie stood with her in the street and watched the funeral cortege go by.

A week later there was a knock on the door. A young man, very smartly dressed in a stiff white collar and dark suit, stood on the doorstep. He had a wad of papers in his hand.

'Mr Rupert Degraves to see Mrs Thomas Whiteley,' he said. Paddy knew, without even asking, that the young man was a bearer of bad tidings.

Ten minutes later, Paddy heard Eddie and the young man arguing fiercely in the hallway.

'Get out, damn you,' shouted Eddie. 'How dare you march in here with your legal claptrap and threaten a vulnerable old woman. Sir Gilbert meant for Mrs Whiteley to have a home here always. They had a clear understanding.'

'There is no paperwork to show any such "understanding" with Mrs Whiteley. Our family never condoned a relationship that implied illegal "understandings".'

Threateningly, Eddie stepped in close to the visitor.

'Are you trying to imply there was something improper about my stepmother's relationship with Sir Gilbert? Because if you are . . .'

Rupert Degraves put his hands up in the air. 'I don't mean any such thing. I'm sure my uncle's motives were honourable. But our family often had cause to regret his soft-heartedness, and as to Charity House, my mother is anxious, now that the property is her own, to realise its value.'

'You mean sell it out from under Mrs Whiteley! Turn the old lady out on the street, after all these years!'

'This is not our intention! We are giving her notice. Thirty days, in fact. Most generous, given that she's never paid more than a peppercorn rent!'

'I'll give you bloody notice!'

Eddie pulled the front door open and shoved Rupert Degraves down the steps.

'This is outrageous,' yelled Degraves. 'Who do you think you are?'

'It doesn't matter who I am. But I know who you are. I know what a blaggard your father was, and you show yourself to be every inch your father's son.'

The young man looked even more incensed. 'After all the generosity my family has shown Mrs Whiteley, we expect to be dealt with better than this!' He straightened his jacket. 'You'll be hearing from our solicitors. If Mrs Whiteley and all her lodgers aren't off the premises in thirty days, the police will be here to evict the lot of you.'

Eddie slammed the door shut, and suddenly all the rage flooded out of him. He slumped against the wall and ran one hand through his hair.

'You handled him well,' said Paddy, wrestling with the problem of having to actually congratulate Eddie. 'What a bloody bugger, wanting to throw Mum Whiteley out!'

Eddie laughed, a dark and bitter laugh. 'And he'll succeed, you can be sure of that. He and his mother own the place now. Sir Gilbert had a sister called Charity Degraves. That snake is her son. "Charity House" – be damned.'

That night, Paddy couldn't sleep. He half expected the police to arrive at any moment and haul them all out into the street. He remembered his mother's stories of the evictions in Ireland, of families on the roadside, of ropes tied to the lintels of the house and the whole structure torn down. He tossed restlessly in his bed.

The next morning, Eddie was in the dining room by ten o'clock.

'I hear you auditioned for Pollard's Lilliputians last year,' he said.

'What's it matter to you?' said Paddy, pretending to busy himself with his porridge.

'Well, Baby Pollard, he's an old mate of mine. He reckoned you might make a good actor even if you were too old for the Lilliputians.'

'What are you getting at?'

Eddie stroked his chin thoughtfully and then pulled up a chair.

'Look, boy. Everyone's got to clear out of here. Mum is going to need some dosh to get her started somewhere new. I reckon you and me both owe her a few bob. Ted Bowman is looking for another player for his troupe. He's already agreed to take me on, and if I put a word in his ear, he'll sign you too. We're heading up to Ballarat tomorrow. You go and see him and tell him I sent you.'

Paddy was too stunned to reply. To have to accept a job from Eddie was sickening and if he won the job, he'd be stuck travelling with Eddie for months. But to be on the open road again, away from the smoke and grime of the city, and with a proper theatre troupe – it was what he'd longed for.

Before the morning was out, Paddy was riding the tram down to the Queen's Theatre. He found Ted Bowman backstage, packing up gear for the tour.

'Now you know, boy, a touring production needs everyone to pitch in and work. It's not like being in town. I only want lads who are hard workers, willing to turn their hand to anything and everything.'

'I've worked with a travelling circus. I think I can turn my hand to most tasks, and I'm good with the horses.'

'But I need players who can turn themselves to most parts too. Eddie told me you can do a fair Irish accent, is that right?'

Paddy laughed. 'Now, you'd best be believing it! I'm as Irish as a leprechaun!' he said in his broadest brogue.

'You can speak like an Australian too, I hope,' said Ted Bowman.

'Lord strike me fat! I can speak like a larrikin as good as the next bloke and I'm no gutless wonder, neither. Game as a piss-ant if anyone tries to poke borak,' said Paddy, pleased with himself that he could mimic Nugget Malloy so well.

Ted Bowman laughed. 'Well, you won't need to play the larrikin but I do need someone to take the role of the Irish policeman in *Lightning Jack*. Tom Barrens, who played it for the Melbourne season, won't leave his family behind, so a boy like yourself is just the ticket.'

'Do I need to audition? Do you want me to recite something?'

Ted looked him up and down appraisingly. 'No, I don't think that will be necessary. I trust Eddie's recommendation.'

Paddy couldn't believe anyone would trust Eddie for anything but he wasn't about to argue.

'I'll pay you five shillings a week plus your board. We leave tomorrow to play Bacchus Marsh on Saturday night and then to Ballarat. Then we'll show in Geelong and after that Colac before we take the road all the way to Portland.

We'll be on tour for months. Are you prepared to be away from the city for that long?'

'I'm looking forward to being back on the track.'

'You organise your tack and be here tomorrow morning at ten a.m. sharp. Eddie has a copy of the script, so ask him to show you your lines. You can read, can't you?'

'Of course I can,' said Paddy.

'And see if you can make sure Eddie is on time. Damned if I'll hold the whole troupe up for his sake.'

Paddy didn't like the sound of having to be Eddie's nursemaid, but he wasn't going to worry about that now. Walking back along Bourke Street, he wanted to shout with happiness. He grinned at every passer-by, not caring that people frowned back, puzzled by his giddy delight.

Paddy was so wrapped up in thoughts of the future that he had almost forgotten about the trouble at home. But when he turned into Atherton Road, he stopped dead in his tracks. Sitting outside Charity House was an old horse and cart, and piled up high on the back were all Bridie's possessions. A crowd of showgirls and all the lodgers were fluttering around the cart, tying pots and pans in place and fussing over Bridie, who sat on a chair that someone had placed on the footpath. She was drinking from a cup of tea that Flash Bill had brought her. Despite the air of carnival, she looked tired and defeated.

Eddie came staggering down the steps with Bridie's clothes dummy in his arms.

'What are you doing?' demanded Paddy.

'Moving Mum,' said Eddie.

'But we've fixed everything,' said Paddy. 'We've both got jobs. We can pay Rupert Degraves rent and Mum can stay.'

'I wouldn't give him the time of day, let alone cold hard cash. Anyway, you fool, don't you realise it wasn't about money? There's bad blood, and no amount of money can make up for that. I've found the old gal a room in the city. She won't have to run after this lot,' he said, gesturing towards all the other actors, 'and she won't have to walk so far to the theatres.'

Bridie's new lodgings were on the third floor of a dilapidated old building in Exhibition Street. They consisted of a small bedroom and a parlour where she could work. There was no proper kitchen, just a tiny sink and bench in one corner of the parlour. Bridie's pots and pans sat piled up on the floor, strangely out of place.

The furniture at Charity House had belonged to Sir Gilbert, so there were only a few wooden chairs to sit on. When all the other helpers had left, Paddy laid a fire in the small grate and put the kettle on. Eddie looked about the room with irritation.

'It was the best I could find, at short notice,' he said, defensively, even though no one had spoken.

'It's lovely, Eddie,' said Bridie. 'But there's not much room for you boys.'

'You won't have to worry about either of us,' said Eddie. 'We're off on tour with Bowman & Lytton first thing tomorrow morning.'

'Both of you?' said Bridie. 'Not Billy as well? Eddie, what have you done?'

'Don't put that tone in your voice, old woman. I've got the bludger a job, that's what I've done.' He snatched up his hat and stormed out of the room, slamming the door behind him. A dusting of dirt and plaster drifted down onto the bare floorboards.

'Mum,' said Paddy, putting his hand gently on the old woman's arm. 'It's what I want. It's a chance to act. Why do you disapprove?'

Bridie lifted a hat box off a chair beside the window and sat down. 'Come and sit here, beside me.'

Paddy pulled up an upturned crate and sat with her in the fading light.

'The first time I saw you, with that rascal Nugget, I saw you had a good heart. You reminded me of both my small brothers and of Ireland. One day, you'll find that your homeland stays in your heart like a long-lost love.'

Paddy put his head in his hands, trying to listen patiently. 'Sorry, Mum, but I don't see what this has to do with me being an actor.'

'Ireland is a land of saints and scholars. You're no saint, Billy. You have a quick mind and you have courage, but without learning you won't be able to make your mark.'

'Actors can make their mark.'

'But it's such a hard life. It wasn't a life I wished for Eddie and I don't wish it for you, Billy. I've seen how this old world works. There's no steadiness in the theatre. Sure there's the likes of Williamson and Tait and Coppin – old George Coppin, there's a good and great man for you. But the law, that's where a man can truly make his mark.'

'Mum, I've read you Mr Brodzky's columns. It was solicitors and their like that broke this country. I couldn't be a man of the church for my mam and I can't be the man you want me to be either. But I think, perhaps, if I could get the chance, I could be a good actor.'

'You're a worry, Billy Smith,' she said, shaking her head.

The shadows had fallen quickly and it was almost dark in the small room. Paddy lit a paraffin lamp.

'You wait, Mum. One day, I'll be starring at the Princess Theatre and you'll be sitting in the front row and you'll shake your head in wonder and think to yourself, "Why, Billy has become a great man after all!"'

For the first time since Sir Gilbert had died, Bridie smiled.

28

Perfection

They took the road west out of Melbourne, and the open fields either side of the road were wide and golden. Paddy felt his heart lighten as soon as the city receded. For the first time in months, he felt he could breathe again.

The sets for the play were loaded into two wagons, and another carried the actors' trunks and all the equipment they'd need when they had to camp. The last wagon was the one Ted Bowman called 'the omnibus'. Most of the cast travelled in the omnibus, including the three women – Mrs Lorimer Lytton, Mrs Clara Bowman and her daughter Kate. Paddy sat up front with the driver so that he could jump down and tend the horses when needed.

Mr Bowman had booked a two-week season of the show in Ballarat, and from there the troupe would head south to Geelong. Paddy spread the script open on his lap as the wagon rolled west. When he finally came to the role that he was to play, everything suddenly made sense. The Irish policeman he was to play was a buffoon. Apart from shouting 'Stop, in the name of the Queen!' his single biggest moment on stage would be when he tried to kiss the heroine, who would then be rescued by Eddie playing

Lightning Jack. Paddy couldn't help but groan when he read the lines. Now he knew why Eddie had said it was a perfect role for him. Night after night, Eddie would punch Paddy in the face and save the beautiful heroine. Paddy looked at the stretch of road ahead. It was going to be a very long tour.

They arrived at Bacchus Marsh in the early afternoon and Paddy leapt down to unharness the horses. When he'd finished, Ted Bowman called him over.

'You need to have a go at rehearsing your part. We'll do a complete run through as soon as we've organised the gear and got the community hall set up, but in the meantime Eddie and Kate can put you through your paces.'

Paddy met the other two actors in the yard behind the community hall. Kate was the Bowmans' daughter, and although she was only just turned sixteen, she looked older. She wore her thick brown hair piled up under her hat, like a grown-up woman. Her skin was silky white and there was a quiet grace in the way she moved that Paddy found strangely fascinating. It was hard not to stare at her. He felt weak at the knees at the thought of trying to kiss her. He put his hands in his pockets and tried to look relaxed and professional.

'All right, now,' said Eddie. 'You've memorised your lines, then?'

'There wasn't a lot to memorise,' said Paddy, grinning at Kate.

Eddie frowned.

'Pay attention, boy. The thing you have to understand is that what you say isn't nearly as important as how you move about the stage. That's what will reveal your character. For instance, in my role as a misunderstood and wronged gentleman fallen upon difficult times, I move like the noble creature that I am.' Eddie strode across the dusty yard to emphasise his point, then spun on his heel and walked back towards them, with a confident, forceful step and clear gaze.

'You, on the other hand, must move like the grovelling ignoramus that you are.'

When Paddy bristled, Eddie smiled. 'Come, come my boy, I meant as the character you are portraying, the ignominious and corrupt police officer, Constable O'Grady. Now, Kate is already on stage and you enter from stage left – over there. Let me illustrate.'

Eddie stopped in front of Kate. 'Now you have to show your arrogance by hooking your thumbs through your belt and perhaps tilting your head thus, sizing up the vulnerable girl you are about to molest. What are your lines?'

Paddy took a deep breath and recited. 'Look here, I know that Lightning Jack is hiding near here and we both knows you knows his whereabouts. I mean to nab him and it's straight to the gallows for the wretch. There's a reward that would make my life an easy one. But a pretty miss like yourself could easily turn a man's head from his duty. Why, if you could see your way to be loving, you know, a man could even turn a blind eye so your friend could clear off. But there'd have to be something in it for me, eh?'

'Said with no feeling, nor any credibility,' said Eddie disparagingly. 'Come here, stand close to the girl and try again.' Paddy stepped in close to Kate. He could feel the warmth from her body and smell the clean scent of soap and linen. He'd never stood this close to a girl before, except Violet, who definitely didn't count. It made him feel hot all over. He looked into her dark blue eyes, leant close to her and spoke his lines again.

'How dare you!' she said, looking at him with outrage. Paddy knew she was only acting, but he wanted to apologise immediately.

'No, no, no, boy!' shouted Eddie. 'You have to say it as if you believe it! You are a lecherous scoundrel, not her paramour.'

Eddie stood in front of Kate and said Paddy's lines with a convincing leer but when she rejected him, he went on to the next line. 'C'mon, give us a kiss then.' He grabbed her by the wrist and slipped his arm around her waist as if he was really about to kiss her, but then quickly stepped away.

'Now you do it.'

Paddy repeated his lines and then closed his hand around Kate's slim wrist, drawing her close to him. In that moment, Eddie's hand fell heavily on his shoulder and spun him around and his fist flew straight at Paddy's face. But he didn't make firm contact with Paddy's nose. It was the shove to the shoulder that unbalanced Paddy and sent him sprawling in the dirt.

'That was fine, boy,' said Eddie, standing over him with his hands on his hips, looking pleased. 'Let's run through it again.'

Paddy got to his feet and dusted his clothes off.

'What about the other scenes and my other lines?' asked Paddy, hoping they could move away from this scene that involved so much dust and humiliation.

'We'll come to them,' said Eddie. 'This is the scene that really needs attention, don't you agree, Kate?'

'I'm sorry, Billy, he is right.'

Paddy sighed and got ready to run through the scene again. Much as he hated to admit it, Eddie was very good at what he did. When he was in character, he was no longer the drunken oaf that Paddy loathed. He handled the fight scene deftly with just enough roughness to make Paddy fall to the ground but he never hit so hard as to leave a mark. For his part, Paddy started to understand how to fall just as the blow came. By the end of half an hour, he had managed to develop a proper leer when he leant towards Kate, but he couldn't like the scene.

Next they moved on to another scene in which he was supposed to chase Eddie across the stage and slip, landing flat on his back. By the end of the afternoon Paddy was sore and dirty, but he knew he would make it through the evening performance.

'You did very well,' said Kate as she dusted off the back of his jacket for him.

Paddy smiled and turned around to face her.

'I hope I wasn't too rough when I grabbed you,' he said shyly.

'Of course you weren't. You were perfect,' she said. 'I know you'd never hurt me on purpose.'

'Never,' said Paddy.

29

Lightning Jack

That night, all the local farmers came into town to watch the show. The community hall was jammed with men, women and children.

Paddy felt a stab of stage fright as he watched the audience take their seats. He was glad to be in costume. The dark wool was prickly and hot, but at least he looked like a policeman. Mr Lytton had stuffed some extra wadding into the front of the trousers to make Paddy look fatter and Mrs Lytton aged him several decades with deft make-up.

The fight scene went smoothly, though Paddy felt his nose tingle and his eyes stream when Eddie's fist made contact with his face. As he fell, he heard the audience cheer and he felt a crushing sense of humiliation. Even though he knew it was important to be able to play a villain, he longed to be the hero and hear the audience cheer for him.

It wasn't until the curtain calls at the end of the show, when he and the other bit-part actors bowed deeply, that Paddy felt a swell of pleasure. The applause fell around him like warm rain and he drank it in. Then Eddie and Kate Bowman stepped forward to take a bow and the audience cheered even more.

In Ballarat, Ted Bowman had booked the hall of the Mechanics Institute. Eddie stormed up and down on stage during rehearsals complaining that they should be at Her Majesty's, while Ted argued it was impossible and that the hall was a far better venue in which to stage *Lightning Jack* than any other available. But no amount of argument would settle Eddie's bad temper. Paddy and Clarence Lytton, Mr Lytton's fifteen-year-old son, rolled their eyes at each other. They snuck into the Institute's billiard room for a game while Eddie and Ted Bowman shouted at each other.

Clancy played three different characters in *Lightning Jack* and shared a room with Paddy in the old hotel that the troupe was staying in.

'By God, I'm sick of these country tours. One day, I'll go to London, and get a proper job,' Clancy said as they lay in bed after the opening night's performance, listening to the noise in the pub downstairs.

'Why would you want to be doing that?' asked Paddy. 'Won't you take over the company one day?'

'Not jolly likely,' snorted Clancy. 'I've got plans. I want to be rich. Do you have any idea how often my old man has written a play that's flopped and we've lost everything again? No, sir, the theatre is too much like gambling for me.'

Paddy laughed. 'But that's exactly what I like about it! You go out not knowing if the audience will love you or hate you, and then every night you take that risk all over again.'

Clancy groaned. 'You sound like Eddie. That's the sort of piffle he goes on with.'

Paddy sat up and glared at Clancy. 'I'm nothing like Eddie. He's a drunken sot.'

'He's a damn good actor.'

'Anyone would look good when they're playing opposite Kate Bowman. She makes him look much better than he is. If Kate was a boy, she'd take on the company for her father, you can be sure of that,' said Paddy.

Clancy laughed.

'If she was my daughter, I would have sent her off to boarding school years ago!'

'Clancy, how can you say that! She's so . . .' Paddy could think of a hundred different ways to describe Kate but he didn't think Clancy would appreciate them. 'She's so talented!' he said, finally.

'Look here, I've grown up with Kate and she's like a sister to me, but the stage isn't the place for a girl like her. My mother only took to it when she was a married woman. I want better things for Kate.'

Paddy turned his back on Clancy and punched the old feather pillow into shape. 'Clancy, is she really like a sister to you?'

'You make sure you think of her that way too, Billy.'

'Well, I certainly think about her a lot,' said Paddy.

'Then stop it. Shut up and go to sleep.'

There was something about Ballarat that brought out the worst in Eddie. He was like a coiled spring. When it came to the play's fight scene, Eddie hit so hard that Paddy saw stars and blood spattered across his chin. Backstage, Paddy sat on a stool while Clarence put a cold compress across the bridge of his nose.

'I guess he hates me,' said Paddy.

'He's only acting,' said Clancy mildly.

'Only half the time. I reckon he got me this job so he could hit me twice a day.'

'I imagine if you hate someone, you'd want to get as far away from them as possible.'

Paddy snorted and his nose began to bleed again.

'Look what a pig he's been to me ever since we got to Ballarat.'

'It's nothing to do with you. Kate told me he has good reasons for being unhappy here. She says he'll buck up when we leave.'

'What reasons?' Paddy hated to think of Kate taking Eddie's side.

'Apparently Eddie's father, Tom Whiteley, had a theatre called the Palace here in Ballarat. His first wife was a wild type, came to the goldfields with an English lord and then got herself mixed up with a band of bushrangers and ran off and left him. Old man Whiteley took up with a young girl who was one of the stars of a touring show and they had Eddie but then the Palace burnt down and between the scandal and the fire, Eddie's old man was ruined. At least, that's what he told Kate. He said Ballarat is "steeped in tragedy".'

'It sounds like codswallop to me. I bet he made it up to make Kate feel sorry for him.'

Clancy shrugged. 'Seems to have worked, then.'

Paddy stayed backstage after everyone else had left the rehearsal. When he was finally alone in the hall, he walked out onto centre stage.

'Fight or deliver, pray which do you choose?' he said to the rows of empty seats. He raised an imaginary gun and cocked the pistol, as if he really was playing Lightning

Jack. For a moment, he could imagine the place full, every seat taken, the house lights dimmed and hundreds of eyes watching him with rapt attention. It made his skin tingle, to think that he could be the hero at the centre of the story.

When he turned and saw Kate standing in the wings, he blushed and self-consciously ran his hands through his hair. She smiled, which made him blush even more.

'You'd make a fine Lightning Jack,' she said. She came out onto the stage and spun about, then put her hand to her forehead, pretending to be Ida Golightly. 'Oh, Jack, you truly are a gentleman and not the rogue they think you. If only Father understood that you are a victim of such cruel injustice!'

Paddy took Kate's hand and looked into her blue eyes. 'Beautiful Ida, when I see you and think of the happiness that I am denied, I want to challenge the whole world in a fight to the death!'

Kate started giggling and Paddy smiled. When they stood this close to each other, he was aware of how much taller than her he was, of how fragile her hand felt in his. He kept hold of her hand until she blushed and pulled away. She looked at him as if she was puzzled and the silence between them shimmered with things unspoken.

30

Rustlings in the dark

The Ballarat season finished and the company packed up the wagons and set out for Geelong. They took the road south, winding down the long midland highway.

The first night away from town, they pitched camp in an open paddock, under the stars.

Once all the tents were up, Paddy and Clancy built a bonfire and they settled down for a game of cards, but every now and then, Paddy glanced through the flames to where Kate sat beside her mother. Her cheeks were flushed from the heat and when she met Paddy's gaze, firelight reflected in her eyes like gold.

When the fire burnt low, Paddy and Clancy crawled into the small tent they were sharing with two of the other men. It was hot, with so many bodies underneath the thick calico, and Paddy couldn't get comfortable on the narrow camp bed. Finally he gathered up his swag and stepped out into the night. He drew a deep breath of smoky, gum-scented air.

The bonfire had burnt down to a mound of dull, glowing embers and the sky was awash with stars. Around the camp the darkness was thick, except for a stand of giant gums gleaming silver in the starlight.

Paddy heard a rustling sound and then a horse whinnied. He wondered if an animal was fossicking among the camp supplies and he crept closer to the source of the sound. He glimpsed a swirl of white fabric behind one of the wagons. As he stepped nearer, he saw Eddie and Kate, heads close together, whispering.

Quickly, Paddy stepped away, his thoughts racing. Surely, Kate couldn't be interested in having anything to do with Eddie? No, she was above reproach. It was probably a coincidence. Wasn't he wandering around in the dark himself? Maybe the heat had drawn them from their tents and they had simply crossed paths. Paddy felt a little ashamed. He walked away from the camp and spread out his swag in an open field.

A slight cooling breeze rippled through the long grass. Paddy lay on his back under the blaze of stars and wondered what he would have whispered to Kate if it had been him and not Eddie that had bumped into her in the dark. He'd never thought about wanting to talk to a girl before. He imagined Kate was the sort of girl you could tell everything to. She would sit and listen with her head inclined and that half smile on her lips that made her look so beautiful. Paddy tried to imagine talking to her as if she were his sister, as Clancy had instructed, but Paddy had never been able to tell Honor any of his thoughts or dreams. It would be different with Kate.

In Geelong, the troupe took rooms in an old hotel in Ryrie Street. When they'd finished helping unload the wagons, Kate, Paddy and Clancy hung over the balcony and watched the passing traffic.

'It's good to be out of the scrub and in a decent town again,' said Clancy.

'I rather liked the scrub, myself,' said Paddy.

'No audiences in the bush, old bean,' said Clancy.

Kate looked at them and laughed. 'You two boys are like Tweedledum and Tweedledee. You never seem to agree about anything. Do you think you could agree to accompany me on a walk? I rather fancy seeing the bay.'

'I think we could definitely agree on that,' said Paddy.

Kate was very quiet on the long walk down to the beach but she listened attentively as Paddy and Clancy argued about which was better, the city or the country.

When they reached the Eastern Beach, they discovered there were two bathing pavilions that stretched far out into the water. If there was nothing else they could agree on, both Paddy and Clancy agreed they should all go for a swim. They walked Kate down to the Ladies' Baths and then raced each other to the men's.

Paddy's hired bathing costume fitted him perfectly but Clancy had trouble keeping the straps of his from sliding off his shoulders. Paddy knotted them at the back so they could both dive off the deep end. When Paddy hit the icy seawater he felt as if he was going down forever, the blue green drawing him deep. As he kicked himself upwards and broke the surface, he felt the pull of old memories. He could almost imagine Dai would haul him out of the sea and onto the deck of the *Lapwing*. It was months since he had thought of Dai, and the memory caught him off guard. He still couldn't think of the past without the darkness threatening to swallow him. He swam to the rusty iron ladder and scrambled back onto the boardwalk.

'We'd better put our duds back on,' he called to Clancy. 'We told Kate we'd meet her outside the Ladies' Baths at three.'

'But we'll be early,' complained Clancy.

Paddy ignored his complaints and hurried back to the change room.

They wandered down the length of the beach towards the women's baths. Suddenly, Clancy went pale.

'I think we should go back to the hotel,' he said.

'Why?' asked Paddy, shielding his eyes from the glare.

'I don't think Kate would appreciate us interrupting.'

'What do you mean?'

'For god's sake. Look over there, you dunce,' said Clancy crossly, grabbing Paddy by the arm and pointing.

Paddy stared, his heart sinking. Ahead of them was a long jetty and beneath it, in the shadows, two figures were locked in a passionate embrace. It was Kate and Eddie.

'Wait. We should rescue her!' said Paddy.

'She doesn't look as though she needs rescuing,' said Clancy.

'But the police, if they see them behaving like that in broad daylight, they might arrest them!'

'Good,' said Clancy, dragging Paddy away. 'Come on. Let's go. It's none of our business.'

That night the backstage area was electric with tension. As they took their places on the stage, Kate and Clancy argued fiercely, in breathless, angry whispers.

Kate started singing to cue the beginning of the scene, and the curtain started to rise. Suddenly, Kate's song turned into a scream and the audience roared with laughter. Then

Paddy saw what had happened. The hook at the bottom of the curtain had caught on Kate's dress. Though she struggled to free herself, the dress rose inexorably along with the curtain until her skirts were up around her head and her bare stomach was exposed to all the audience.

Eddie rushed to Kate's side and ripped her skirts down. There was a tearing of fabric and Mr Bowman began shouting at the stagehands. The curtain descended again and the audience started booing while Kate was led offstage, weeping inconsolably.

'At least she didn't catch fire,' said Clancy, with a touch of malice. 'Minnie Muggeridge took fire – dancing too close to the gaslights at the foot of the stage and poof, her dress went up in smoke. Terrible.'

'Don't even talk about it,' said Mrs Bowman. 'You'll bring worse upon us.' She shuddered and reached over to touch a nearby chair. Paddy couldn't imagine that things could get any worse than this.

Later that evening, after the show had finally run its course, Paddy found himself alone with Eddie in the men's dressing room. They didn't speak, silently removing their stage make-up, ignoring each other's presence.

Finally, Eddie spoke. 'You hate me, boy, don't you?'

Paddy pretended to be busy removing his pencilled eyebrows.

'Hate's a very strong word,' he answered, trying to sound indifferent, though he knew his voice bristled with dislike.

'I don't care what you or that Lytton brat think of me,' said Eddie. 'And you can tell your weasely mate that if he thinks he can bully Kate into avoiding me, he'd better think again.'

'One word to her father and you'll be out of this company, and good riddance to bad rubbish,' said Paddy.

Eddie laughed. 'And where would the company be without me? Without Lightning Jack? Without me and Kate, there is no show.'

'Mr Bowman wouldn't care. If he knew what you were up to, he'd be glad to see the back of you.'

'So you're going to tell him, are you, you and that bloody Clancy. You'll ruin everything out of sheer malice.'

'You're the one that's ruining everything,' shouted Paddy. He felt tears of rage threatening to overwhelm him. He leapt to his feet, pushing his chair to the floor. It happened in an instant. His fist caught Eddie on the cheekbone with a satisfying smack.

When Clancy came into the dressing room, he stared in amazement at the figure of Eddie Whiteley, sprawled unconscious on the floor. Paddy stood over him, his face pale, his eyes blazing.

'Good Lord, old bean!' said Clancy. 'You haven't killed him, have you?'

31

Becoming Billy Dare

Ted Bowman wasn't happy about his leading man having a black eye, but neither Eddie nor Paddy would explain how he came by it.

When the Geelong season finished, the troupe moved on to Winchelsea. Even though it was only November, the days were blazing. Every performance was a torment for Paddy. Dressed in his thick woollen uniform with layers of padding to fatten him up, he dripped with sweat. And each night, when it came to the scene where Eddie punched him, either his lip or his nose dripped blood that mingled with the sweat. By the time they reached Colac, Eddie's bruise had faded but Paddy was sporting a seriously swollen lip.

Farmers from all over the district were in Colac for the agricultural show and Mr Lytton was busy all morning, selling tickets for a week's performances. After the tent was erected, Paddy and Clancy went into town and gave out handbills advertising the show to the people who were milling at the showgrounds. When they arrived back at the camp, they found it in uproar.

Everyone was gathered around the campfire where Mrs Bowman sat weeping.

'The scandal, the scandal,' moaned Mrs Bowman, putting her head in her hands and bursting into tears. 'My poor Kate, my poor, silly child.'

'We'll have to go after them. Get her back before they do anything rash,' said her husband.

'It's too late for that,' moaned Mrs Bowman. 'They've caught the train at least two hours ago. They'll be in Melbourne by now.'

'Damn the girl,' roared Mr Bowman. 'What about the show? I've already sold out for the first three nights. Half the bloody town will turn up tonight and we've nothing to give them! They'll tear the tent down. Damn that Eddie Whiteley! I'll have his hide when I catch them.'

'We can't afford to not do anything,' said Lytton, taking off his hat and running his hand through his thinning hair. 'It would be the ruin of us.'

Clancy stepped forward and put a hand on his father's arm.

'Father, we can still do the show without Eddie and Kate. Paddy and I know all their lines.'

'And which of you will play Ida, may I ask?'

Clancy sighed. 'I will. It's not as if I haven't played a girl before. You know Mother can make me look at least as pretty as Kate.'

Mr Lytton managed a grim smile.

'You might make a fine Ida, but Paddy's too young to play Lightning Jack. He's just a strip of a boy.'

'He can, Father, I know he can. He's taller than me. He's easily as tall as Eddie. We could pad out his jacket a little and he'd be a better Lightning Jack than Whiteley ever was.'

'The handbills all have Whiteley on them and the posters.'

'We'll make an announcement. Billy Smith in the role of the bushranger Lightning Jack.'

'Clancy's right,' said Paddy. 'I can do Lightning Jack just as well as Eddie. But not as Billy Smith. Call me Billy Dare.'

'Splendid!' said Clancy. 'That's a smashing stage name. Father, there you go, you can announce a special performance by Billy Dare as Lightning Jack and I'll play Ida Golightly. You can call me Clarinda Lytton, if you like.'

'And who's to play your own roles?' asked Mr Bowman, looking faintly amused.

'I'm never on stage at the same time as Ida Golightly so I can do both.'

'You'll run yourself ragged, boy!'

'I suppose I can play the policeman,' said Mr Lytton, sighing. 'Though I can't say I fancy all that falling about. I'm too old for it. And are you positive, Clarence, that you are not too old to take on a girl's role?'

'Nothing to it, old man!' said Clancy. He touched his chin with the tip of his finger. 'C'mon, Billy Dare, kiss me right there, c'mon. Are you man enough, old chap?'

Paddy laughed. Harry Bowman and Charlie Lytton looked at each other questioningly, but before they spoke Paddy knew what their answer would be. The show would go on. Even Mrs Bowman rallied at the prospect.

'We can't have him going out there with that golden hair. He looks more like a young angel than a bushranger,' said Mrs Lytton. 'Clancy, fetch my bag.'

They sat Paddy on a stool near the campfire with a bit of old calico around his shoulders. Then the two women set to work, mixing a thick black sludge and working it through Paddy's red-gold curls.

'It's a shame to change the colour, but if we darken you up, you'll look more of a man.'

When Mrs Lytton held up a hand-mirror to Paddy he hardly recognised himself. Even his eyebrows and lashes were darkened with a touch of dye. His eyes looked like pieces of sky, they were so blue beside the black curls.

Paddy grinned. When he slipped off the stool and changed into the bushranger's outfit, he was no longer the shipwrecked Paddy Delaney nor even the runaway Billy Smith. It was as if he had shed his past, sloughed it off like an old skin. In a matter of moments, he was transformed from a boy to a bushranger.

'What do you think?' he said to Clancy.

The other boy laughed. 'I think you'll become a legend, Billy Dare.'

That night, a summer storm moved in over the landscape. Flashes of lightning illuminated the tent as the audience took their seats. Paddy thought the rain might drown him out, but when he was on stage, he discovered he could make his voice swell louder than any thunder. As long as he was on stage, he really was Lightning Jack. It was like magic. It was exactly what he'd dreamt he would feel as star of the show. For three acts, Paddy forgot the past. For ninety minutes, while an audience watched his every move, Paddy was the bushranger Lightning Jack, defender of the weak, a rebel soldier against tyranny and injustice. And when the makeshift curtain fell and he stepped out to receive the audience's roar of approval, he was more himself than he had ever been. He was Billy Dare.

32

Limelight man

At the end of the week, the whole troupe was exhausted. Mrs Bowman had spent most of her time in the post office, wiring telegrams to Melbourne in the hope of finding Kate. Clancy was worn out from having to make three costume changes every evening and was having trouble remembering which character he was playing at any given moment. Old man Lytton limped around the camp, having injured his hip on the third evening of playing Officer O'Grady. Ted Bowman announced they were folding the tour and heading back to Melbourne. They'd made enough to cover their losses and the Bowmans wanted to go home.

'We have to find Kate. There's still a chance we may be able to cover it all up. The marriage isn't legal without our consent. We'll have it annulled and get our Kate back.'

Clancy rolled his eyes and leant close to Paddy.

'They've never fathomed Kate. They don't know how stubborn she is,' said Clancy. 'I've known her all my life. If she's mad enough to run away with Whiteley, she's not likely to come back. She'll make a fist of it, will Kate. And everyone will just have to get used to the fact that she's Mrs Eddie Whiteley from now on.'

Paddy winced. Clancy might have known Kate for a long time but he didn't know much about Eddie. Paddy couldn't imagine Eddie sticking with anything, let alone marriage.

On the morning that they were to leave Colac, Paddy walked away from the camp and into the bush. Dappled sunlight cut through the gum trees and the air smelt sweet and dry, with a tang of eucalypt. Paddy took a deep breath. He plucked at a gum leaf and crushed it between his fingers. He shut his eyes and tried to imagine what it would have been like to be a bushranger, to be Ned Kelly or Ben Hall or a character like Lightning Jack, and roam across this huge, open land. And then he thought of the night of the storm, his first night in a starring role, and he felt a sharp happiness.

When he opened his eyes, he found Clancy standing beside him.

'We have to go,' said Clancy. 'Father says we're to take the train back to Melbourne with Mother and Mrs Bowman. They're going to drive us to the station now. What are you doing wandering about like this?'

'Just saying goodbye,' said Paddy. 'I wish we could keep on touring. I wish we could have made it to Portland.'

'Well, I'm ready to go back to town,' said Clancy. 'I've never liked touring. All the spiders and the heat and the mud. I wish we could go on tour on a boat and sail home to England. That would be real touring. This gallivanting from one drought-stricken town to the next, it's simply not good enough.'

'I don't want to go to England. It's not my home.'

'Well, I'm looking forward to being a proper British

citizen and going to England one day. You're as bad as Father, with all his republican ideas! If I was old enough, I'd sign up and go and fight for the Queen, to show I'm really British.'

All the way back to Melbourne, Clancy and Paddy argued about which was better, England or Australia. Eventually, Clancy had had enough. He pushed his cap forward over his face, folded his arms and slumped lower in his seat, pretending to be asleep. Paddy looked out at the blue sky arching above and the great expanse of dry fields. A stand of golden wattle glowed on a distant hillside. When had it happened? – that moment when he realised he belonged in this landscape?

At Spencer Street Station, Mrs Bowman and Mrs Lytton organised a porter to load their trunks onto a carriage.

'No hard feelings, old bean,' said Clancy. 'Hope to catch you round the traps. I'll watch out for those "Celebrated Star Artist – Melbourne Idol – Billy Dare" posters.'

'And I'll keep an eye out for those headlines, "Colonel Clarence Lytton, hero of the empire",' joked Paddy. They shook hands and punched each other in the shoulder.

'But seriously, I'll send news if I hear anything at all about Kate and Eddie.'

The city smelt hot and sour after his months in the country. Paddy walked down Bourke Street feeling as if a huge weight was settling on his shoulders. He didn't want to go back to tell Bridie about what had happened. He could just imagine the look on her face; the crushing shame and disappointment when he told her about Eddie Whiteley eloping with Kate Bowman.

He turned into Stephen Street and stopped. The road

was almost blocked with bird fanciers who were buying and selling their birds. One man had a big black-and-yellow cockatoo in a cage and its screeches were so loud, they hurt Paddy's ears. Another man had a sulphur-crested white one that he claimed could talk. There were hundreds of different pigeons changing hands. Paddy looked up at the copper-coloured evening sky. On a windowsill on the third floor, a flock of sparrows had gathered. Bridie was definitely at home. Paddy drew a breath and turned into the narrow stairwell.

The lodgings smelt of sour cabbage and rancid meat. Shifting his duffel bag and swag onto his shoulder, he trudged up the stairs of the building.

For a split second, Bridie stared at him, bewildered.

'Billy Smith!' she exclaimed. 'What drove you to turn those golden curls black as coal?'

'It's a long story,' said Paddy. 'And I'm not Billy Smith any more. I've changed my name again. Billy Dare.'

'Billy Dare?'

'Remember? Sir Gilbert, he told us about a character he knew once, a boy called Billy Dare who shot a bushranger? I thought it made a good stage name. *I dare do all that may become a man, who dares do more is none.*''

Bridie wiped tears of laughter from her eyes and clapped her hands.

'Brave words, Billy Dare.' Then she peered over his shoulder into the darkening hallway. 'But where's Eddie? Did he come back with you? I've missed you boys. The pennies have kept the wolf from the door but I've missed the pair of you every day.'

Paddy felt the words stick in his throat as he tried to

explain what had happened. Bridie leant forward in her chair, frowning a little, as if he were speaking a different language and she had to concentrate hard to understand him. But when he'd finished she simply nodded. She took Paddy's chin in her hand and turned his face towards her.

'You mustn't judge him too harshly, Billy. You mustn't judge if you don't know his story.'

Paddy couldn't stop himself. 'I don't need to know his story to know he's a scoundrel.'

Bridie turned away and hobbled over to the window seat where she had left her work. She picked it up and returned to sewing sequins onto the costume. She would never hear a word said against Eddie.

'Well, I'd best be getting on. I have to find lodgings before dark,' said Paddy, hitching his swag back onto his shoulder.

'Don't go, Billy,' said Bridie, looking up from her work. 'I know it's not as comfortable as Charity House. All I can offer is a place to roll out your swag and a cup of sweet tea in the morning. I don't have any work for you and no sixpences to spare. But you always have a place here, with me, if you choose it. I promise you that.'

Paddy stood with his hand on the door handle.

'Even if I'm an actor?'

'Even if you're an actor. But you must promise me one thing.'

Paddy hoped it wasn't a promise he couldn't keep.

'What?'

'I want a front-row seat when you open at the Princess Theatre.'

Paddy laughed. 'First I have to find a theatre that will take me!'

'You're too late to find a part in the Christmas pantomimes. I'll have a word to Tom Wannan, down at the Bijou. He's the limelight man there and I've heard he's looking for a boy.'

'But I want to be on stage, not behind the limelight.'

'I know, and you will be, but you can make a start there. You'll meet everyone you will ever need to know. All of Melbourne goes to the Bijou.'

All through the long hot summer of 1898, Paddy worked at the Bijou, running back and forth from the footlights to backstage, scurrying along the underground passages beneath the stage.

'Mr Hugarde!' Paddy called. 'Five minutes, sir!'

Hugarde nodded and led his six soldiers into the wing, waiting for their final cue. Even after weeks of watching it, Paddy hadn't discovered how the man defied death day after day. Hugarde strode out onto centre stage and delivered his usual speech, his team of soldiers behind him. Then he moved to the left of the stage and the six soldiers lined up on the opposite side, guns at the ready. At a signal from Hugarde, they opened fire one by one. With a movement so quick, so deft that Paddy could never see it, Hugarde caught the bullets, holding them up between thumb and forefinger for the astonished audience to see.

Joey Windsor the ventriloquist and McGiney, his Irish dummy, were next up. Joey was always late but he usually blamed McGiney. They'd come on stage arguing furiously. McGiney was meant to be a stupid Irish dolt, but somehow, the dummy always managed to get the last word in.

Paddy watched them impatiently, waiting for the last

joke that was a signal to him to run and line up the other acts. Jugglers, impersonators, shadowists and escapologists all crowded in the backstage dressing rooms, waiting for Paddy to give them their call. The stage manager panicked whenever anyone was late.

The second-last act was Georgia Magnet. Paddy felt the stage shudder as she lumbered past him. Georgia Magnet's act traded on the sheer strength of her presence. She was so powerful that no one could drag her from the stage. The audience roared as men were invited to step up from the stalls to try and move the giant of a woman. Three men with ropes couldn't drag her away.

Finally, Chung Ling Soo, the magician, took the stage. Chung wasn't really Chinese, but when he was on stage he carried an air of Oriental mystery that convinced the audience that he was from the heart of the East. He was a master of smoke and mirrors, bewildering everyone with illusion. Objects floated across the stage, a goldfish materialised out of thin air and Chung Ling caught it in his hand. Paddy hated it when he had to run under the stage to help Tom with the lighting. He couldn't bear to miss a minute.

After the show, Paddy met Nugget at the pie and tea shop in Little Collins Street. The boys squeezed into a corner booth and ordered a pie floater each.

Nugget packed his pipe while they waited and looked at Paddy appraisingly.

'Glad to see you got rid of all that nancy-boy hair. You was starting to look like a right freak with that black and gold mop. You look like a man again.'

Paddy ran one hand over his scalp. A thin stubble of blond hair was all that was left. Nugget had given him such a hard time about the black curls with blond roots that he'd had the barber shave it all off.

'I wish I did look like a man. I can't seem to get the parts I want. I've auditioned for a couple of shows but when I tell the directors that I'm fifteen, they say I'm too young to play a man and too old to play a child.'

'You should spin 'em a yarn. Say you're nineteen. No one's gunna snitch on you.'

'No one's going to believe I'm nineteen, either.'

Nugget mashed his pie into his bowl of pea green soup. 'Give it time, mate. I reckon you was born lucky. Never seen a man land on his feet like you do. Reckon you must be half cat. No matter how far you fall, you always come up trumps. How you going with the old girl? Still bunking down on her floor?'

'For the moment,' said Paddy.

'She's a great old bird, Mum Whiteley,' said Nugget, shaking his head. 'She's helped a lot of us out. Always willing to feed a cobber, if she's got anything to spare. It'll be a black day when she passes in her marbles.'

'What do you mean?' asked Paddy.

'You know, drops off the twig, croaks it, kicks the bucket, mate. She must be more than sixty years old. She won't be around forever.'

Paddy shuddered. Was this really where Bridie's life would end, in those two dark rooms in Exhibition Street? Bridie said everything changed, whether you wanted it to or not. But Paddy felt they were both marking time. He was waiting for his big break, the role that would take him out of the wings and put him in front of the audience. Was death the only thing Bridie was waiting for?

33

Welcome strangers

On a hot afternoon, Paddy staggered through the front door of the lodgings with an armful of costumes from the Bijou for Mum to repair. Standing at the foot of the stairs was a dark-eyed, black-haired girl in a pale blue dress.

'Hello there,' she said in an American accent. 'Could you help me? We're looking for Mrs Bridie Whiteley. We were told she lived in this building, but Gramps has already knocked on every door and we can't find her.'

'I'm going up to her rooms right now,' said Paddy, trying to smile at the girl over the crumpled fabrics.

'Gramps,' she called excitedly, 'come quick, this young man knows where she lives.' An old gentleman appeared from down the end of the gloomy hallway. His pale blue eyes crinkled into a smile when he saw Paddy.

'Good afternoon to you,' he said, raising his hat. 'Lead on, young man.'

Paddy took them upstairs. 'Could you knock for me?' he asked the girl. 'It's a bit tricky, with my hands full.'

The girl turned to the old man. 'Are you ready, Gramps?'

Paddy looked curiously from the girl to her grandfather. The old man's hand trembled as he knocked.

Bridie opened the door and the old man stepped forward as if to introduce himself, but all he did was stare. Bridie looked back warily. Slowly, tenderly, the old man raised one hand and touched Bridie on the cheek. Her eyes grew wide and she trembled.

'Even after all these years, blood knows blood, eh, Bridie girl?' said the old man.

Then Bridie and the old man were hugging and crying and Paddy was so embarrassed he didn't know where to look. The dark-haired girl glanced across at Paddy and laughed. 'I'm Annie O'Connor. And that's my grandfather and my great-auntie. They haven't seen each other for a long time.'

'You mean that's Brandon?' asked Paddy, incredulous.

The old man turned around and stretched his hand out to Paddy. 'Doc O'Connor. It's a long time since anyone's called me Brandon. Only my bossy big sister can get away with that.'

Paddy stared at him in wonder and then, thrusting a hand out from beneath the armful of costumes, shook the old man's hand.

That evening, the O'Connors and Bridie went to the Bijou and afterwards they all met Paddy in the Grand Saloon at the Victoria Coffee Palace for supper. Doc O'Connor made sure they had the best table.

'Now you order anything you fancy, Bridie, Billy. And I've been thinking, I'm not happy about your lodgings. You two should come over to the Grand Hotel and stay there with me and Annie until Bridie's sorted her business.'

'You're not staying at the Grand Hotel?' said Paddy. The

Grand was the most luxurious hotel in all of Melbourne.

'Brandon, you can't be paying for us to stay at the Grand,' said Bridie. 'A night in the Grand would cost as much as we earn in a month! Besides, I don't want to move out of my lodgings. Billy, can you imagine what Tilly Dunne would say if I asked her to come to the Grand Hotel for a fitting!'

Paddy couldn't help but laugh at the thought of a parade of showgirls trotting in and out of the foyer of the Grand Hotel.

Doc leant across the table and covered Mum's hand with his. 'I don't want you worrying about stitching for a living any more, Bridie.'

Bridie smiled, but Paddy could tell she was uncomfortable.

'Billy,' said Doc, 'me and Annie, we owe you. If you hadn't written those letters, we never would have come for Bridie. I'm right grateful to you. You want to stay at the Grand, don't you?'

Before Paddy could answer, two men stopped at their table.

'We're real glad to see you here in Melbourne, Doctor O'Connor,' said the taller of the men. 'Tim Madigan and Jim O'Leary. You're an answer to our prayers, sir, if you don't mind me saying it.'

Doc shook hands with each of the men.

'We've heard you can turn a no-hoper into a real goer,' said O'Leary. 'Our syndicate's got the finest filly you ever saw, but she needs a gentle hand. You could have her ready for the Spring racing carnival, you could have her take the Melbourne Cup.'

Doc laughed but Paddy could see his sharp blue eyes taking the measure of the two men. 'Well, I could take a look at her, if you like. But I'm only here for a short visit, then I'll be taking my family here back home.' Doc spread his arms expansively to encompass the whole table.

Paddy stared at Doc, bewildered. Was the old man including him and Bridie? Maybe he thought Paddy was really Bridie's grandson.

While the two men tried to persuade Doc that he at least had to see their horse, Paddy tried to catch Bridie's eye but she was intent on the conversation between Doc and the punters. Annie took her spoon out of the bowl of strawberry icecream and licked it clean, staring at Paddy with her unfathomable black eyes. 'It's going to be real fun getting to know you better, Billy Dare,' she said.

Early the next morning Annie, Doc and Paddy went out to Flemington. Paddy was meant to be showing them around but Doc didn't seem to need much help. He simply hailed a cab and ordered it to take them straight to the track.

Annie and Paddy wandered from one stall to the next, looking at the racehorses while Doc went off to inspect the new filly. Paddy hadn't realised how much he'd been missing the scent of horseflesh. Annie seemed to be thinking exactly the same thing. When a mare came to the front of the stall she reached up and slipped her arms around its neck. The horse nuzzled her and she stroked it with tenderness.

'Back home, I ride every day but I haven't been on a horse since we took the damn boat out here,' said Annie. 'I told Mr Madigan and he says he's gonna give me a pony. I'll be riding her as the Spirit of Erin in the St Patrick's Day parade at the end of the week.'

'What, you got given a horse? Just like that?'

'It's not because of me, silly. I told you. Gramps is famous. He's the finest horse doctor in all of California, probably in the whole US of A. C'mon, let's go see what this pony of mine looks like.'

Paddy caught his breath when Annie led the horse into the stable yards. Annie's new horse was called Tara's Pride and she was no mere pony. She was a big, black mare and as sleek as a panther.

'They don't have any side-saddles. And they won't let me ride her without one,' said Annie, looking sulky.

'Could I ride her? Just to see how she handles?' asked Paddy.

Annie laughed. 'Do you know how to? You don't look like a horseman to me.'

'There's a lot of things about me that you don't know,' said Paddy.

Paddy put his hands on the mare's neck and then, in one swift movement, he swung himself onto her bare back. Annie watched as Paddy rode Tara's Pride around the stable yard. Suddenly, she caught the horse by her bridle.

Paddy smiled, questioningly.

'I want to ride up front.' She called to a stablehand to help lift her onto the horse's back. Tentatively, Paddy reached around her to take the reins again. Annie's warm, sweet perfume enveloped him. For a moment, she rested one white-gloved hand on his arm to steady herself. 'C'mon, Billy Dare,' she said. 'Let's see how she handles.'

Afterwards, Paddy and Annie wandered across the lawns. They passed by the rose gardens, and then climbed up into the wide grandstand. Up amongst the eaves, small birds wove in and out of the trusses.

In the shadow of the grandstand, Annie suddenly turned to Paddy, put her hands on his shoulders and kissed him. He stepped back in surprise.

'What did you do that for?'

Annie laughed and then blushed. 'You looked real handsome for a minute.'

Paddy laughed uncertainly. Annie looked at him expectantly for a moment and then scowled. 'Don't take it so serious. I just felt like doing it, didn't I? Don't get any dumb ideas. It don't mean anything.'

She flounced away, her white skirts swirling around her as she crossed the wide green lawns. Paddy watched her disappear and then put his hand to the place on his cheek where her lips had touched him.

34

Wherever green is worn

St Patrick's Day dawned bright and cool. Paddy was up before sunrise, pacing outside the stables of the Grand Hotel, waiting for Annie and Tara's Pride.

Annie rode out of the stables with Doc beside her. Paddy felt breathless at the sight of her. Ever since the kiss in the grandstand, just being near Annie made his heart beat faster, made every sinew of his body feel taut and hot. He thought about her kiss and tried to recall exactly what it had felt like, wishing she'd try it again.

Bridie had sewn a costume for Annie of emerald green and she wore her long black hair loose over her shoulder. She looked like a dark fairy, something from a poem rather than a real girl. Paddy couldn't imagine a more beautiful Spirit of Erin.

Paddy followed Doc as he led Tara's Pride into the street and down to St Patrick's Hall to take their place in the procession. People were flooding into the city from every direction. A huge banner of St Patrick was raised above the crowd. Everyone wore sashes of green. Men in kilts were tuning up their pipes and the bodhrans set a drum rhythm that rippled through the crowd. Paddy walked beside the

Spirit of Erin float, watching Annie ride just ahead, waving to the cheering crowd like a princess.

Bridie waited at the top of Swanston Street, beaming as Annie came into view. She was wearing a new dress and a fancy, wide-brimmed hat trimmed with green. It was as if none of the terrible events of the past six months had happened – Sir Gilbert's death, the eviction, Eddie's betrayal. The weight of all those things seemed to have lifted and Bridie looked more like the feisty old woman who had given Nugget Malloy a good shaking and set Paddy on his feet.

That evening, Bridie insisted that they all go to mass at St Patrick's Cathedral to give thanks for being reunited. Paddy had always managed to avoid mass, quietly disappearing with Nugget on Sunday mornings, but this time there was no getting out of it.

Annie arrived in a long white dress, looking as if she was going to her first communion. Doc and Paddy walked a little behind the women as they sauntered up Macarthur Street.

As Paddy passed through the gates into the cathedral yard he felt a sinking sensation in his stomach and all the blood drained from his head. He wouldn't be able to enter the church. He couldn't take communion. He hadn't been to confession since he'd run away from St Columcille's. Doc looked at him shrewdly.

'Here, Bridie girl,' he said. 'You and Annie go in ahead. This boy and I need to have a little talk.'

Doc took him by the arm and led him out into the street.

'Listen, Billy, I'm not a man for the church any more. I'm

sure the Lord will be happy enough to have two O'Connors thanking him without us adding to all that praise.'

Paddy laughed.

'Sure, it's a nice town, this Melbourne, but you can tell there's been some bad business and folk have had the stuffing kicked out of them.'

'Mum says the depression tore the heart from the city,' said Paddy. 'But things are getting better.'

'Are they better for her? Living in a couple of old rooms, stitching her fingers to the bone?' Doc shook his head.

Paddy felt uncomfortable. He'd always thought of Bridie as someone who loved her work, who laughed at the showgirls and took pride and pleasure in the fineness of her handiwork, but Doc was right. She was getting old and the rooms in Exhibition Street weren't like Charity House.

Doc led the way into an arcade in Swanston Street and up some marble stairs to the Celtic Club rooms. He ordered two long glasses of beer. Paddy looked into Doc's pale blue eyes as they raised their glasses.

'To you, boy, with thanks. It's a grand thing you've done, bringing me here to Bridie. I was at my own club back home when I saw your letter in the *Irish Times*. My own sister's name in print, bold as brass. It was as if the clouds parted, son. I knew exactly what I had to do. I'll always be grateful to you for that.'

'I don't know that I really thought it could work. I mean, when I sent the letters, it was just a lucky toss. It seems such a long time ago.'

Doc laughed. 'It doesn't seem so long ago that Bridie and I were in the workhouse back in Ireland. I remember the night she came and told me she was going to Australia as if it were yesterday. We'd lost our brother and our parents but for me, losing Bridie, that was the greatest blow. I lost hope for a time, lost faith that I'd ever see her again.'

'Is that why you left Ireland? Because there was nothing to keep you there?'

Doc smiled. 'That's a story! After Bridie left, I stayed on at the workhouse for another year until they found me a place with a blacksmith. I worked like a slave but he wasn't a bad master. He let me sleep by the forge in winter and he could see I had a way with the horses, so he didn't flog me often. Then one day, the local lord came in with his horse. It had lost a shoe and this fancy-pants wanted it fixed right away. I worked on the horse while the lord sat in the smithy's, warming himself by the forge, drinking from a jug of ale he'd ordered from the pub. Now there was a girl who brought him the jug, Maureen was her name. The most beautiful girl in the whole of Ireland. At least, I thought she was. But the lord treated her like a trollop. Disrespected her. Acted as if she were no better than a whore.

'I can't bear to see a woman or a horse mistreated, and judging by the state of this lord's horse, he had no respect for either creature. I was only a whip of a boy, no older than you, but I wasn't going to stand for it. When he slack-jawed Maureen, I told that fine and mighty lord that there wasn't to be such talk in the forge.' Doc laughed at the memory.

'Did he mind you?' asked Paddy.

'Mind a fifteen-year-old smithy's apprentice? He brought out his horsewhip to thrash me. But I was damned if I'd let him get away with it. I took the branding iron out of the forge and split his majesty's face wide open. And then there was nothing for it but to run. There was no safe place for me in Ireland from that day. The first ship I could find – I was bound for America. I found work in New York, at the track, working as a stable lad. Best start a boy could want. I've had a lifetime working at the track. Found my way out West later. Have my own ranch now, breed the finest racehorses on the west coast. I've had a grand life, for all the hard times.'

'But listen, Billy Dare, I haven't brought you here to jaw on about the past. I want to talk about the future. You know that I want to take Bridie home with me, back to California, but she keeps telling me no. I don't want to stay in Melbourne any longer. I need to be getting home. I was thinking, seeing as you're like her own grandson, that maybe you'd be able to talk the old girl around. She's got no family, there's nothing to keep her here.'

Paddy, took another mouthful of beer. He didn't know how to answer.

'We could take you with us, boy, if that's what's worrying her.'

Paddy looked away. A flock of silvery-grey pigeons winged past the arched windows. America. Doc really did want to take him to America.

'There's nothing to hold you here,' said Doc, leaning across the table. 'I could give you work on the ranch. Real work, man's work, not like this errand-boy stuff you do down at the Bijou.'

Paddy blushed. As much as he loved horses, he didn't want to work on a ranch. If he explained he was waiting for the right part to come along to put him in front of the footlights, and not behind them, he might sound pathetic. And then there was Annie. The thought of being near Annie every day, for months, for years. It made his head swim. He wasn't sure if it was the beer or all his whirling emotions.

'I'll see what I can do,' said Paddy, swigging down the last of his beer.

Late that night, when Paddy came back from the Bijou, Bridie was still working beneath the glow of a gas lamp. She looked oddly pale and was frowning as she knotted the last stitch in the seam of the costume.

'Mum, are you not feeling well?' asked Paddy

'Billy,' she said, smiling ruefully. 'I'm having to ask you a favour.' She reached into her black bag and pulled out a letter.

'This arrived this morning. And I'm worried. I'm worried 'cause I'm not knowing what it says. I can pick out some of the words, but I can't make the sense of it.'

Paddy sat down beside her and opened the letter. It was from Eddie. The temptation to tear it up was strong, but he drew a deep breath and read it word for word.

Dear Mum,

I hope this letter finds you well. I'm writing to you from lodgings here in Sydney, where I am staying with my wife, Kate. I married Miss Kate Bowman last November. We are hoping to come to Melbourne soon, as my wife is with child and expecting to be delivered in August.

'Oh, Paddy. A baby! Eddie's to be a father.'

We were hoping that it might be possible to stop a night or two with you at your lodgings until Kate has ascertained the exact circumstances of relations with her parents.

'I knew he wouldn't write unless he wanted something,' said Paddy, looking up from the letter.

Bridie sighed. 'Can you read me the rest of the letter, Billy.'

'That's all he says. The rest is only the address of his lodgings in Sydney.'

'Will you pen him a reply from me?' asked Bridie, putting away her sewing and hurrying over to the cupboard where Paddy's writing folio was kept.

'Mum, there's something else I want to talk to you about,' said Paddy, folding up Eddie's letter. 'About Doc, and Annie. About going to America.'

'Has Brandon been at you?' asked Bridie, suspiciously.

'Why don't you want to go with him?'

'How can I ever be leaving Australia if I'm to be a grandmother?' said Bridie, taking the letter from Paddy and looking at it as if it were a precious gem.

'But Eddie's not your family. Doc and Annie, they're your kin, not me, not Eddie.'

'Brandon has put you up to this. I've told him, I can't go to America.'

'He only wants what's best for you. He said he'd take me too, if it meant you'd go with him.'

Bridie looked up sharply.

'That's not why I'm talking about it,' Paddy went on. 'I haven't made up my mind what to do. Tom says Bland Holt has a new production coming up. I want to audition for it. If I got the part, maybe I'd stay. I don't really want to work on the ranch, I want to be an actor. It's hard for me to know what's the right decision. But it's different for you.'

'It's not different. You want your own life. This is my life, here. I love that old man just as much as I loved him when he was a boy but I can't go and be part of his world any more than he can stay and be part of mine. And now this news from Eddie! A baby!'

'But Doc's your family, your blood. Eddie . . . he's . . .'

Bridie crossed the room and took Paddy's hands in her own.

'I know you think badly of him, but Eddie is as much my son as any son I could have borne myself. I loved his father and as difficult as Eddie can be, he will always have a place in my heart.'

Paddy pulled his hands away and shoved them deep into his pockets.

'And so will you, Billy Dare. Maybe, one day, when you're as old as me, you'll understand. No matter how much you love your kin and homeland, in a long life, there are always other loves, other places that become a part of you. The memories that you store up in a place, they're as precious as gold. Fifty years I've lived in this colony. I've seen the best and the worst of it. I belong here now. Brandon's heart is in America with the life he has made there.'

Paddy stood by the window and looked out into the

darkened street. He knew he'd never be able to talk Bridie into leaving.

'Billy, you could go with Brandon and Annie. If I ask, he'll take you with him. You're young. You have your whole life ahead of you. But I have to stay with my old life and welcome the new life that's coming into it,' she said, looking down at Eddie's letter and smiling to herself. 'Lord knows, it's the little ones that give you hope, that make you keep faith in the future.'

Faith in the future. Paddy put his head in his hands. He wasn't sure where his future lay, his faith, his hopes and dreams were all caught up in a whirlwind of impossible longings and confusing possibilities. Suddenly, through the darkness of his indecision, he had a vision of Violet – Violet with her small, trusting hand in his and her unshakeable faith. If he left Australia, would he ever see her again?

35

The great rescue

There was a crowd of actors waiting at the stage door for the audition. Paddy leant against the warm brick wall and studied the lines of the scene over and over.

'Well this is a jolly surprise!' came a voice. 'If it isn't Billy Dare!'

Paddy looked up in surprise. 'Clancy Lytton! What are you doing here!'

'Auditioning, old man. What else?'

'But what about the Bowman-Lytton company?'

'Washed up, I'm afraid. Perhaps Father will get a new production up later in the year, but we need some dosh to tide us over so here I am. I say, you're not auditioning for the part of Lawrence Hargreaves, the trusty young companion of the hero, are you? I wouldn't stand a chance if you were.'

'I'll take it if they offer it, but I'd really like to play Percival Hurricane.'

Clancy laughed. 'Always aim high, don't you?'

'I know I'm a bit young, but they say you have to be a good horseman for the role so they're willing to take all comers. Did you see *The Scout* when it was at the

Alexandra? The lead in that was only nineteen. He won it because of his horsemanship as much as his acting ability. I didn't spend all those months chasing those circus ponies for nothing.'

'Well, I must say, it would be a lark if we both got the parts we want. I'd rather like to play your mate instead of your true love. No hard feelings, old chum, but I don't think I ever want to have to kiss you again.'

It was bright in the sunlit laneway and when the stage door finally opened it took a moment for Paddy's eyes to adjust to the gloom backstage. Clancy and Paddy joined the throng of performers milling in the wings, waiting for their call. An actor was already out in the centre of the stage, reading the part of Percy Hurricane.

Paddy listened to the actor and mouthed the words himself. There was something strangely familiar about the voice. It was rich and deep and reverberated through the backstage area. Slowly, Paddy edged his way into the wings and grabbed a handful of the curtains, clenching it tightly. Eddie stood centre stage, his hair cropped short, his profile strikingly handsome.

'By Jove!' exclaimed Clancy, standing behind Paddy. 'The blaggard is back. I'm surprised he'd show his face in Melbourne again.'

'You know he's married Kate and . . .' Paddy couldn't bring himself to tell Clancy all the news.

'I know,' said Clancy, grimly. 'She'll never escape his clutches now.'

Eddie finished his reading and climbed down into the stalls. When Mr Holt's assistant called 'Billy Dare', he looked up with curiosity.

Paddy drew a deep breath. He wasn't going to let Eddie's presence distract him.

'*Death has been about me since first I set foot in this dry land. I have woken with his voice at my ear, each day since I ran away to find my fortune, taunting me, telling me failure is my fate and the grave but a heartbeat away. I have been to the brink of despair. I have heard his dry whisper and oft I've thought to listen. But now, there is a new voice. Her voice, and her need. What sweetness to have found my purpose in life.*'

There was silence when Paddy finished.

'Very fine work, Mr Dare,' said Mr Holt without looking up from his notes. Then he stood and turned to the crowd of actors who sat waiting expectantly.

'Messrs Alec Rickards and Edward Whiteley please stay in your seats, the rest of you gentlemen may go. Your services will not be required for the moment, though Miss Coppin will be in contact, as some of you may be called upon to fill smaller roles or audition again.'

Paddy turned away, feeling the weight of disappointment heavy on his shoulders.

'Oh, and Mr Dare. Would you please stay where you are. We haven't finished with you yet.'

Clancy came out from the wings and grinned at him. 'I'll stay and watch, if you don't mind. Be your lucky mascot, eh what? You have to crack it, Dare. You can't let Whiteley best you.'

Mr Holt came on stage with Eddie and Alec Rickards behind him. Eddie nodded at Paddy but Paddy stepped away, keeping his distance. Mr Holt put his hands behind his back and looked at the three men thoughtfully.

'You know, gentlemen, Sarah Bernhardt herself said my last show was the sensation of the century. When she was here in Melbourne she came by just to see how true spectacle can really capture an audience. So there's a reputation to uphold, a legend, no less. This show could top all that we've ever done before.

'There are four acts, ten yells, three plunges and a shriek to set your spine tingling. You have all read with flair and competence, but there is more to this show than mere dramatic ability. The scene I would like you to attempt now is at the end of Act II. Your character is being pursued by ruthless men who wish to steal the great nugget he has found – the Golden Dream. But you escape, plunge into the river and gallop away to glory. We've had a tank set into the stage – ten feet deep, ten feet wide. I want each of you to attempt to leap from the bridge on horseback and into the pool – which is a river from the point of view of the audience. Then you are to swim to the side and scramble ashore. There's a mechanism that you must activate to allow a ramp for the horse to extend into the pool and you must emerge together.

'As was advertised, this role is for performers who are also accomplished horsemen. Our steed has been trained to make the jump, but if she senses your fear or incompetence, she may shy. There is a serious element of danger. If at any stage you wish to withdraw, that is perfectly understandable.'

Paddy and Clancy settled down in the back of the stalls, waiting for Paddy to be called. Mr Holt's secretary led Eddie backstage where the trained horse was waiting in the wings.

Alec Rickards attempted the jump first. It was obvious

from the moment he rode the grey mare on stage that he was uneasy in the saddle. Before the horse had even mounted the scaffolding, he had lost his seat and lay sprawled on the stage.

'Would you like to attempt the jump again?' called Mr Holt. Alec stood up and dusted his trousers, shaking his head mournfully.

Clancy elbowed Paddy as they watched Eddie walk backstage to take his turn.

'Let's hex him, so that he breaks his neck,' said Clancy in a whisper.

'Let's not. I don't want Kate's baby to be an orphan.'

Eddie came cantering in from the wings but when the mare reached the top of the scaffolding she stopped, hesitating at the brink of the jump.

'Bring her down again,' cried a voice from the wings. 'She'll take the jump this time.'

It was difficult to make the horse turn on the scaffold but Eddie managed to guide her down. They came at the scaffold again and this time the horse galloped unhesitatingly to the brink. It was the force of her sudden stop that catapulted Eddie over her head and into the pool. The grey mare backed down the scaffolding as a plume of water rose up into the air. Clancy chuckled. Eddie swam to the edge and climbed out. He stood by the pool, dripping and muttering angrily to himself, while a stage attendant handed him a towel.

Undeterred, Eddie tried again. Again he rode the horse up the scaffolding and again it shied at the summit. This time he managed to stay in the saddle, but the horse refused to take the jump. He dismounted and led the horse back down.

'Your turn to show them how it's done,' said Clancy, slapping Paddy on the back. 'Good luck, old bean.'

Eddie was standing holding the reins of the horse as Paddy walked into the backstage area.

'I'll be damned if I'll keep making a fool of myself,' he said angrily. 'That horse hasn't been trained!'

A dark-haired man stepped forward and snatched the reins from Eddie.

'There's not a problem with the horse. She'll jump for any competent rider,' he said, his voice bristling with aggression.

Paddy blinked. 'Jack Ace!' he said, disbelievingly.

For a moment, Jack didn't recognise Paddy. 'Billy Dare?' he said, offering Paddy the reins. 'She's a docile mare. You be confident and she'll do the stunt, no worries.'

Then the smile fell away from his face.

'You,' he said. 'I'd hoped you'd starved in the bush, you and the brat.'

'You'll never get your filthy hands on her again.'

Jack Ace lunged at Paddy. In an instant, his hands were around Paddy's neck, squeezing the breath from him. Paddy drew his body away, as if resisting the attack and then with all the force he could muster rammed his head forward, straight into Jack's face. Jack let out a cry and loosened his grip. For a moment he was stunned, his hands cupped beneath his bleeding nose. Then he lunged at Paddy again. But this time, Eddie, Alec and one of the stage hands grabbed Jack by his arms and held him back.

'Settle down, mate,' said Eddie. 'The lad's about to audition.'

'Not if I can help it,' said Jack, straining against Eddie's grip.

Mr Holt's secretary, Miss Coppin, tapped her clipboard. She was a small, sweet-faced woman but her voice was steely. 'I am sorry, Mr Ace, but we cannot allow this sort of behaviour in our theatre. We have already paid the full purchase price of this horse and as it is obvious that your presence contributes nothing to her performance, we no longer require your services. You will kindly restrain yourself or leave.'

Jack stopped struggling against the hands that held him. They let him go.

'I have unsettled business with this bugger. You let me take him outside for ten minutes and then you can go on with this audition caper.'

'I don't think that would be at all appropriate,' said Miss Coppin.

Jack grabbed Paddy by the front of his shirt. But before he could do anything more, Eddie stepped between them, shoving Jack away and threatening him with his fist. 'You heard what the lady said. Clear off.'

Jack grabbed his coat and left the theatre in a rage.

Paddy couldn't bring himself to look at Eddie. His head was spinning from the force of the blow he'd dealt Jack, and everyone was staring at him.

'Mr Dare,' called Bland Holt, oblivious to the dramas backstage. 'We are waiting!'

'Get on with it,' said Eddie. 'Pull yourself together, boy.'

Paddy turned to face the horse and realised with a thrill that it was none other than Tattoo.

'Hello, girl,' he said. She stepped closer and nuzzled his chest.

When Paddy swung into the saddle, Tattoo pawed the stage restlessly. He leant forward and stroked her neck.

'Don't worry, girl,' he whispered. 'Everything's going to be all right now.'

At a sign from the stage manager, Paddy urged Tattoo forward and they raced up onto the bridge. In a flash, she leapt over the edge. They seemed to fall through the air for ever and then a wave of white rose up around them. Paddy felt a rush of fear as the water closed over him but Tattoo was swift and sure beneath him, kicking her way upwards.

When they broke the surface of the water, Paddy slipped off Tattoo's back. He swam to the side of the tank, releasing the mechanism that made the ramp unfold into the water, and then rode the horse up out of the pool. As they emerged from the water, all the stage hands and actors applauded wildly.

'Excellent, my boy,' called out Mr Holt. 'I think we may safely say we have found a new Percy Hurricane.'

Paddy couldn't believe it. His head was still throbbing and water streamed from his clothes but he laughed out loud. Clancy raced down the aisle and leapt onto the stage, cheering. He slapped Paddy so hard on the back that water shot out of his nose.

'What a crackerjack, Billy Dare!' he said, sounding as pleased as if he had won the part himself.

Tattoo stood calmly beside him as the stage hands came out to towel her down. Paddy turned and threw his arms around her neck. 'Thanks, old girl,' he said.

Backstage, Eddie was sitting with a towel thrown around his shoulders, his wet, tangled hair pushed away from his face.

'Congratulations,' said Eddie, extending a hand towards Paddy. 'I didn't think you had it in you.'

'Thank you,' said Paddy. 'I didn't think you had it in you either. You know, to help me out and . . .' He stopped, embarrassed.

'It's all right, Smith. You've had reason to doubt me before but things are different. I've Kate and the baby to think of. I've changed.'

'I've changed too,' said Paddy. 'I'm not Billy Smith any more, or Paddy Delaney, or any of the boys I used to be. I've become Billy Dare.'

36

Bright thresholds

It was like a parade as the cabs and carts wove their way down St Kilda Road and turned into Fitzroy Street in St Kilda. The bay shimmered in the autumn sunshine and there was an air of festival as everyone piled out of the carriages and waited on the kerbside for Bridie and Doc to join them. Some of the men were already starting to unload Bridie's possessions and carry them up the path of her new home.

Doc had announced that if Bridie wasn't coming with him, then she wasn't staying in the rooms in Exhibition Street either, but what he was planning had to be a surprise.

Doc had more than one surprise to share that day. Paddy nearly fell over backwards when a horseless carriage came veering around the corner with Doc, Annie and Bridie inside it.

'Damn newfangled gadget,' said Doc, as he climbed out of the automobile and slammed the door. 'Don't know why I let you talk me into that, Annie. Give me a horse any day.'

'You like it, Gramps, you just don't want to admit it.'

— 248

But Doc wasn't interested in arguing with Annie. He was watching Bridie closely as she stood on the pavement outside her new home.

'I hope it's the right place, Bridie.'

The house was on a narrow strip of land between two grand brick mansions, and the white gravel driveway that led to it wound through an old, overgrown garden.

They all followed Doc and Bridie up to the front steps of her new home. Paddy thought it looked like a doll's house. It had high gables with weathered, silvery-grey timber fretwork all along the eaves. The old stone walls had been freshly painted a golden yellow. The door was red and a sheet of bright copper had been nailed down over the front doorstep and polished until it shone. Above, etched on the fanlight in beautiful scrolling letters, was the name of the house, *Beaumer*.

Bridie stood at the threshold, her hands pressed together as if in prayer, her face streaked with tears. For a moment, Doc looked worried but Bridie turned to him and smiled, speechless with happiness.

'Your silver and gold house,' said Doc. He put his arm around Bridie's shoulder and then kissed her on the cheek.

Inside, the house smelt of new polish and old stone. Paddy and Annie explored every corner of it. There were three rooms upstairs and three down as well as a walk-in pantry. There were a couple of out-buildings in the back garden too, but they were almost covered with a cascade of autumn roses.

By three o'clock even more people had arrived for the housewarming: Eddie and Kate, Flash Bill, Wybert Fox and a crowd of showgirls and old actors. Even Nugget

Malloy had turned up, looking uncomfortably out of place squashed on the chaise longue between the Tallis twins. There was barely room for everyone to fit in the front parlour and the guests spilled into the hall and out onto the front lawn.

Paddy and Annie slipped out through the front gate and into the street. The sharp, salty scent of the sea blew across the Esplanade.

'Sure was cosy in there,' said Annie, taking off her hat and shaking her black hair loose. 'Let's go for a promenade. I want to feel the sea breeze.'

They crossed the road and walked along the beach front. Annie wanted to walk the length of the pier to the pavilion at the end, but Paddy took her arm and led her further along the beach. On a smooth stretch of sand, a small stage was set up with the flat waters of the bay as its backdrop.

Harlequin and Columbine were dancing across the boards while Pierrot sat on the edge of the stage, strumming a mandolin. The makeshift theatre was surrounded by a low picket fence and a second melancholy Pierrot stood by the gate, holding out a hat to passers-by. Paddy dropped some pennies into it and followed Annie through the gate. They sat side by side on the low benches before the stage. Paddy had meant to watch the performance but he found himself watching Annie. She laughed at the trickery of Harlequin and cried out with sympathy for the poor, melancholy Pierrot. Every time she applauded, she would glance across at him and smile. It made him wish the performance could last all afternoon.

When the show had finished, the actors passed the hat

around again and Paddy emptied his loose change into it.

'I can't believe you and Auntie Bridie aren't coming to America,' said Annie as they walked back along the Esplanade.

'We're playing a one-month season here in Melbourne. Then we go on tour. We're up to Sydney and then inland from there,' said Paddy. 'And by then you'll be halfway across the world.'

Annie laughed. 'Didn't Auntie Bridie tell you? We're staying on a while longer. Gramps got talked around. He's training a new colt for your Melbourne Cup. We're moving on down to the George Hotel this week, right here in St Kilda, so we can be near Auntie Bridie. Those two old coots never run out of things to talk about!'

'Does that mean you'll be in town when *The Great Rescue* opens?'

'Sure does,' she said, grinning. 'Gramps has already booked us a box.'

'Well, I guess I should give this to you anyway.'

'What?' she asked.

'Something for good luck. It's not so much to use as to keep – a keepsake so you don't forget me.'

'I'm not going to forget you in a big hurry, Billy Dare.'

Paddy had wrapped the present in a piece of blue silk and tied it with gold braid. Annie took the gift and unwrapped it carefully. The pale red wood looked striking against the sky-coloured fabric. Annie put the love spoon against her cheek.

'Where'd it come from?'

'I made it,' said Paddy. He leant towards her and pointed out the band of chains that coiled around the handle of the spoon. 'It's the first spoon I've made out of Australian wood. It's red gum. These Australian timbers, they're hard to carve, but they last forever. See, it smells like the bush.'

'And the flower, and the chains? What do they mean?' asked Annie, tracing the pattern with her fingers.

'They're part of the design,' he said, reluctant to tell the full truth.

'Does this mean you want me to kiss you again, Billy Dare?' asked Annie.

Paddy blushed. Did he want her to kiss him? Is that why he'd given her the love spoon? The price of a kiss. He looked at her laughing brown eyes and smiled.

'I don't mind if you do,' he said.

Author's note

This is a work of fiction, but in writing it I hoped to shed some light on an important era in Australian history. Although I had to use my imagination to create Paddy Delaney, the world in which he lived was a real one and the events of his life are based on fact. Despite the depression of the early 1890s, by the time Paddy Delaney arrived in Australia, the colonies were soon to become a federation. It was the era of Henry Lawson and the awakening of a distinctive sense of national identity. Just as Paddy Delaney reinvented himself as Billy Dare, Australia was inventing itself as a nation.

In the late nineteenth century, Australia's entertainment industry was one of the most vibrant in the world and Australians began to define their separation from the old world by producing hundreds of locally inspired productions. Melodramas that romanticised the earlier era of the bush-rangers, like *Lightning Jack*, were hugely popular. Circuses and touring theatre troupes were as important as television is today.

Now that we live in a more secular age, it's hard to appreciate the importance of religion in the nineteenth century. My great-grandfather, David MacNamara, ran away from a seminary in Ireland and was subsequently ostracised by his family because of it. He shovelled coal to make his way back to Australia, the country of his birth. Some aspects of Paddy Delaney's story were inspired by his impulsive personality.

Many of the characters in *Becoming Billy Dare* are composites of men and women of their time, but a number of them are real people and I used their real names. The actors mentioned as performing at the Bijou Theatre were famous in their time – including the death-defying Hugarde, the ventriloquist Joey Windsor, the magician Chung Ling Soo and the immovable Georgia Magnet. The Lilliputians theatre troupe that Violet joins was a genuine 'children's' company. It was run by the Pollard family and for many years toured Australia, New Zealand and south-east Asia. Jim Crilly was a famous showman of his day who really did exhibit a 'living skeleton' in Swanston Street. Bland Holt was one of Australia's most famous theatrical figures of the nineteenth century. He was an actor, manager and producer of the country's greatest stage sensations. He really did produce a play called *The Great Rescue*, though it differed slightly from the one in which Paddy wins the starring role. Other real people who either appear or are discussed in the pages of this book include William Lane, George Coppin, Miss Coppin, Mr Brodzky and Messrs Tait and Williamson.

It's now over 100 years since the events described in this story. Almost no one who lived in that era is alive today but when I was a child, many elderly people described that time as if it was only yesterday. Time moves so quickly that sometimes we can forget how our lives have been touched by those who came before us. One day our own stories will echo as loudly to the generations that follow.